A Child's War

Richard Ballard

To Rob,
With all good wishes,
Richard
23 April 2010

MY Books

AN MY PUBLICATIONS
PAPERBACK

First published in 2005

A CIP catalogue record for this title is available from the British Library

ISBN 09547280-2-5

Published by
M-Y Books
Hertford
England

For Alexander, Lydia and Serena,
in case they want to know

1

"Did you see it last night, Edna? The plane coming down in Richmond Avenue?"

"George and I certainly heard it. We were on our way to the shelter with Alex when it happened."

"They say it got two houses. In one the family were in their beds and killed outright, and the others were down the shelter. It was a Jerry bomber and the pilot and crew couldn't get out."

"Poor devils. I don't suppose most of them want all this any more than we do. They can't all be fanatical Nazis, can they?"

"In the Luftwaffe they can. Apparently old Goering likes them to be."

This exchange took place in the street outside Edna's house in Raynes Park, London SW20 on a sunny morning towards the end of September 1940. The houses there had all been built at the beginning of the twentieth century. They had bay windows upstairs and down ornamented with mouldings, and were fronted by little gardens edged with decorative iron railings. The pavements on either side of the road were lined with trees whose leaves were getting tired now. It had been a quiet road until Hitler decided to bomb London instead of the southern English airfields, and remained so during the day. There was not much traffic beyond the horse-drawn milk cart each morning, the butcher's boy making deliveries on a bicycle with a large basket over its small front wheel soon after the housewives had had their breakfast on a Saturday, the dustcart at mid-day on a Wednesday and the occasional deliveries from department stores such as the ones made in a green and gold motor van to George and Edna Ryland at number 74. Very few of the residents in Chestnut Road had cars of their own, either at that time or before war broke out, so there was virtually no kerbside parking.

Four-year-old Alex Ryland became excited when he heard his mother go to the front gate to greet her best friend. He saw that she had left the front door wide open, and in his eagerness to run outside he caught his foot on the door frame and fell on the corner of the stone step as the two women watched.

"Good Lord, he's split his chin!" cried Edna.

The child yelled with pain and rage. His blood was all over the front of his clean jersey, provoking annoyance from his mother and concern from her friend. He was soon gathered up and, still screaming, was carried off to the kitchen where a sticking plaster was found and ineffectively administered. When Edna realized that the plaster was of little use, she rushed to the mirror by thc front door and pushed her thick but short black hair into place. She turned round, dragged her brown coat off the hallstand and quickly put it on. After another look in the glass, pouting because she did not like her appearance in her newly acquired horn-rimmed glasses, she reached into the cupboard under the stairs - which at that time contained a mattress to sleep on during an air-raid as an alternative to the Anderson shelter in the garden - to find Alex's redundant pushchair. It had been carefully kept in fear lest there might be any more accidental births. She dumped him none too gently into it and took him to the casualty department at the hospital a few streets away.

She sat fretfully with her child in the waiting room for half an hour, doing her best to ignore the demands he expressed in between the little sobs he kept making that he should sit on her lap. In the end, the woman nursing her swollen thumb on a chair facing Edna across the room made sympathetic smiles towards Alex and shamed her into lifting him up and holding him close. He sniffed and whimpered by turns for five more minutes until the receptionist called her name.

II

"A split chin like that will need several stitches," said the young doctor who pulled a long face as she saw it. "I think it would be best, Mrs Ryland, if he stayed here with us."

"No child of mine is staying here with these bombs falling night after night," was the reply. "Would you let me use a telephone, please?"

"Of course," said the doctor, "Sister will show you where there is one."

After the call had been passed round the underground regions of the big department store where her husband worked as Chief Maintenance Engineer, George was finally found. He wiped his hands on a cloth, on his greasy overalls, on the cloth again, and then through his thinning hair which had fallen over his face while he was working. He did not like being called to the telephone while he was involved in some tricky operation that involved skill and swearing. However, being told that it was his wife and knowing that she would only ring him at work if there were a real emergency at home, his greeting was almost kind as he took off his glasses to scratch his head,

"What's up, girl?"

"I'm at Merton Hospital. Alex has split his chin badly and they want to keep him in overnight. I don't want to leave him. It's dangerous enough in the shelter at home during the air raids, let alone in the children's ward on the top floor here."

"What do you want to do, then?"

"I'd like to take him to stay with the Pattersons in Oxford, where he'd be safe. The only thing is that the journey with him in this state will be difficult on the train or the coach."

"The only other way's a taxi. Do you want to do that?"

"Cost the earth, though."

George realized that he had smeared one of the lenses of his glasses with his dirty thumb as he put them on again, and that there was nothing in the pockets of his overalls that resembled a clean handkerchief with which to clean it. He did his best to suppress his irritation as he replied,

"If it's an emergency we shall have to find the money. Ring Graham Patterson at the dairy from where you are and if it's all right with them get a car and go. I'll come up on the coach on Friday night and stay the weekend."

Edna used the telephone twice more to do what George had suggested and then, after the doctor had sewn Alex's chin together and covered her work with a huge and effective plaster, he suffered the indignity of the pushchair again to go back home. His mother spent a furious half hour packing what both of them would need for a short stay away and nearly split her own chin while getting a suitcase down from the top of the wardrobe.

There was a knock on the front door, and Alex saw to his delight that a huge black taxi had arrived. While he sat once more in the push-chair waiting to get into the taxi and Edna made sure that the house was properly locked up, the thing that registered most in his mind was the shiny metal hubcap with a decorous copperplate capital A for Austin on it that graced its wheel. His mother picked Alex up and set him down in the back of the car while the driver registered her anxiety and responded to it with his own. He packed the suitcase and then the pushchair in the boot.

"If we go now," he said, "I can get back before the raids start to-night, or my wife will do me the honour of going up the wall with worry."

"How far is Oxford?" asked Edna.

"A good four hours each way. At least, that's what my boss says."

With that he started the engine, and Alex sank into the brown leather upholstery of the back seat alongside his mother who was irritably looking through the hand luggage she had about her, making sure she had what she had convinced herself that she had left behind. She was dressed in her Sunday best black coat now and was wearing her newest black hat festooned with spotted veiling. When at last she was still, she took off her glasses to wipe them with her little lace handkerchief, sighing and biting her bottom lip.

The two greatest impressions upon Alex's memory, since he was not tall enough to see out of the window, were the overpowering smell of the treated leather and the smooth motion of this great big car. These soothed him after the distress of the morning. He did not understand why his mother would not let him rub the plaster over the stitches in his chin when it started to hurt severely but, once she had set him on her lap and they were being driven along the Great West Road, he fell into an uneasy sleep, only to be woken as they crossed the bridge at Henley because he was giving his mother excruciating cramp and she was telling him so as she moved him to one side.

For the rest of the journey, the little boy drifted between sleeping and being woken up by the throbbing pain in his chin, hoping that it would not hurt forever. His mother tried to make a joke out of the great bruise that covered his lower jaw around the plaster but he was in no mood for such ill-judged pleasantries, especially when she showed it to him to him in the small mirror from her handbag. He knew on the basis of past experience that he was irritating his mother, but he could not help crying for a while until he fell asleep again.

When he woke up next, it was because his mother was talking to the driver.

"Go through the city centre," she was saying, "and make for the station. When we've gone under the station bridge we are nearly there."

"That's all very well," the driver replied, "but I've never been here before and don't know how to get to the station."

By this time they were going across a bridge that had a large tower on the right hand side before joining a main street.

"Keep straight on here and, when we get to Carfax, I'll tell you where to go from there."

"You're in charge, ma'am," was all the man could think of to say and he followed his nose and her directions, sensing that she was not a frequent traveller in cars and was very likely as confused as he was. He was not far wrong in this: she had only been to the city twice to see her friends since they had moved to Oxford at the start of the war for the sake of their twelve-year-old son. On both those occasions she had come on a coach with George showing her the way after they had arrived at Gloucester Green, not far from the railway station.

Alex was annoyed by not being able to see out, and knelt up on the seat to see what went by. There were at first gardens with impressive gates set back from the road, then large stone houses, a row of shops, then more stone buildings. He noticed that these had small windows, interspersed with one or two arched doorways that appeared vast to him. A great many people were walking to and fro on the pavement, including little groups of young men wearing strange-looking gowns over their tweed jackets, who all seemed to be laughing together. When he turned round to see out of the window on his mother's side, he saw two buses, one in front of a green lorry and the other behind it, which were not quite red and not quite brown with the word OXFORD painted on their sides in large gold letters

The fact that Alex started whimpering again because his face hurt as he turned his head did not sweeten the temper either of Edna or the taxi driver. A hostile silence was maintained until at last his mother recognized the crossroads at Carfax and shouted out,

"Straight on here!" while the driver very nearly went though a red light in his eagerness to comply. Alex's whimpering turned into loud crying until she muttered under her breath at her son, "For God's sake, shut up. If it wasn't for you we wouldn't have to be doing all this."

None of the three in the car was gladder than the driver to see the road descend under the railway bridge with a Great Western engine puffing over it, pulling a long line of carriages. He could now deposit his charges and get home to Wimbledon and his wife and daughter and grandchildren before the night's anxiety at Hitler's hands should begin. His son-in-law had been called up for military service whereas the father of the child now in his taxi had not. That added to his resentment of his passengers, as well as the mother's haughty attitude during his attempts to start a conversation while the child had slept.

They were going over the canal bridge when Edna said, "You see that church on the left? Then the road goes over another bridge, and where we are going is on the right hand side of the road opposite a shop, number fifty-six." That was the final direction and having complied with it the driver moved smoothly across the road and braked at the kerb, facing the oncoming traffic. He got out and discourteously opened the offside passenger door first so that Alex could scramble out, leaving his mother to gather up all her miscellaneous hand luggage herself. Then he fetched the big suitcase and the pushchair from the boot.

The final snapshot in the little boy's memory of his evacuation from the London blitz was of his mother rummaging in her handbag for the wherewithal to pay the driver, who thanked her, touching the peak of his cap in a salute to her before pocketing the money. Alex watched as he went forward on the wrong side of the road before turning round in a side street and roaring off home as fast as he could before the blackout could make unaccustomed rural travel really difficult.

Hearing the taxi stop outside, Joyce Patterson opened the door and greeted her friend warmly. The two women were in total contrast to each other in looks. Joyce was tall with greying, wavy hair, a clear complexion and a neat dress for the afternoon. Edna appeared crumpled and defeated, with her face powdered and her lipstick wearing thin after nervous movements of her mouth all the way in the taxi. She evaded the embarrassing embrace as soon as she could and, picking up Alex to be kissed in turn, followed Joyce who was carrying their luggage into the house. Edna put Alex down as they stood in the hall.

"Here is the reason we are imposing ourselves on you for a week or so until he's better," she said in a rather mournful voice.

"He does look as though he's been in the wars, doesn't he?" remarked Joyce, looking down at the child's swollen, discoloured chin with its large plaster covering the wound.

"Well, we all have had six whole nights in a row in the shelter – and that followed a fortnight of having to go down to it in the middle of the night when those terrible air-raid sirens began their wailing sound. They were enough to wake the dead, let alone the sleeping," Joyce laughed.

"George set up a place under the stairs for us," Edna went on, "for when he was on nights at the store, but luckily he was on days this week so he was able to carry Alex down the garden while he was still asleep."

"What you need is a real rest then, Edna, by the sound of it. Come on; don't stand about in the hallway. You take your hat and coat off and go upstairs. The room you are in is the first on the right upstairs. There's a double bed and a single for this little chap. Leave the push-chair there by the hall stand, and go and put your case away while I make the tea. I've already put the kettle on; it's just about to boil so it'll be ready in a second."

Alex watched his mother go up the stairs and sat on the bottom one to wait for whatever happened next. Talk of the shelter in the garden reminded him of the time when he had watched George and some of his neighbours excavate and cover it and then go on and help the rest of the neighbours in their turn. The government, George told him, supplied the two curved walls made out of corrugated iron and the rails they were bolted to. He also told him that the government minister responsible for supplying two and a quarter million shelters was called Anderson, so they were all known thereafter as Anderson shelters.

George was looking forward to a time when, if he and his family survived, he would be able to teach things to his boy with higher hopes of him understanding all he said. He would have been pleased if he knew that Alex was remembering it all now, as he waited in a daze for Edna to finish tidying herself up. Alex remembered that a lot of shovelling of earth and digging up of earth had to be done because the walls had to be put up over a pit three feet deep and the completed shelter had then to be covered with soil to a depth of eighteen inches. By the time the bombs started to fall there was many a marrow coming to full size on the top of the shelters along Chestnut Road. Most of the residents had bought their shelters a year before, since they earned rather more than would qualify them for free ones. They all agreed that it was probably ten pounds well spent, since a family of six could be kept safe from the blast that might take away the houses, provided that the shelter did not receive a direct hit itself. They all felt sorry for the people who lived down near the docks or in central London without gardens in which to build the shelters. At least in the western suburbs they were consoled by the idea that if death came to them, it would come to family groups huddling together and not to a communal shelter full of people who would be strangers to each other.

When Edna came down again, she was very distressed to find a wet patch underneath Alex on the stair carpet, though Joyce did not seem to mind at all and produced a bucket of water and a cloth to deal with it. He was none too gently dragged upstairs for a wash and some hastily found clean clothes. Before she married George, Edna had worked for a short time as a nurse in the children's ward of an infectious diseases hospital. She knew how to be efficient, and her son now felt the full force of that efficiency.

III

When she rang him at work, George knew that Edna was under more strain than she usually was. He had accepted years ago that she would never turn into a gentle and imperturbable woman, and recognized his own tendency towards anxiety well enough. So while he agreed that she should visit their close friends in Oxford on account of her tense state, underneath he was glad of the chance to have a proper reason for getting her to a safe place without her seeming to have run away, or appearing to be trying to escape himself at the weekends.

At the time they had married in 1923 he had been twenty-two and an Engine Room Artificer in the Royal Navy, handsome in his fore-and-aft uniform and his cap worn at a rakish angle in the style of Admiral Beatty. She was twenty-one, with appealing brown eyes and hair like the feathers of a raven. Nothing wrong with all that, though his parents thought there was, and her own mother had been dead four years or she might have made some remark about repenting at leisure. Edna's father had become dispirited since his bereavement and expected his middle daughter to look after his youngest one, a responsibility to which she had not taken very kindly. Edna was not very fond of the idea of children nor, indeed, of their reality in spite of her job looking after some of them. George was a kind man, and had felt sorry for the attractive children's nurse he met at a dance. He was willing to outface his mother and father when she accepted his proposal of marriage. He offended them even more by arranging his wedding by special licence in a short period of leave when he was meant to have been initiated to a lodge of freemasons during his father's year as its worshipful master. His father, who was also in the Navy, had high hopes for his elder son, which did not include an early and probably improvident marriage to a girl who had no more in her stocking than her obviously fetching leg. David Ryland was more surprised than pleased when his daughter-in-law did not give birth to a child during the next nine months nor for that matter for the next thirteen years. By the end of that time hope of having grandchildren had overridden his earlier misgivings about his son's marriage. Nevertheless, the doubts of George's mother still lingered and erupted into unpleasant scenes from time to time when she and Edna met, which did not happen very often.

George and Edna themselves had become used to their lack of diminutive dependants and forgot the risk involved in their contentment with each other one barmy night towards the end of 1935. Alex was born after a difficult pregnancy and a horribly long time in labour, which precluded the possibility of other children, as Edna would tell anyone who would listen for many years to come. Although George was thrilled to have his son and heir, as he incessantly called him to his friends, Edna found the joys of motherhood overrated. She was ashamed to remember the occasion, before the war started, over eighteen months ago, when Alex had not only been singing while she wanted to sleep after lunch on a fairly cold day, but had also been playing with his wooden bricks, causing clicking sounds. She had threatened to throw his bricks on the fire if he continued. He did not stop and being a woman of her word, she threw three of the offending bricks into the flames. This neither facilitated her sleeping process nor provided the hoped for silence from her son. Time had to be spent in quenching his rage as his bricks burned in the grate, despite her remorseful attempts to rake them out of the fire. As Edna saw things, in her generation, parents were not required to apologise to their children - so she had not done so.

When the little so-and-so fell over and split his chin, something gave way in her. Relations had been strained between them for some time because he would still sing his tuneless songs while he played after lunch at the side of her chair when she wanted to have her five minutes' sleep and in recent days her internal clock had failed after all the sleepless nights caused by the air raids. She considered that even Tommy Handley could not have seen the funny side of what she was going through. George considered that she laughed more loudly than was justified by his 'It's That Man Again' programme on the wireless because of a desperate need to be cheerful when she was far from being so. Historians say that revolutions are caused by the agitation of those who have something to lose. George saw the corollary of that argument. Having worked hard, after many years of disappointment, he had become a conformist in order to keep what he had eventually gained. He had been born in 1900. In July 1917, after being embarrassed for several months by girls in the street looking at his tall, rugby-playing frame and wondering why he was still a civilian, George had volunteered for the Navy as he had long intended to do in any case. He was glad to become what was called a 'boy tiffy' at H.M.S. Fisgard in Portsmouth because of his dread of ever being placed in the special care of his father who had a responsible post at the Naval Detention Barracks in Chatham. He had gained his promotions in the engine room of a destroyer and then of a light cruiser. He suffered a fall on board ship, which resulted in a hernia. This was confirmed in medical language as a right inguinal bubonocele on account of which he was granted a hurt certificate in April 1927. It was graciously conceded on the document that he was sober at the time. However, George refused to submit to surgery. He was transferred to a shore establishment where he was discovered to be in need of glasses for his recently developed short sight, which he discovered when he was drilling a party of sailors who found it difficult to accept his order to march straight through a wall. The final entry on his certificate of service in the Royal Navy said that his character was very good and his ability as an Engine Room Artificer Third Class was superior. He was then invalided out of the service with a gratuity in the summer of 1928.

In eleven years he had learnt pretty well all there was to know about turbines so, after months and years of uncertainty, he had landed an extremely good job as Chief Maintenance Engineer in the spacious basements beneath a prestigious department store very near to Knightsbridge underground station. On the strength of this, he had taken out a mortgage in 1938 and bought a house in the tree-lined road in Raynes Park, where he hoped to settle for the rest of his life to grow roses, just as his father did not very far from Chatham in the years after completing his own pensionable service.

When the second war, as his generation called it, began George did not have a great deal of regret about not being called back to the Navy: a Chief Petty Officer wearing a surgical truss might be a liability in an engine room. As the conflict went on he would find his engineering skills of great value to the war effort, and his loyalty to King and country was never in question. In personal terms, the threatened destruction of life and property in the blitz was about the worst thing that could happen: George had a great deal to lose. He had not wanted to put his wife and son at risk and so he secretly congratulated Edna upon finding a way of keeping herself and the boy safe for a while as the guest of his friend Graham Patterson. When the bombing had finished, all being well, they would come home again.

Graham was older than George, who had become a close friend as well as a colleague at the department store until, at the end of what people later called the phoney war in order that his wife and twelve-year-old only son should be safe, he left to take an engineer's job at a dairy in Oxford. This carried with it a fairly good sized tied house in a short terrace in Botley Road close by. What convinced him that this was a sensible course to take had been a newspaper article that assured him that Hitler would never order the bombing of Oxford because he wanted it for the training of British Nazis after a putative successful invasion. Graham was protective of his own enough to be spurred into action by the first idea, while his patriotism denied the possibility of the latter. He had let his house in Motspur Park on an open-ended basis, intending to return there when Britannia ruled the waves and the air space again.

His friendship with George was initiated by the fact that he had also served in the Navy, though he and George had never been shipmates. His wife Joyce was an outgoing person, who was more than willing to help someone through a difficult patch in their life. A woman who looked as out of sorts as Edna did and a little lad who was so distressed as to forget his toilet training were fit objects for her genuine compassion. Alex was glad of this, though his mother, now that she had arrived where she had chosen to be, resented having to put herself under someone else's control.

IV

Alex went to sleep in a big armchair and had disturbing dreams. There had been a great deal to feed such dreams lately. The nightmare he remembered was about a London tram on fire after being bombed during an air-raid in a city street. They had trolley buses where he lived, but he had heard George telling Edna about a seeing a tram that had been hit by a bomb as he made his way along to the station from work one night. In the dream people could be seen upstairs and downstairs inside the tram, pushing to get out and having to run through flames that seemed to rise from the street itself. Like many dreams, it recurred with variations while the boy slept. After watching him shake his head with his eyes shut and hearing his little noises of distress for about ten minutes, Edna woke him up, put him beside her on the settee and cuddled him while he fell asleep to dream again. This time he was standing at night in the back garden in Raynes Park, waiting for George to open the Anderson shelter while there were noises in the sky, which Edna told him were fireworks going off, though he could not remember ever having seen real ones (This was the same idiom as she would use many years later to try to reassure a grandchild that thunder was caused by someone moving grand pianos in the sky). One of the fireworks appeared behind a large shadow and was followed by a great explosion a few streets away. Neighbours, who were also in their gardens on their way to their shelters, were asking anxiously of each other: "Ours or theirs?" or "That must have come down over Merton way!" - words which may as well have been said in Mandarin for all the sense they made to Alex both at the time and when his mind was sending them up again to disturb his traumatized sleep as a result of his painful chin. He heard the agonizingly mournful wailing sound of the air-raid siren in the final dream before he woke up and when he did, he found it metamorphosed into his mother's voice as she tried to soothe him by singing to him:

Do you want the moon the play with
Or the stars to run away with?
They'll come if you don't cry . . .'

He had never liked that song, especially its nonsensical and unbearably distressing chorus that went, 'Lulla lulla lulla lulla bye bye'. When he heard her singing it he began to cry. Great sobs came out of him and he was inconsolable while Edna became more confused and unable to be calm herself, because she too had been ground down by the same ordeals as he had in these last weeks. Joyce, with her arms round both of them together, eventually brought calm, but she realized it was the calm of exhaustion rather than recovery.

Not long afterwards, Graham came over from the dairy and his son John arrived home from school. At teatime good things were prised from carefully garnered pre-war tins and put on the table for them to eat. Joyce made sure that there was enough whisky in Edna's teacup for her to fall sound asleep in the front room after the meal, while she put Alex to bed, now self-promoted to an aunt. She made him laugh by telling him funny things and then reading to him out of a dog-eared story book found by John and illustrated with black and white line drawings of lovely trees. These images, still sombre but beautifully so, took over from the earlier ones in his mind as he fell into restorative sleep. When his mother came to her bed three hours later he was sound asleep. During the night he woke up and needed a pee. He found the china pot and gratefully relieved himself, then returned to bed and slept again. This time, his dream was of lying on the crown of a tree with his injured face held up towards therapeutic and happy sunlight.

He woke to hear his mother as she sat up in bed and took the teacup she was offered, saying to Joyce,

"How lovely it was to be able to stay in bed all night!"

The trees that lingered in his waking memory disappeared at her next sentence:

"I hope George was all right at home." Then his chin started to hurt again, only worse than before.

V

In a few days' time, with his chin getting better and his mother a little less inclined to tell him off for everything he did, Alex found he was enjoying himself. He liked his new surroundings and the family with whom Edna and he found themselves living. Edna had given Graham avuncular status towards Alex to go with his wife's new rôle. He was a stocky, jocular, easy-going man with a small moustache, grown after he had left the Royal Navy, and greased down hair, worn short in the fashion of all ex-servicemen. John emerged as admirable because his toys and games were interesting to the four-year-old, though careful prohibitions were issued about touching anything for which specific permission had not been given. Sharp words were to be said on the rare occasions when Alex did so. Nevertheless, Alex soon found in John a model to follow, being so much taller than he was, dressed smartly in his grey school suit, or casually in a sports jersey and short trousers at weekends after Saturday morning school. Alex was left to himself a good deal. The only rule issued, with terrifying sanctions attached to it, was that he should not open the front door by himself but since he could not reach the Yale lock it was of little importance to him. He was free to come and go in all the downstairs rooms and the garden where, again, only those who could reach higher than three foot eleven inches could open the back gate.

Other people's houses are just as exciting to explore as other people's bread and jam is better to eat. There were three rooms downstairs that could properly be called such, as well as a scullery off the kitchen, and a lavatory you reached by going out of the back door. There was an oblong hallway, with the stairs taking up half of it. Then, first on the right, was the front room as it was called, with the best furniture and some rich velour curtains now lined with black to comply with the air raid precautions, which were very strictly observed. The Pattersons practised such hospitality as they were able to in straitened times in this room. The next door off the passage belonged to what they called the living room, which was where most things happened around the big table and there were armchairs on either side of the fireplace. A birdcage hung near the window and a canary called Joey made his presence known at all hours of the day. Joyce talked to the bird incessantly as if he were John's baby sister. She insisted that its name was short for Josephine but Graham was well aware that it was a male bird. John was now of an age to wonder how he knew. There were two pictures hanging in this room, both landscapes, one in spring and the other in autumn, bought with a staff discount from the store's picture gallery when Graham worked there. The square carpet had seen better times, but they had had to leave their better carpets in the Motspur Park house in order to get a good rent as long as they were away from it. A single window at one end of the room looked out past the kitchen and lavatory towards the garden. The dairy buildings could be seen on the other side of a five-foot brick wall at the bottom of the garden.

Straight in front of you as you came to the end of the passage from the front door, you went down two steps and found the kitchen with a large black enamelled range on which the cooking was done and the kettle was incessantly boiling. A shift of a lever on the range would mean that you could have a bath upstairs in twenty minutes on hot days and an hour in the depth of winter. There was a table placed under the window between the scullery wall and the back door. The window looked out over the path and dividing wall to Mrs White's window, next door. The kitchen was where most meals were eaten. The range was alight on most days: a coal allowance was part of Graham's remuneration from the dairy because a great deal of it was delivered for the propulsion of the machinery and there was always some to spare, even in those days. The last room in the house downstairs was the scullery off the kitchen with a large stone sink, a concrete floor and a copper for the washing. Joyce had put a gas stove in there, which, now that there were two families to cater for, was to be used more than ever before.

Monday was a hot day for everyone because lighting the burner underneath the copper was a major task and in the time just beginning neither Joyce nor Edna was prepared to do that more than once a week. If the clothes you wanted had not been washed in this contraption on Monday, then you had to wait for them until after next wash day. Through the scullery window you could see the garden again, all down to grass with just a few flowers by next door's wall. A huge Ewbank mangle stood outside ready for use after the copper had performed its function with the soap flakes and blue bag and what seemed endless rinses. All the washing had to be mangled in between the rinses. The garden was thirty feet long, and that allowed for a single washing line between two posts to cope with one family's washing. Now that there would be more washing, the ex-naval personnel on the Saturday after the first wash-day that involved both the Pattersons and the Rylands and in anticipation of the next, rigged lines and tackle until the garden faintly resembled the shrouds of Nelson's flagship in their imaginations. In fact there was much amusement with a couple of signal flags that emerged from Graham's souvenirs at the inauguration of the lines. It was regretted that neither of the two chiefs had or knew how to use a bosun's pipe.

During the early days at the house Alex liked the garden. It was still warm enough to play outside and quite safe there. Since his mother knew he was all right, she left him to his own devices, which he liked even more. He also had an assortment of 00 gauge Hornby railway lines and rolling stock that John had grown out of, but he was not allowed to touch his valuable locomotives. There was also a small wooden tunnel and a length of station platform. Since Alex could not remember having gone to a real main line station at any time, these mysterious objects made him more imaginative than he would have been had he merely accepted them as replicas.

Upstairs was a prohibited area for him, apart from the room he slept in at first and the bathroom. This was a decision partly affected by the fact that on the second day in the house he fell down the stairs from top to bottom, crashing round the bend at the top end, and making his chin bleed again. He saw the point of this ban himself and for some days pretended to be asleep while he was being read to downstairs, all ready in his pyjamas and dressing gown, so that he would be carried up to bed when the time came. Stairs to a nervous four-year-old are not unlike a pile of sand to a stag beetle. The bedroom that he and Edna used at this time was the middle one of three. Graham and Joyce had the front one. The one at the back that looked over the garden was John's, and one morning after a night of rain, he looked out to see that his rails and carriages had not been brought in when Alex had finished with them the evening before. The next day, all they would let him have to play with outside was an old pie dish, which he filled with mud. Edna saw him from the scullery window as he was about to eat what he had imagined himself cooking with a garden trowel he had found in the unlocked shed. So they locked the shed and frowned at him.

Edna became more and more exasperated with Alex, and told George endlessly in bed about his wrongdoings, wasting precious time on the second night of the week-end by complaining, thinking that Alex was asleep. He persisted with the pretence of being asleep because his mother made him feel vulnerable with her complaints to his father. After their talking had stopped, he found it very puzzling when his parents appeared to be moving rapidly against each other. Fortunately for all three of them, he did fall properly asleep by the time he might have asked any awkward questions, and in the morning he had forgotten about it along with all his other dreams, pleasant and unpleasant alike.

On Sunday morning, the two families settled round the kitchen table for breakfast. Alex was pleased that last night's diatribes about his misconduct had not changed his father's attitude towards him. George seemed anxious to draw Alex into the conversation that went on and he did his best to respond though there was not much he could say. He listened with amusement as George gave fictitious characters to his fellow passengers on the coach on Friday night, claiming that one of them was Funf, the German spy from Tommy Handley's wireless programme. The laughter broke out and this gave Edna her cue to start gathering up the plates and cereal bowls. When all of them stood up from the table, George took Alex out into the garden and solemnly inspected the pie dish with him

Alex and Edna, with the addition of George at the weekends, expected to live in this manner for no more than a month in the autumn of 1940.

2

George had dutifully brought up thicker coats and other things they needed for colder weather as long as they were malleable enough to carry on the Black and White coach from Victoria. He stayed at a colleague's flat near the store during the week but went back to their house in Raynes Park now and again to see if all was well and collect what he could for them.

On a Thursday morning at the time of the year when a first cold chill is felt, Edna and Alex went on the bus to Elliston and Cavell's store, "Just to get out for an hour or two," as Edna told Joyce. She took Alex to the Cadena Café in the Cornmarket and they had coffee and an orange squash. The departments of the store were beginning show wartime shabbiness by now, since there was a limit to what could be sold imposed by government regulations and by the new clothing coupons. Edna went next to book seats for the variety show at the New Theatre for the Saturday matinée to which all three of them would go, leaving Graham, Joyce and John the freedom of their own house for at least half a day.

Edna realized they were just round the corner from Gloucester Green where the coach from London arrived and deposited its passengers.

"That's where your Dad will come in tomorrow night," she told her son.

Then they had walked back up to Carfax and waited for the Botley bus to return to the Pattersons' house. They went upstairs and sat in the front seat on the left. The bus had been especially built low so that it could get under the railway bridge without having its roof ripped off like the lid of a tin of sardines, which they would see happen to an ordinary sized one some time later. On this one, you went up the top of the stairs into a low trough at the right hand side and stepped up into the long seats.

Struggling all the way to the front at Alex's insistence produced irritability in his mother. As the bus went along, Alex saw the grim-looking castle keep and asked Edna for an explanation of it, which she gave but not so as to satisfy him. She was more at ease pointing out the marmalade factory and yet another 'Puffing Billy' as she called it on the station bridge with the carriages lined up at the platform. Then came Osney Bridge and the view down the stretch of water. St Frideswide's Church was duly designated by Edna as the 'house of God' and then they got up to make their way back to the stairs. They got off just past Haines's fish shop, crossed the road, and were in front of the house, when Edna suddenly stopped, making Alex, whose hand she was holding, fall backwards against her. She had seen her husband in his best suit at the front window, holding back the net curtains, waiting for her and their child to come back. He looked pale and anxious. After seeing them, he clumsily left the window and went to open the front door.

George was a few inches taller than Edna, and he put his arms right round her, reaching down to pat his son's cap saying, in as firm a voice as he could manage,

"It's gone, girl: direct hit on the back bedroom the night before last. Only the front room was still standing and there are a few bits of the furniture from there left; I got them taken to the firm's depository. The only good thing was that you were both here and I was on nights. The Anderson shelter might have kept us safe, but there was nothing left of that place we made under the stairs as an indoor shelter."

They stood together on the doorstep for what seemed a very long time to Alex until a shared handkerchief wiped the first of the tears away from his parents' faces, and they went indoors. Joyce did not disguise the whisky this time, but gave it to her friends neat. She took Alex off with her to get something from Mr Haines's, making their absence last as long as she could. However, Alex really wanted to be with his parents just then, much as he enjoyed being on his own with Auntie Joyce.

II

"What can we do to help, George?"

"I know we've probably outstayed our welcome, but can we stay on here until we can see our way forward a bit clearer, please?"

"That goes without saying," replied Joyce, having discussed it all with Graham at his workshop in the dairy when she had gone over the yard to see him there an hour before he came home.

Edna, who had gone round and round her emerging plans with George all afternoon, added, "What we mean is can we carry on as we are now?"

"Yes," put in George, "with me coming and going at week-ends and Edna and the son and heir staying here with you all the time. Put like that, it does seem as though that's a lot to ask of anybody."

"You're not asking it of anybody," replied Graham, "You and I've been friends for a good few years now since we both took a fancy to the same set of generating equipment and saw it installed together. You're asking it of Joyce and me, who have offered it anyway."

"Well . . . , thanks very much," said George, with Edna sadly nodding as the words slowly came out. "When you've lost nearly everything you owned, it is reassuring to know that people stand by you."

"I'd like to make a suggestion," said Joyce, breaking the awkward silence. "You're all three upstairs in the middle bedroom now. You need your own room at the weekends, and I expect, Edna, you don't want Alex round you all night as well as all day. So what I suggest is that we bring the divan he is sleeping on down to the living room, and he can sleep there. He goes to bed at eight, and we can come in here then and light the fire - coal isn't a problem in Graham's job, and we won't have to wake him up early in the morning because nobody goes in there until Graham has come back for his breakfast from over the yard. What do you think?"

Edna looked at Joyce gratefully and agreed to what she had said. So Joyce went on.

"Good," she said. "That will be better all round for all three of you. The only thing is that he won't have to mind Joey chirping at him when it gets light - oh, I forgot, we have to have the black-out up in there too, don't we, so it won't get light until I let the sun in after Graham's breakfast!"

George cleared his throat in embarrassment now.

"There is something else to talk about before we make too many decisions. We can't let you put us up like this without us agreeing on a proper rent."

"I thought you'd bring that up, George, knowing you," replied his friend. "Let's not talk about it as rent. This place goes with the job and with the rent from the other place, we are not doing so badly - John goes to a private school, even, don't you, son?"

"What are you paying them to teach me, then?" joked John, who, like Alex was all ears to what was being said, in spite of a show of imparting the mysteries of the draughts board.

"If we can share what the ration books entitle us to, and you put something in the kitty each week, we shall get along very well, I think," decided Graham. "We'll be eating like lords," he added, with a smile on his face and a circular motion with his hand on his girth, which was ample already under his Fair Isle pullover.

Both men had had a certain formality trained into them. They stood up and warmly shook hands. Edna sat chewing her lower lip, until Joyce came over to put her arm round her and kiss her cheek.

When he had seen his father sit down again, Alex climbed on his lap and asked him to read him a story. So, for the next half an hour, George read to everyone from the book of bedtime stories he had brought up from the still intact house on the Friday of last week. Each time George finished one of the yarns as he called them in the manner of seafarers, Alex called out for another one. George read well and everyone was attentive.

"Just one more, then that's it," George said at last.

The final tale he turned to was The Three Little Pigs. No one else remembered what was coming, but they all understood why Edna got up and left as George could not find a way of avoiding the words "I'll huff and I'll puff, and I'll blow your house down." For the sake of the youngest listener George persevered to the end of the story, thinking it was sad that Edna had not waited for the reassurance offered in the rest of it. When it was over, Graham and Joyce and John looked away as Alex put his arms round his father's neck, and was hugged back by him as he also gave way to his grief. Then he handed over his son to Joyce and went to find his wife who was sobbing in the scullery.

III

George had come a day early, and they had until Sunday evening to work out the implications of what had been decided upon. The suggestion to put the divan bed Alex slept on in the sitting room was gratefully accepted, and Graham and George carried it down on Friday afternoon before it was next needed. Alex was also provided with a little cupboard to keep his things in and a promise was exacted from him that it would be kept tidy. He liked going to bed there because the fire was still warm from earlier in the day and there was usually a warm glow reassuring enough to hold the dreams off. In fact the dreams became normal in a very short time and were not memorable at all. His recovery after the shock of the split chin was also aided by the fact that no one woke him until about half past nine when either Joyce or his mother pulled the curtains and told him his breakfast was ready in the kitchen.

This had happened only twice when his father had to go again, so as to be at work on Monday morning with the shift that began at eight. He had to be there at half past seven, whatever holes in the road Goering's airmen might have put in his way. After he had gone, Alex did not ask for stories to be read, but leafed through his books on his own. George had made sure he was generously provided with well-illustrated books and he spent a lot of time during the day trying, with some success, to copy things from them with a 2B lead pencil given him by John, which he used in preference to all the wax crayons he had received from other people. He soon understood the value of shading to achieve the effect of motion and on the occasions when he decided not to copy a picture but draw something of his own instead, using no more than component images at second hand, he found that the composition of the whole drawing was something that came naturally.

He was grieved by Edna not being particularly interested in these creations, and he carefully put them in his cupboard to show to George when he came home on Friday night, although he would not see him until Saturday. Alex knew what his father would do. He would look at the drawing, then turn it over to see if there was anything on the other side, look at it again, and say what had always been said to him when he was a boy and had achieved something of real worth: "Not bad, boy . . . Not bad at all!"

An appointment had been made to see the Pattersons' doctor about the stitches in Alex's chin. Every time Alex stood on a chair in the bathroom to clean his teeth, he noticed with relief that the bruising was less and the new plaster that Edna put on each day was becoming smaller. He was glad of this because, having been a nurse, she never worried that the unsticking would hurt while she tore the plaster off without any apology and called him a baby if he protested.

Fortunately he had no constipation such as he had been having at home because Edna was very keen on regularity. There had been days when she seemed to him to think of nothing else from Alex's point of view. He found it difficult to feel at ease with her, especially as she looked so sad all the time and would not go anywhere without him. This meant that he spent hours walking round with her whenever she decided to go out so as not to be in Joyce's way. They often went to the recreation ground on the other side of the dairy, which Alex enjoyed because a wide stream ran through the back of it and there were ducks which she did not stop him feeding so long as he did not go too close to the water. If he did, an interminable cry of "Don't fall in, will you?" was set up. Edna certainly adopted the Mosaic principle in bringing up her little boy: it was as though 'Thou shalt not' was held up on a placard before him on all necessary occasions - and on many unnecessary ones as well as it seemed to him.

These conditions led to Alex preferring his own company. Apart from the special circumstances of that first evening on which they knew about the house being bombed, John always had his homework to do in the hour before Alex went to bed, so Alex spent the time very happily leafing through a pile of Meccano Magazines that John had been collecting every week since he was nine. The illustrations fascinated Alex. He did not understand the models to be built, because he did not yet know what Meccano was, but there were endless illustrations of locomotives and the recently new rolling stock for the electrified Southern Railway. He found he could read some of the captions to the photographs, having looked at the text his father was reading to him at bedtime for as long as he could remember. He often helped Alex do this by running his finger along the line as he read it to him. So 'An L.N.E.R 2 - 4 - 0 leaving King's Cross drawing carriages in their new livery' would be hieroglyphics he could almost decipher for himself, though he had no idea what a livery might be or what the numbers stood for. He knew what L.N.E.R. was, because it had been explained to him that the country was divided up into four areas by the major railway companies, which was why most people could not get where they were going in time, even without the harassment of an enemy. As has been said earlier, he had never been on a main line train, but he liked these illustrations.

There were many occasions when either Joyce or Edna accompanied housework with listening to the wireless. They listened to songs from which they then sang snatches. Edna's favourite was 'Stormy Weather' which she alternated with 'On the Sunny Side of the Street' and the appeal of both of these to her was obvious. One stated the problem:

'My guy and I ain't together.
Keeps rainin' all the time,'

while the other suggested an antidote:

'Get your coat and get your hat,
Leave your troubles on the doorstep . . .'

Which partly explained this endless traipsing round she did with her diminutive companion in tow.

A good deal of the time, however, Alex could be found listening to the wireless by himself when it was left switched on for him in the living room. It occurred to him that most of the songs he heard were curiously sad and the contemporary pre-Sinatra way of singing added to the sense of depression he received from them. A recent hit like 'A Nightingale Sang in Berkeley Square' was one that particularly catered for this black mood. He once caused Joyce much consternation when she came into the room as one of these songs finished and, not knowing he was overheard, said out loud, "Oh, how sad everything is!" He had thought he had no one except the canary to talk to at that point, so he was a ready listener to his own opinions. Often he expressed what he was thinking to Edna, who told him not to 'air his knowledge', and he did not understand what she meant. She had a terror of precocious children and feared that she had given birth to one.

One survivor of the bombing was real treasure for Alex. George had served on a light cruiser, H.M.S. Danae, which once went on circumnavigation of the globe in a special service squadron – George enjoyed saying that - showing the White Ensign to as many as wanted to see it. The newly built H.M.S. Hood was the squadron's flagship. The commemorative photograph album for this was a thick book with blue velvet covers and the pictures that George had chosen at the time were stuck on black card with handwritten captions in white ink in a neater hand than his. Alex spent hours with this album, looking at group photos of the whole ship's company posed beneath the guns of the main armament, or of the captain and commander, complete with telescopes under their arms and their heads clamped to their bodies with great high collars. There were snapshots of places where the ship had called in. Others showed his father and one of his friends with a wallaby they brought on board at Melbourne as a mascot. George told him it slept in his hat box and used to chew the strings of his hammock. It was put ashore at Sydney in consideration of its own health as well as the well-being of George's mess deck. Both back in Raynes Park and now in Oxford, George was always pleased when he saw Alex with the book and would sit down with him and reminisce. There were incongruous pictures of George in his number one uniform riding a donkey up a mountain in China, or posing beneath exotic trees in Dar-es-Salaam, or as a passenger in a rickshaw with a friend called Frank Collins - always known incomprehensibly as 'Jumper' - who, with his wife, shared a flat in Valetta with George and Edna for a happy year when they were not away at sea.

He would say, “Ah! Adelaide, that’s where all the flappers tried to take the gilt buttons off our summer jackets,” and Alex, who knew his cue well after a few times, would reply, “What’s a flapper, Dad?”

George would never make this comment if Edna was not there, because he always enjoyed her saying, “Harrumph! While I was back in Malta wondering what you were up to!” The question Alex had asked was never answered owing to the amusement this regular pleasantry caused his parents even in their present distress. A few years later, Alex found out what a flapper was from his father’s younger brother, back from spending the war years in a dockyard in Ceylon; he taught him a song, which included the verse:

‘Ruth, she was a flapper of a very modern type.
She wore short skirts and rode a motorbike.
She wore an awful lipstick, and her eye was of the glad,
But the Salvation Army saved her from the bad.’

It lightened the load, that souvenir album, in their involuntary exile. In later life, Alex regretted that it disappeared when Edna died, along with a good many other reminders of his father.

IV

The arrangement with Alex sleeping in the sitting room worked fairly well, though there were occasions in the early days when Joyce could not leave him asleep because she found she had left something vital in the cupboard by the fireplace, and the bird cascaded its song all over her as she tried to find it. When she had gone and the room was in darkness again, it continued to make disconsolate chirps until the blinds were drawn back and the reality of daytime was incontrovertible.

One morning in his second week of sleeping there it was Edna who woke him up and told him to get dressed quickly because they were going out. She helped him into his shorts and jersey in haste and then took him up for a wash in a manner that was none too gentle. After he had sat down at the table, she remembered that he had not used the lavatory as she always insisted on him doing when he first got out of bed, and dragged him to the outside one despite the cold, telling him to hurry up.

He was only just given time to eat his piece of toast and dripping and his spoonful of government-sponsored thick orange juice (war-time fare for giving strength) when he was bundled into his coat and made to run holding Edna's hand to the bus stop. Once they were on the bus, he said to Edna,

"You haven't changed my plaster this morning."

"You won't need it much longer," she replied.

"Why not?"

"Oh, I didn't want to tell you where we are going in case it worried you. You are going to have the stitches out if you must know."

The cause of all the bad temper was that Edna had overslept after arranging the appointment with Joyce's doctor who had her practice in Holywell Street, for half past nine and, if they missed the ten past bus to the city centre, they would be late for it. Edna had lost her ability to organize things since she had been uprooted from her home. She was never very keen on motherhood. Now its nuisance value was becoming more and more apparent to her. This was having a deleterious effect on Alex, she noticed, because he was often morose when he was with her. She found there was nothing she could do about it and all her attempts to be kind to him were artificial even in her own eyes. She needed George to prop her up, and he had to be in London because he had to earn their living. She knew that there were plenty of women managing by themselves, like Joyce's neighbour Mrs Wilson, who was bringing up her two girls on her own because her husband was in the regular army: he had been allowed home for a few days after getting back from Dunkirk, but was now heavily involved in training men who had been called up and she never knew when she would see him. Even so, after all the years of going without, Edna and George had had a comfortable way of life in a place they had chosen for themselves - and it had all been snatched away by this awful war.

She let her resentment fall on Alex as he sat on the seat beside her. Looking at the top of his head, she did not stop herself thinking, "If it weren't for you and your split chin, perhaps I could have prevented our home being destroyed; or if George and I had been at home, we could have stopped the worst effects of the bombing and had something more to rebuild."

Self-recrimination is often sterile, but Edna found it impossible not to give way to a measure of self-pity now. She had become a lodger in someone else's house and she did not like it. She was thirty-eight years old, had been married for sixteen years and had thought her lodging-house days were over. Her reverie continued all the way until the bus conductor called out, "Magdalen Bridge anybody?" and she returned to awareness of her whereabouts, bundling Alex off on to the pavement where he turned his ankle on the kerb and began to cry.

"This is all I need," she muttered, and made a hasty attempt to dry his eyes with her handkerchief. When she rang the doctor's doorbell she was two minutes late. The fact that the waiting room was full and they had to wait an hour did not make up for anything. It was hard to keep such a fidgety child quiet in a room full of mainly elderly people. She would have preferred to believe that they were the kind of solid provincial citizens who saw evacuees like her and her child as a threat to their well-being, whereas most of them were simply concerned for the little boy with a plaster on his chin and signs of recent crying. They kept smiling at him and at his mother.

Edna's prejudice about the people in the waiting room was coloured to a great extent by something that Joyce had told her a few days before. Apparently it was common knowledge that the Majestic Cinema further up the road from where they were now living had ceased showing films when war broke out, and had become filled with evacuee mothers and their children from the East End of London. It was being said that there were getting on for a thousand of them in there and the stink from the doors was terrible because all they had in the way of washing and lavatory facilities were those provided for cinema-goers. Many children had contracted head lice as a result and the women had given up on basic cleanliness. They had nowhere else to seek shelter and it was said that the local people shunned them and offered them nothing in the way of help or comfort. What made Edna more resentful was that if any of the East-enders had come looking for shelter in SW20, she would have reacted with the same kind of respectable apprehension as the people up the road had - and yet she was sharing the fears that had made her an evacuee in Oxford too. Edna made attempts at self-composure, but did not respond to anybody in the waiting room who tried to open a conversation with her.

Alex found that the pile of old copies of Country Life contained pictures from outside the range of his imagination, but went through a good many of the magazines because he did not want to talk any more than his mother did. When he did sit still, as he was constantly being told to do in a loud whisper, he found he was interested in the elegance of the room with its oddly pointed windows, its blue and white decor and two large lumps of shiny, flecked stone with the oddest handles coming out of the top them on either side of the fireplace.

He was deeply considering the possible uses of these when the receptionist called out, "Master Alexander Ryland." He did not recognize that as his own name and it took a long time for it to register with Edna. The woman was about to pass on to the next name on her list when realization dawned and Edna stood up, took Alex's hand and dragged him into the consulting room where the skirts of a large white coat over thick stockings at a desk was all he could see at first. Then the elderly head above it and eyes behind gold-rimmed glasses loomed down over him and a voice, later discovered to be Scottish, said, "Oh, little man, we'll soon have those wretched things out for you. Would you take that seat, Mrs Ryland, while I see to your brave boy."

Alex did not consider himself to be brave: that was a word that Alvar Liddell and other announcers on the wireless news used about soldiers, sailors and airmen, and he soon discovered that he was not. The doctor's hand ripped away the plaster with even greater energy than his mother did, and set about cutting the stitches with some oddly shaped scissors before pulling them out of his face. After six loud protestations by Alex, which made Edna wince, the doctor said, "There! That didn't hurt at all, did it?" and Alex said, "Yes, it did," but nobody took any notice. Then, to his surprise, the doctor put a new plaster on, "To keep it clean, you see."

After a few hortatory words to Edna, the doctor opened the door and said, "I shall not need to see him again. It's all healing very well," and mother and son were ushered into the street by the receptionist before Alex could ask what those weird stones in the fireplace were. He asked Edna, but she did not know and was in no mood for such questions in any case.

They were soon in Broad Street, and Edna made her way to the end of New Inn Hall Street past the theatre where they had gone on Saturday afternoon.

"We can walk home from here," she said, and they did eventually, after Alex wanted to go to the lavatory, which meant retracing their steps all the way back to the Ladies in the centre of St Giles: an underground structure full of polished brass and white tiles which impressed him greatly as it provided him in his imagination with a vision of the engine rooms on board ship that his father talked about to him. How he did miss his father - and worried about him too. Even a four-year-old knows what happens when large buildings are knocked down with people in them and

George spent his working days underneath one such large building. Alex could not persuade himself that bombers were only active during the night and had forgotten that George was often doing maintenance work in the store at the time the Luftwaffe infested the skies over London.

He was very tired when he was at last brought home and made a decision that remained with him for life over the lunch that Joyce set before him. He would not eat fish however many of the children who were starving in China would like to have it instead of him. He did not know where China was and did not know any of the children who lived there. He did remember other children though, with whom he used to play in the quiet street from time to time at home, and gave himself some solace by thinking about them. There was the boy a little older than himself who one day, at the end of a game of oranges and lemons, brought out an axe from his father's shed, coinciding with the chant, and advanced towards Alex, making great slashes with it as the others all sang:

'Here comes the candle to light you to bed:

'Here comes the chopper to chop off your head!' which would have become a reality if Edna had not seen what was happening through the front room window and rushed out to protect him. Afterwards, she went to denounce the aggressive boy to his parents.

Edna now wanted to send Alex to bed as a punishment for refusing good food and offending Joyce; Alex wanted to go to bed himself because he was tired out after the walking he had been made to do and Joyce wondered whether she had done the right thing in being so generous as to take her husband's friend's wife and child in. However, there was no bed for him to go to because Joyce had lit a fire in the living room for herself and Edna to sit by and so he went out into the garden and told himself how unhappy he was for a good hour until it was too cold to remain there. Towards evening, he was told off again when it was found that he had pulled several ferns out of the earth where they grew under the living room window. His defence that he thought they might have been weeds cut no ice with his Medusa of a mother. She would have preferred a stone child at that point. Garden gnomes don't tear up other people's plants.

V

George was late in his arrival that weekend. He had left the store behind time and had missed the coach he usually caught in the early evening. He found there was another one at nine o'clock and when it came in at Victoria Coach Station he sat on it to read the newspaper and doze off. The air-raid warning sounded but he did not want to lose his seat and did not go to the shelter as some of the other passengers did. The raid was close by and the blast damaged the glass roof of the coach station. When he did get to Oxford in the middle of the night, he was still very alarmed indeed. He kept on telling his wife and his friends who had anxiously waited up for him, how he had sat there listening to the glass crashing down onto and around the coach, wondering if this was where he was going to meet his end. When the all-clear sounded he had lent a hand to sweep a path for the coach to get out on to the road. He tried to repeat the story again and again and it took a drink-induced sleep to make him calm down.

By the morning the memory of his fear had become an exciting story to tell his son and, having sensed that Edna would like a break from looking after Alex, he decided that he would take him out for a walk. He asked Graham to tell him a pleasant route that would occupy an hour or two. Graham suggested Binsey Lane as far as the Perch and the river, so he got Alex into his coat and cap and, at Edna's insistence, put on the woollen leggings she made him wear over his short trousers and socks to keep him warm. They buttoned up at the sides of his legs causing them to fit tightly and Alex's own protestations that they itched were ineffective. George put on his long black overcoat and took his bowler hat from the peg on the hall stand and off they went.

The outward journey was amusing. George had things to tell Alex, and Alex had things to ask George. It was George who cleared up the mystery of the large stones with handles in the doctor's fireplace by explaining that they were curling stones used on frozen ponds in a Scottish sport. He knew this because of going ashore at Rosyth once during a short visit by courtesy of Grey Funnel Line. That led to a long explanation of the difference between the colour used on home fleet ships and those, which were painted in the more comely Mediterranean Grey, and how captains of ships in time past had been responsible themselves for having their ships painted. It was on this walk that Alex first heard of Nelson, the British admiral with an eye and an arm missing who in spite of his disabilities had destroyed the sea power of someone called Bonaparte who ruled France a hundred and fifty years ago, and about someone called Pétain who had taken power in part of France now and whose ships had also been sunk by the Royal Navy in order to keep them out of German hands in a port with the intriguing name of Mers-el-Kebir. Alex noticed that George's delivery of these lengthy pieces of information made him a little out of breath. When Alex commented on this, George replied, "Yes. I'm getting a bit like the guide who used to be at Rochester Castle when we used to go there as boys: if anyone asked him a question, he had to start his speech all over again because he had learned it by heart and couldn't stop in the middle of it without forgetting what he was saying"

"Did you learn all that about Nelson by heart, Dad?" asked Alex.

"I suppose I did when I first learnt it." George replied. "You heard the bit about Marshal Pétain and the ships at Oran for yourself on the news, though, didn't you?"

"Where's Oran?"

"On the northern coast of Africa in a country called Algeria which has been a French colony for more than a century."

Then followed explanations about what colonies were, and how Great Britain had many of them and therefore needed a strong navy, which was now being eclipsed by American sea power . . .

When Alex became tired, George took off his bowler hat and lifted him onto his shoulders to carry him part of the way. The hat was entrusted to Alex's safe-keeping for this, although George was a little anxious that it should not get out of shape at his son's hands. After a quarter of an hour, George asked Alex if he felt like walking again.

"No, but I will," he said, and he was lifted higher before being put down. "These leggings do itch. Can't I take them off, Dad?"

"No. Your mother told me expressly to keep them on you, so it's more than my life's worth to let you take them off."

"Will she know?"

"You can't keep secrets from her, you ought to know that!"

So the leggings and the itch stayed, but a huge glass of squash was set before him on a seat outside the Perch and George set a pint glass before himself on the table before them.

"I bet this tastes better than that," said Alex.

"Try it, then," said his father. After one mouthful Alex said he had not had enough to make up his mind and after three reserved his public judgement, glad that his father had treated him as an equal.

When they began to feel the cold they got up to go. The way to the river led past a patch of open ground where the landlord of the Perch was keeping some geese for eggs at present and for the table later on. One of the huge birds came towards Alex and began to peck the buttons of his leggings. This was frightening at first but became very amusing after a while. In the end George pulled him away, the goose tired of unrewarding pecking, and father and son thought holy thoughts as they looked into Godstow Abbey ruins before going home.

The way home was very long and very slow. George decided to go ahead as far as he could, at one point hoping that Alex would increase his speed. When he did not he had to go back for him. George exhorted him more than once with variations on, "I thought you were coming for a walk with me, not a sail in line astern!" Alex caught up but was fast asleep in George's arms by the time they turned the corner into the dairy yard to find the back gate. Alex was wearing both his cap and his father's bowler, the latter well down over his eyes. He fell asleep again over the apple pie that finished lunch so, since the adults were going to spend the afternoon before the front room fire, Edna laid him on his bed still asleep.

VI

Christmas was coming. "I feel sorry for the poor buggers in the Midlands," Edna announced after the Home Service news one dinnertime had reported that industrial centres there were being bombed. Alex was bound to ask who these poverty stricken people might be and was once more unsatisfied with Edna's answer. Joyce did not help by saying that the other word he asked about meant "souls" in this instance.

George was home (as it now was) for the best part of a week around Christmas. He had brought things with him about which he was very secretive, and discovered to every one's amusement (or not, depending on the time of day) that he could still whistle in spite of his full dentures and did so with great determination. One morning Alex found him in the garden with his jacket buttoned up over his thick cardigan, a scarf round his neck and his hat on, completing the picture by wearing one of Edna's pinafores and sitting on a kitchen chair on an old sheet found for him by Joyce, plucking three diminutive chickens one after the other. The whistling prevented the smaller feathers getting into his mouth as he worked, but they either settled on every feature of his attire with very few actually reaching the sheet beneath him or blew about in the wind before sticking to the rough wood of the fence, the frost-damp rollers of the mangle and the decaying weeds in the flower bed beside it. Afterwards feathers grew in the garden for several days until Graham decided he really must get rid of them before anyone looking over the wall from the dairy yard asked awkward questions about where the birds had come from and how they had been obtained.

George brought the naked and headless creatures into the kitchen and began the grisly task of removing the giblets. He whistled once more in order to avoid the expected stench and Alex, who had watched the process so far with enormous interest, withdrew when he discovered for the first time what the inside of a chicken smelled like. It reminded him of a morning about a week ago when he had evaded Edna's demands that he should "do his duty" and to her unexpected amusement, considering her disciplinarian stance in these matters, he had broken wind spectacularly, provoking her to comment, "Good Lord, Alex! It's as though something had crept up you and died!" Luckily he had forgotten this foul aspect of the preparation of the chicken when he came to eat his Christmas dinner.

When the great day came, Alex could not remember having had chicken to eat before or having had a taste of a drink that the others called Sauternes. There was a Christmas pudding too: "We aren't going to let a man with only one ball dictate to us what we eat at Christmas!" Graham said as he emptied the last of a bottle of pre-war brandy over it in the dark and Alex imagined the entire German nation unable to play more than one game of football or tennis at any given time. He had been shown Germany on the map in John's school atlas and was worried because, instead of being on the other side of the world as he had supposed since they had to use aeroplanes to bring bombs from it, it was not very far away after all. His gloomy thought was interrupted as the lighted match set off the blue flame of the burning brandy and a general cheerfulness broke out.

After dinner, everyone went to the front room where there was a good fire and the blackout was already up at half past three. Alex's present from George and Edna turned out to be better than any toy he had had before. He watched his father assemble it for him on the floor, for which transaction a fairly large space had to be cleared. None of the presents given and received that year in that house had wrapping paper on account of the war effort but the store still had a toy department with a good deal of stock in it and a long cardboard box from which all labels had been removed was duly opened for the components of Alex's present to emerge one by one. George had been through the box before and arranged its contents so that they would come out in an order that would heighten the sense of wonder. First there was a circular piece of metal with a central socket which was put down as a base, then an upright, nine or ten inches high, with a bracket at the top of it. Next a longer metal bar was produced, with a bracket two-thirds along its length to be fixed horizontally so that it swivelled round on the upright. A weight was attached to the shorter end.

"This is the tricky bit," said George, as he connected a wire with a small screwdriver from the still vacant end of the horizontal bar through the swivel where the two bars met, to run down to the floor inside the upright, whence it was led away to a large battery at a distance. Alex was attentive to every move and he could not guess in advance what would happen next.

"Now for the thing itself!" said George, and he produced from the bottom of the box something carefully concealed in a piece of cloth. He took the cloth off as if he were a magician and revealed a model aeroplane made of light metal. George explained that it was a fixed wing monoplane and he rapidly attached it to the vacant end of the horizontal bar by means of two nuts and bolts with the aid of a diminutive spanner beside which his engineer's fingers seemed gigantic. The last job was to connect everything to a switch that he had fixed to a small piece of wood to keep it steady.

"There," he said, "Now all keep back and we'll see if it works."

Alex was told to come over to where the switch was and to take hold of the small knob in one hand and steady the piece of wood with the other.

"That's right. Now switch on!"

Alex did, and squealed delightedly as the propeller on the little aeroplane began to rotate and take it round the central pillar in a circle until it was going fast enough to leave the ground and fly, balanced by its counterweight.

The flying hours of that monoplane were countless. It flew for the best part of the next hour and it was brought out at least once a day well into 1941, still making appearances when anyone remembered to obtain a new battery for it for several years after that.

However, George had not finished. At five o'clock he asked Alex to turn the aeroplane off and gently dismantled it, putting it in its box and explaining to Alex how he would be able to get it out for himself on subsequent occasions. Then he, Graham and John moved all the chairs to the side of the room opposite the front window. The table had been brought in from the living room after the washing-up had been completed and was now moved forward to allow George to stand behind it in front of the curtains. Then he asked everybody to close their eyes and not to open them until he said so. All obeyed, including Alex, and they waited while they heard George moving about behind the table.

"All right. Open your eyes now!"

There on the table was a beautiful model theatre. John switched off the light in the room. A string was pulled and the curtain went up to reveal a lit stage with scenery and a frenetically dancing harlequin. The curtain descended and rose up again and this time there was Mr Punch. With Graham behind the table as well, four characters were possible: Mrs Punch, the policeman, the baby and the crocodile all appeared in turn and the script was read out by two distorted voices by the light of a torch held by a clamp in a stand constructed for the purpose. Everybody joined in at "That's the way to do it!" and it did not occur to them that there was any cruelty involved in Mr Punch's violence. George's own voice then announced an interval, and a tray of drinks was produced from behind the table with something appropriate for everyone present.

Then, after ten minutes, George and Graham were ready to present two figures in ballet costume for a version of a pas-de-deux, with the music played by the two fathers on kazoos. The curtain fell and rose again and as a finale Harlequin appeared once more to wish all present a prosperous New Year and, God willing, more peaceful times. The curtain descended and rose for the last time and then the two controllers of the straight wires that supported each of the cardboard figures with knotted joints produced a curtain call appearance of the whole cast amid the acclamations of all four in the audience. Alex was making most favourable comparisons between this show and the ones he had seen on his Saturday visits to the New Theatre.

To maintain the magic, Joyce ushered everyone to the kitchen on a pretext all understood except Alex, while the two men quickly took the component parts of the theatre upstairs and restored the front room to its normal state except for the large table. The reason for leaving the room was to pick up little cakes, which were then brought back on plates and eaten. Christmas was kept until ten o'clock, by which time Alex was dozing off and bedtime was decreed.

VII

In their room, George and Edna reviewed the day

"Thank you for this dress, George. I like it very much indeed."

"I'm glad you do. You look nearly as good in it as without it."

"Go on! Don't start all that: these walls are very thin."

"Thank you for these gloves, too. Just what I need for those cold nights on the coach when the heater fails, as it usually does just past High Wycombe. And this tie is just what I like."

"I'm sorry there wasn't more. They were very strict about clothing coupons in the shops here."

"A bit of black market comes in handy from time to time if you know the right contacts!"

"And you must've to get a silk dress like this!"

She gave one last twirl before she took it off and carefully hung it up. George wished she wouldn't wear corsets. Gone were the days when she ran to fat and her friends called her "Pudding" or "Pud" (to rhyme with mud) for short. Since they had come here she had lost a good deal of weight and her jet-black hair had begun to go grey, "To match mine," he thought to himself.

"I haven't seen Alex so happy for a long time," she said to him with a lot of feeling. "He really enjoyed the aeroplane, didn't he? And the theatre: those lights you made for it were marvellous."

"It's wonderful what a lot of torch bulbs in the right sockets can do!" he modestly replied. "But what about your curtain? That was the best bit!"

"You must take the credit for getting hold of the theatre itself, though. I bet it cost a pretty penny."

"It did, but not so bad with staff discount. Anyway, the best thing was seeing his face through the proscenium arch!"

"The what arch?"

Then the mood of happiness suddenly evaporated. The strain of what had happened overcame them and making their own necessary preparations in isolation from each other they quietly got into bed with their teeth out, after switching off the light and drawing the blackout back a little so as to be able to breathe. There was not much difference between age of this house and its outlook and the one they had lost. That one, however, had been their own, not a friend's like this one, nor tied up with someone's job. They missed the quiet and the trees. This house was on a main road with buses often passing and an increasing amount of military traffic. An odious comparison between the houses was always being summoned up in their minds.

"At least we're all three alive," said George, trying to take a positive line against his present disposition. "We must see what the solicitor has been able find out about the possibility of rebuilding number seventy-four."

But a great sadness had taken over in Edna, and all she could do in reply was take his hand in both hers to hold it desperately.

3

In the New Year things went on very much the same. The air raid warning sounded in Oxford when the Luftwaffe was making its way to bomb the midland cities. George and Graham often burst out into verbal imitations hostile to Hitler, balanced by imitations supportive towards Churchill. When John, who was still too young to see the point of this, tried to imitate the King's stutter, the adults thought what he did was in very bad taste:

"The poor man can't speak very confidently at the best of times, but he does try to rally us, and I think he has," said Joyce.

In time, when the penny dropped on the patriotic nature of these imitations, John took over for himself the stereotyped schoolboy's Hitler imitation, which involved strutting about in a goosestep with the first finger of his left hand held under his nose and his right hand aloft. Since the only German word John knew was "Achtung", that was spluttered out many times, mixed in with a great deal of gibberish which must have made Goethe and Schiller turn in their graves. John's school had gone for xenophobia full steam ahead. Nobody said "Nazis" anymore. It was always "Germans". Under Graham's roof no objection was raised to that. On the contrary, Alex time and time again heard his parents and his adoptive uncle and aunt talk about "unfinished business from twenty years ago", which was a very dark saying to him and raised the question whether you had to have a world war like this every couple of decades.

The two sailors were wrapped in grief and mourned the loss of H.M.S. Hood with very nearly her entire ship's company. On the Saturday in May after it happened, George told Alex to go and get the World's Cruise book. He opened it at the picture of the battle cruiser that had been the flagship and pride of the Special Service Squadron. She was a magnificent ship and George wept for her loss as he sat there with the book on his knee. He thought of the men in the engine room, such as he would have been if he had still been in the service, not a few of whom would be his age. He thought bitterly of several men he knew from way back who were at risk now. Alex watched and thought he nearly understood. George quietly remarked that many of them must be at sea with the knowledge that their wives and children were living where the bombs were falling. He was glad to know from his father and mother who still lived near Chatham that not much was happening there in the way of bombing but news reports of much of Portsmouth being totally destroyed were very frightening - and the Hood was a Portsmouth ship.

On Sunday afternoon the two fathers and their sons went up to Graham's allotment to see if the runner beans were above ground. As they stood there they heard the faint noise of aero engines and looked up to see an aeroplane, which John identified with the help of a small book he always carried, as a Witley bomber. Its progress across the sky was so very slow and George became reflective.

"That plane is like us," he said. "We are digging for victory and using Shanks's pony and our clothing coupons and ration books, accepting shortages and blackout, and we haven't started to fight back yet."

"Don't forget we did sink the Bismarck," said Graham. "They're not having it all their own way." The pessimist in George still thought the worst was about to happen, only for Graham to assume the part of the optimist who reckoned that it already had.

Alex, nevertheless, accepted the presence of runner bean shoots three inches in the air above the ground as his symbol. They had looked very inert as mere beans a little while ago, yet the sticks had been put up in the expectation that the plants growing from them would be as tall as a man before very long.

There wasn't much to do on the allotment now. Some desultory draws were given with a Dutch hoe along the ranks of potatoes around the shoots that were showing above ground. Graham fairly quickly made two drills and put some broad beans in and then all four of them simply stood there in the calm light hoping for better things, but not expecting too much. The reverie lasted until John told his father he was getting hungry and they walked home. Each father and son formed a pair to go out of the field which had been divided up to provide the allotments and along Helen Road with its terraced houses on either side towards the main thoroughfare. As they passed the open outer doors of the chapel on the corner they heard a hymn being sung.

"What are they doing in there?" Alex asked George.

"You can hear. They're singing."

"Why are they singing?"

"Because it's Sunday."

"But we don't sing on Sundays like that. Why should they?"

"Because they believe that if they sing hymns it will be pleasing to God."

"Why should God be pleased if they sing hymns? It sounds awful to me."

"It does to me, too. Come on, don't let's hang around here any more, or they'll be coming out and asking us to join in."

"Would they really do that? "

"Come on, will you? Shake your feathers!"

Alex did move along but he was not going to let the question go.

"I can't see why, because they believe in God, they have to sing hymns." Then came his real question:

"Do you believe in God, Dad?"

George realized that there was no smart answer to this that would let him off his son's hook. Now that they were out of range of the singers and very near home he stopped. He thought carefully about his answer. His response to his son was: "I don't know whether there's a God or not. But I do know that when you're at sea with a mile or so of water between you and the bottom, you hope there is." His own private thought was that there was more than one kind of sea.

With that he took the last two strides to join Graham at the front gate and went indoors. Alex heard Graham say to George as he went out of the back door to go to the lavatory,

"I thought you answered that well. Who said being a father was easy?"

II

Fresh eggs had become hard to get. Edna asked discreet questions of her new acquaintances and neighbours about where a plentiful supply of new-laid ones might be available. Gossip among the women she was getting to know, backed up by the information channelled towards her by Joyce, led to hard information and her quest narrowed to an out of the way chicken farm at Old Marston. On a showery day she poured Alex into his coat and pulled a hat with flaps down over his ears before leading him out to the bus stop. Alex's own view of this was that she had perforce to lead him because he could only see the ground a few feet in front of him until she realized that in covering his ears she had covered his eyes as well. He consoled himself with the idea that at least there was no need now for the itchy leggings she made him wear in the winter.

There was not much room downstairs when the bus came along and Edna decided not to see if there was more room on the upper deck. She found a seat for herself next to a young woman wearing slacks and a scarf as a turban who was smoking a cigarette despite all the notices to the contrary on the lower deck, unseen or ignored by the bus conductor. Alex was dragged on to Edna's lap and she held him tight around his waist to keep him in place since the lack of room between Edna's bunched up overcoat and the next seat made his slipping down to the floor in front of her a strong likelihood. She held him in place with the aid of her old shopping bag, which he noticed was made out of quilted patches. Many of the stitches that should have held the patches together had split apart from one another. It seemed that the perpetrator of his discomfort had found an accomplice at the same time as he squirmed round to complain to her, because a tube of smoke issued from the double mound of lipstick six inches beneath the turbaned scarf and met his nostrils, giving him an unwelcome share of the young woman's breath and second-hand tobacco smoke. His unrestrained coughing embarrassed Edna, who began apologising to her fellow passenger. Alex considered his mother's words to be unfair, since the woman should be apologising to him.

When the bus reached the station, the young woman stood up, asking Edna to excuse her while she got off. Edna took away the bag, picked Alex up, stationed him violently in the gangway, and stood herself to let her out. When Alex rushed to take her seat by the window, Edna sat down again close to him, still seeming to him to think it better if he were wedged into his seat by her full-skirted coat and the weight of her body. His intention had been to look out of the window but it was steamed up, and Edna told him off for wiping the moisture away, claiming that this would put indescribable filth on his hand which would soon make his way to his lungs and stomach to cause incurable illness.

It was a relief to change buses in the city, involving a short walk along the High Street and a wait outside one college and opposite another.

"These places aren't houses, are they?" he said.

"No," said Edna.

"They aren't shops either, are they?"

"No."

"Are they offices?"

"No."

"What are they, then?"

"Oh, do stop asking me things," said Edna, and immediately thought better of it. She told him, "They are Oxford colleges."

"I know this is Oxford," he said, "But what's a college?"

Edna gave up worrying about George's absence and not being able to return to Raynes Park. She tried to furnish a reply.

"It's a place where rich young men come to study after they leave school."

"Why are colleges only for rich young men?"

"Because it costs a lot of money to study in one of these places."

"What does 'study' mean?"

"It means reading a lot of dry books and talking posh and going to lectures."

She realized then that she might have to cope with providing meanings for all the three terms she had used and was relieved when all he said was, "That's funny. Why do the books they read have to be dry? I suppose it's because if you drop a book in water you can't turn the pages very easily."

This was a scientific observation based on an experiment of his own which had upset him some days earlier in the garden, involving the old pie dish again.

Edna was very glad to see the bus crawling towards them and said remarkably gently, "No more questions now. Let's get ready to get on." This process involved lifting him up to the height of her waist where he was buffeted by her handbag from one side and completely blinded as the shopping bag found its place in front of his mouth and was sucked over his face. Once on the bus he regained his sight and during the uneventful journey out of the city that followed few words were spoken by either of them. Edna planned her strategy for her first foray into illegitimate food purchases, which necessitated bringing her growing child with her in order to excite the poultry farmer's sympathetic feelings, instead of leaving him at home with Joyce. Alex considered the likelihood that his father would give him a fuller explanation of what the rich young men got up to in their colleges and decided to ask him at the weekend.

Edna was surprised how easily the black marketing had been achieved as she dragged Alex back to the return bus stop, keeping the now valuable shopping bag at arm's length from her leg. She made him hold her hand so as to keep him on the pavement and he showed a dangerous tendency to disturb her balance as he skipped about at her side. As they waited, with no one else about to hear, Edna said,

"Now, listen. I don't want you to say anything about what's in this bag while we're on the bus going home."

"Why not?"

"Because you'll get me into trouble with the authorities if you do. So it will be best if we don't have any chatter at all."

Alex took her at her word and did not answer, though he would have liked to know what an authority was and why, together with others, it constituted a threat to his mother.

"Do you hear what I say?"

"Yes."

"Why didn't you answer me, then?"

"I thought you told me not to!"

Edna bit her bottom lip and hurt it to add to her problems. She was glad to see that when the single-decker bus stopped, Alex had enough sense to take hold of the rail and step on to it by himself.

Edging her fragile and precious bag in front of her, she followed Alex to the only vacant seat, and motioned him to take a place by her as she sat down.

"You'll have to stand in the gangway," she whispered in his ear.

"I don't want to," he muttered.

"Keep quiet now. Remember what I said."

Edna did a balancing trick with shopping bag, handbag and purse to pay the fare while the bus conductor patted Alex's cap, thereby depriving him of sight for the third time that morning. Alex took his cap off. Edna wanted him to put it on again lest he dropped it and it got dirty, but remembered in time that she had enjoined silence upon him and kept quiet herself.

He was only four and was weary with travel and frustration at not having his questions answered to his satisfaction. He was puzzled by mystery being created round such an apparently simple thing as buying three dozen eggs. He longed to sit down. There were no free seats so, despite her whispered and frantic protests, he climbed on her lap and sat on the shopping bag, hearing the cracking of the shells and Edna's furious gasp, "Oh, bugger!"

Alex saw the amused pity in the eyes of the woman in the other half of the seat. Edna felt the slimy wetness penetrating her coat and skirt and stockings and neither mother nor son said anything for the rest of the lengthy, miserable journey.

Edna found getting off the bus very difficult indeed since she could not avoid egg white and pierced yolk dripping from the bag and from beneath her coat as she went uncomfortably along the bus. She left Alex to make his own way to the pavement, while he was hoping that he would never see her again.

He let her catch up with him soon and because she did not want to foul another bus seat beneath the gaze of fellow travellers she dragged him on foot all the way home from the city centre. Since she still did not want anyone else to know about her nefarious purchase, she said under her breath while she spread the tears on her face with her free hand,

"You silly little fool. Why did you have to sit on my lap? I told you about the eggs and how awkward it would be if anybody found out that I had them. Now they're still dripping all over the pavement and people can see what I've got here and I'll have to take my clothes to be cleaned and the cleaners will see what has happened and wonder where I got the eggs from, besides the fact that my crutch is all wet and sticky - and it's all because of you, you silly little fool!"

"You only told me to keep quiet. You didn't say anything about not sitting on your lap!"

"But I told you there were eggs in the bag and you know that eggs break when you sit on them!"

"I've never sat on one before," he replied and felt her hand in full force on his ear so that he wished he still had his cap on.

He said no more and Edna kept her thighs as far from each other as possible as she went forward, dragging Alex behind her, exciting the interest of those whom they passed with the wet shopping bag dripping alongside her. What they noticed more, however, was the exasperated expression on the face of the limping woman with a wet and slimy coat, whose little boy seemed to share her grief. Fortunately, they were of a mind to pass by and not render assistance. That would have been more than Edna could have borne. The showers had gone now and as they walked the day had become oppressively hot.

When they were home, Joyce tried to stop herself laughing at what had happened, and found two of the eggs undamaged in spite of everything. Edna had a wash down and put on clean clothes. The bag was assiduously cleansed and left hanging out on the clothesline for the rest of the week in order to remind Alex of his misdemeanour.

When George arrived home on Friday night, he produced three full egg boxes in mint condition from his case and one of them was opened on Saturday morning. Alex had forgotten how nice a soft-boiled egg tasted eaten with soldiers of toast dipped into it. Nothing was said about Monday's fiasco in his presence, but George's knowing wink as he took away his eggcup when Alex had finished let him know that what he had done was not held against him. Just then, Edna appeared with a large newspaper parcel. She gave it to George and quietly said to him,

"Thanks for seeing to this for me."

George took it from her, and went out quickly.

He was back after half an hour or so.

"They'll be ready on Thursday," he said. "Here's the receipt. Don't go paying twice."

Edna took the shopping bag from the line and put it in the dustbin.

III

Towards the end of June Alex came to the breakfast table one Sunday morning to hear his father and honorary uncle excitedly talking about the war. There was nothing new in them talking about it: it was the excitement that was different.

"He's bitten off more than he can chew this time!"

"So much for non-aggression pacts made with him!"

"Yes, but the important thing is what the papers say Winnie said."

"You mean, 'any man or state that fights the Nazis has our aid'."

"Yes. I never thought we'd end up in cahoots with Uncle Joe."

"Any port in a storm, George. Any port in a storm."

This discussion was brought to an end by Joyce calling out from the scullery,

"Do either of you want another piece of fried bread?"

As Alex climbed on his chair and put a large tea towel round his neck as was required of him, he tried to decipher what seemed to have happened. He knew who "Winnie" was from the impressions of his speech often made at this table: he went about smoking a cigar and making a gesture with his fingers that Alex was not allowed by Edna under any circumstances to imitate for fear that his version might be imperfect and therefore misinterpreted by the respectable. What a non-aggression pact might be eluded him, as did the possible identity of "Uncle Joe". And someone else had his mouth too full of food that he could not swallow, which had some bearing on the war.

All that became insignificant when Joyce brought his porridge in for him. He was relieved that he did not have to chew porridge, or he might end up like the unfortunate subject of his father's remark.

Before he actually needed to ask, George explained to him that Hitler had unexpectedly sent his army into Russia in force and this meant that Great Britain was no longer fighting him and the Italian Fascists on her own. Edna had not come downstairs yet so it was all right to produce the Sunday paper, breaking her rule against reading at the table, and George showed Alex the map of the invasion and explained it to him.

"No one has ever been able to invade Russia successfully," George said. "You see: this will make a lot of difference. Napoleon was defeated after he reached Moscow. Lenin was able to impose peace on the Kaiser in the first war when the German generals found they could not win a war fought on two fronts. Nobody expected what has just happened because one of the worrying things has been that Hitler and Joe Stalin . . ."

"Oh," put in Alex, "Then that's 'Uncle Joe'!"

"Yes. Swore that they would never attack each other only two years ago and this left Hitler free to keep his attention on us. Now he's turned round and gone the other way. If only the Americans would do a bit more than lease us a few of their old destroyers we could see him off while his back's turned."

"He's still got his U-boats though, George," put in Graham.

Alex noticed that the two men had changed their rôles. George was saying all the hopeful things with Graham putting a damper on him, whereas always before it had been the other way round. But the interesting grown-up men's talk soon stopped when George heard Edna on the stairs and quickly folded the newspaper to make it disappear. He got up and offered her his place, since there were only four chairs at the table and the other one was Joyce's if she wanted it. He went to get his wife a cup of tea from the pot warming on the kitchen range as she came into the kitchen.

Alex said,

"Hitler's invaded Russia, Mum."

"Never mind about that. Just eat your porridge."

George shook his head with a smile at his boy and went off to devour the rest of the paper in peace.

"Morning, Edna," said Graham. "Things have taken an unexpected turn, though. George seems quite hopeful that it will make a difference."

"Yes. Dad says it means we haven't got to fight Hitler on our own anymore."

"It will be a good thing when you go to school and you won't have to fill your head up with things that are beyond you."

This thought about school was to be reiterated constantly over the next three months, hanging over Alex and assuming the proportions of a threat greater than he could imagine. He knew where the school was. He knew that everyone just a year older than he had to go there. But what they did inside that great big building in Ferry Hinksey Road, and why they had to take their gas masks with them every time, were questions he could not answer for himself and was afraid to ask his mother.

Later on in the day he asked George about the purpose of going to school.

"They'll teach you how to read," he told him.

"But I can read. Can't I?"

"Not quite yet," said George, "And there's counting and writing to learn as well. You might as well take what they are offering. Come to think of it, you could read to me for a change."

Edna and Joyce came in at this point, and Graham soon followed. Alex realized that it was time for the great Sunday afternoon snooze and went out to the garden, stopping at his cupboard in the sitting room for some balsa wood off cuts that John had given him and bits of wire and lengths of string. He went into the garden, where he manufactured a fully rigged and armoured warship. Alex saw what he had made as H.M.S. Exeter taking on the Graf Spee, which he had been told about ages ago. Some dirt off the inspection cover made it the right grey and some of the spills used to light the gas oven were fetched and became, in small pieces, signal flags and, in long ones, its main armament. He came in for two cotton reels he knew he had and these became the fore and aft turrets. When it had finished its battle, it limped home and was put into his pie dish, found where he had hidden it behind a scruffy rose in the corner of the garden, and now metamorphosed into a dry dock in which the ship underwent its refit before going on to further triumphs, perhaps to bring help to the Russian navy...

After an hour of self-absorption, he took the whole thing in, pie dish and all, to his waking father, who rubbed his eyes and said what a parent never must: "Hullo, that's good. What is it?"

He had the presence of mind, however, to ask Alex less curtly to explain to him what it was, thus restoring self-respect on the boy's part. When Alex had gone, Edna said,

"You oughtn't to pander to that boy's fancy world so much."

"I don't know. You're not lonely for long if you've got a good imagination."

And there they both left it because George had to go to Gloucester Green for the coach in another two hours and they did not want to be in dispute before that happened. It was important to both of them that the smiles as they parted at the front door each week were unforced so that they could remember them and keep them in focus until the following Friday. Edna prided herself on being practical and left imaginative thoughts to George and, reluctantly, to Alex.

"I'll make a cup of tea," she said and asked Graham and Joyce if they would like one.

IV

When older people talked about "before the war . . ." with a wistful look on their faces, Alex did not understand what they meant at all. He had come to consciousness of reality while the war was beginning. He had emerged from babyhood in an Anderson shelter and he was just about to go to school with others of his age who could not imagine a world without ration books, or in which new clothes and furniture did not conform to a standard of utility which was serviceable but not elegant, and where everything was marked with two circles with a segment cut out of them and the number forty-one.

Edna always looked elegant when she was in her better clothes. She still had many of her pre-war things, since George had brought up a great suitcase the weekend before the house was destroyed. Clothes were worn to destruction if they were liked. In the summer, Edna often wore a thin black coat with appliqué embroidery around the collar and on its facings, held together in front by a row of small covered buttons fastening into loops over her new pink silk dress trimmed at the neck with lace. The hat she wore with this coat was nearly all covered in black feathers over its crown and brim, with a large crimson feather over her forehead resembling a maple leaf. Sometimes she wore the spotted veiling that went with it and sometimes not. The coat was what she had on when she and Alex arrived in Oxford last year and it would see out each wartime summer before it was discarded. She only stopped wearing it then because she could no longer get it on over her increased weight once she had decided to be a matronly figure at the age of forty-three. Alex associated it in his own mind with another garment she often sang a song about, not realizing that he was listening, or she never would have:

'My sweet little Alice Blue gown,
I so often wore it to town:
I wore it and wore it,
Till some blighter tore it,
My sweet little Alice Blue gown.'

George had three suits of increasing age, not bought at the store on his discount but from Montague Burton, as all his braces buttons announced. He also had what he called his sports coat - a fashionable jacket with a half belt at the back and a pleat from waist to neck - and flannels and a selection of collarless shirts, each with at least one spare collar. It was Alex's responsibility most weekends, if his father was wearing one of these, to find his back collar stud when he dropped it from behind, having forgotten to put it in place before he drew the shirt on. As summer warmed up, George more likely wore one of his less formal shirts, even with no tie. All his shirts were coloured. When Alex asked him why he did not wear white ones as many men did, he replied that he always had to wear white ones in the Navy and now he didn't have to he didn't want to. Edna knew this, but made sure that Alex, when dressed for best, always had a dazzling white shirt. Alex was not old enough to wonder why. It was some time before he saw his father wearing the clothes in which he did his work as an engineer.

Alex himself was invariably dressed in a pair of short trousers. He had dark brown corduroy shorts for October to May - one pair on and one in the wash - and three pairs of lighter ones for spring and summer. If more than one pair needed to be washed at once it meant going to bed early - usually to atone for having got them dirty. In days of double summer time this was irksome because no one ever thought of drawing the blackout curtains until it really was lighting up time and the canary thought it was incumbent upon it to sing a protracted evening serenade. On these occasions he would be told by his mother, after she had decreed the punishment, that she was not looking for work and was not going to run round after him when he was so thoughtless. Her attitude to grazed knees was often similar to the one adopted for dirty clothes, depending upon the mood she was in.

On weekdays, a boy in a respectable family wore a jersey with a collar, which usually carried a single line of decoration. The favoured colour for this garment was grey or brown so as not to show the dirt. It usually itched, especially as the underclothes issued with it on colder days were also made of wool.

When it was time for his Aertex vest and pants in spring, Alex considered that day to be a foretaste of the heaven he had been told about in which all our gallant airmen who had been shot down and the sailors from ships in the Atlantic food convoys sunk by U-Boats were to be found in bliss.

"What's bliss, Auntie Joyce?"

"Feeling happy for ever, Alex."

"That would be nice."

V

In September the time came when Alex going to school was no longer a topic to be talked about but one that was actually going to happen. Edna took him across Botley Road and then along Ferry Hinksey Road until the large building familiar from their endless promenades appeared behind high trees. Over two entrances next to each other were carved stones, which Alex could read for himself. One said Girls in beautiful letters, and the other Boys. He soon discovered the redundant nature of these signs since the children were taught all together now and had been for some years, though the coming of international conflict and the registration of increasingly older men for the services had meant that the education of the nation's rising generation was entirely in the hands of women.

The Headmistress was Miss Cook, a stout lady of a certain age at all times dressed in what was then called a costume: a well cut jacket above a skirt nearly to the ankles, beneath which appeared lisle stockings and severe shoes with a strap over the instep buttoning on the outer side. Her ensemble was completed by a silky white blouse, sometimes embellished with a cameo or some other brooch, and sometimes with a necktie. She had a loud voice and did not look very kind, but her looks were deceptive as Alex soon learned.

After a few minutes' discussion about things like the vaccinations Alex had undergone and the unfortunate loss of their home in "the suburbs", as she called the place where Alex's family used to live, the Headmistress took Edna and her son to meet Miss Hill, who was the teacher in charge of the infants' class. She was surrounded already by a number of mothers with their new entrants to the school and while Miss Cook moved away to meet the next pair in the queue outside her own classroom, Edna and Alex had to wait their turn sitting on a large tiled step that went right round the inside of the room. The primary function of this step was to allow the children to reach the slates set into the walls on which they were encouraged to draw from time to time with coloured chalks. Edna found it cold to her posterior, and said so, and was displeased when Alex said out loud that his bum was cold too. The whispered altercation about this was still going on when Miss Hill, from her raised desk, called his name out and added, "You must reply: 'Yes, Miss Hill.'"

Edna nudged him and he said it. They both got up and went to stand before Miss Hill as if she were going to ask him "When did you last see your father?"

What she actually said was,

"Have you brought your gas mask?"

"Yes, Miss Hill."

"Do you know how to put it on?"

"We have shown him how," said Edna.

"He must answer for himself, mother," said Miss Hill, reprovingly.

"Go on then, Alex, tell the lady," snarled Edna, who would have preferred to express her dislike for the woman instead.

"Yes, Miss Hill," said Alex.

"You know that you must never come to school without it, nor must you go home again without it."

"Of course, Miss Hill." This was said through a constriction in his throat and was not distinctly said. Because it was a variation on the approved formula, Miss Hill looked thunderous and replied,

"I did not hear what you said. You must speak clearly!"

Alex had heard "must" from her lips five times by now and had had enough of her imperative mood.

"I said I do know how to put it on," he asserted, and this brought his mother to the side of authority, despite her earlier resentment of it.

"Speak to Miss Hill in the proper way," she said.

Alex had not learned the precept that a soft answer turneth away wrath and knew that he had replied properly in giving Miss Hill the information for which she had asked. All he could do was be silent.

"Very well," said Miss Hill. "Please leave him with me now, Mrs Ryland. Morning school ends at twelve o'clock sharp, so please be here to collect him and bring him back at twenty past one."

Edna also thought that silence was the better part of resentment and left Alex with no more than a pat on the shoulder, which he was left to interpret as a smack. This made him even less willing to be co-operative with this new and apparently unpleasant authority who was taller than his mother and, if she were not so conscious of her need to keep the differentials between herself and her charges, could even have had a pleasant face. As it was, she would not allow herself to smile and seemed to take refuge in being stern to defend herself against parents and children alike.

Miss Hill got up and took him past the other three children and their mothers whose names began with S, V and Y, to a rank of what she called "cubby holes". She pointed to one with the name Alexander Ryland printed in a large hand above it. Still seething with annoyance, Alex almost shouted,

"My full name is Alexander Martin Ryland!"

"We would only need to put that if there were another Alexander Ryland and there is not!" said the offended teacher, realizing just in time that she ought not to stamp her foot down.

She quickly shoved Alex behind a desk and went back to meet Mrs Shergold and Isabel. She turned out to be a nice little girl who did not argue.

Things got worse before they were better for Alex. He found that the lid of the double desk could be lifted up and there was no way of stopping it from clattering down again when he let it go since there was as yet no one sitting next to him. This made all the other children who had hitherto sat in an over-awed silence at Miss Hill's command release their own tension with uninhibited laughter.

When the laughter had subsided and Miss Hill's irritation abated, Alex was no longer the centre of attention, and he found he was not displeased by the seat in the desk alongside him being given to Isabel who smiled at him as she sat down. The seat behind them in the row of desks at the right hand end of the room was taken by James Vaughan and Mary Younghusband. Most of the girls already felt very sorry for Mary, while the boys would soon find her surname too much of a provocation not to leave her in peace.

When all the parents had left, Miss Hill set out her ground rules of silence unless she asked a particular pupil a question and undivided attention at all times to whatever she said to them. During this process Alex heard the word "must" a great many more times, often complemented with "must not".

"Have you all understood?"

"Yes, Miss Hill," came the automatic chorus.

The learning of arithmetical tables by heart began and never seemed to cease until something called playtime was decreed for Miss Hill's class: a different time from the children in the older classes in order to avoid the intimidation that had been known to be offered to newcomers in time past. Once in the open air, the new boys and girls began to speak to each other and form acquaintanceships that, it was supposed, would last as long as the children lived in this little part of the city. This bonding was represented by every book that they used for exercises having

"City of Oxford Education Committee" emblazoned upon its front cover. There had been no distinction made between the children born in Oxford and those whose provenance was peacetime London. That was Miss Cook's school policy. Sadly, it was not always the policy of the children's parents, however egalitarian the children themselves might wish to be in choosing their friends.

After break, there was reading. Alex was astonished by the odd shape of the reading book they were given. It was longer than it was high, looking like the sort of book you stuck National Savings stamps into on your birthday. It was illustrated with little basic line drawings of people out of whose mouths came the words you were going to learn to read enclosed in speech bubbles. For Alex, there was no challenge in this since for as far forward as he was able to turn without Miss Hill seeing him do it, he could read all the words anyway. One or two others did find it difficult to read the simple words out loud: "Run, Nat, see the fun", but Alex had to wait until page fifteen before he found a fence he could not jump. He felt it was better not to appear to have more than average fluency when his turn to read aloud came, because Miss Hill might subscribe to the strong body of adults who did not like children to seem to know very much until they had personally told it to them.

Twelve o'clock came and the children ran from the school door, not having dared to run in the corridors because strict orders against doing so had been issued. Their mothers were at the school gate and Edna's crimson hat feather was conspicuous among other headgear to be seen. Alex was taken away from the gate with the utmost rapidity. The other mothers seemed to know each other, but Edna saw no reason to involve herself with them. It was Alex's day for causing offence. All he could say to Edna was,

"I wish I had a young mother."

This did not, in the idiom used by Edna, make for happiness. Lunchtime was passed in an atmosphere of hostile tension. Alex, caught between the devil and the deep (another of his mother's favourite sayings), was glad when the minute hand on the clock registered a quarter past one and he was led back to the school gate to be herded with the others back into classroom.

A new exercise book had been set in each child's place and the first thing Miss Hill did after she had received the required chorus in reply to her saying "Good afternoon, Class One," was give out a sharpened pencil to each of her charges. As she did this, Alex had the opportunity to observe this new principal participant in his life. She was in her thirties, bespectacled, with hair curled in a ring all round the crown of her head as was fashionable at the time. She was wearing a straight grey skirt into which a satin blouse was tucked. This shiny blouse became an object of fascination for Alex for the next few minutes and something remembered at intervals for a long time thereafter. Its surface drew attention to her underwear, the shape of which could be seen below her high collar. Of greater interest to Alex was what went on below that. From her neck to the waistband of her skirt, there was a vertical row of large, shiny, flat buttons and on either side of it a shape jiggled about independently each time she moved in a way that was infinitely fascinating. When she came near him, bending down to give him his pencil, a beautiful smell was added to what he had been intently watching and one of the shapes lowered itself near his face, making him feel luxurious.

This sense of well being was removed as soon as it had been granted.

"Take your pencils in your right hands, with the thumb and forefinger opposite each other a little way from where the pencil has been sharpened, as you see me do," said Miss Hill to everyone, standing before them behind her desk.

Two problems were created for Alex: first, he could not see her hand on her pencil because Michael Ritson's head was in the way and second, he always held his pencil when he was drawing at home in his left hand and did so now.

Miss Hill turned to the blackboard, substituting pencil for chalk.

"Now," she said, "You must copy the shape I am going to put up, starting at the bottom of the shape as I do, and finishing at the top of it."

She wrote the letter J.

"After you have written it once, fill the top line from left to right in your books with the same shape."

Alex began. His left hand served him very well in drawing the shape. Isabel complained in a whisper that he kept on nudging her elbow with his as he worked. He was protesting that he could not help it when Miss Hill called out,

"Stop talking there! I can see you, Alexander."

Then the heavens descended about his ears. The forms he so much admired came dancing towards him, but for no friendly purpose. Distaste was imprinted on the teacher's face as she wrenched the pencil from his left hand and inserted it in his right.

"Now, do as you have been told, and stop distracting your neighbour."

This was even more confusing because Alex understood his neighbours to be the Wilson family who lived at number 58 and

Mrs White who lived at number 54. It took a long time for him to realize that the neighbour in question was Isabel, who looked at this moment, he was pleased to see, sorry for him.

He tried to reproduce the letters with his right hand, but they were very inferior to the ones he had already supplied and he was grieved that his craftsmanship had been so scorned. After issuing exhortations and rebukes to other members of the class, Miss Hill came back to see what he had done.

"Those are not good shapes, Alexander, but you must go on making them with your right hand because you will never be allowed to use your left as you make your way in life. Try to improve on them in the next few minutes and at least keep them with their feet on the line."

The next few minutes were more and more frustrating, with the pencil constantly slipping between his thumb and finger and the shapes becoming more and more disappointing to one who for a long time now had enjoyed making shapes on paper at home. His father would not say, "Not bad at all," about what ranged across the page now. He also found that the pencil, an indelible one, made purple marks where his tears had fallen. The next half hour was spent in intense misery and playtime gave little relief because the others in the class were quite proud of their achievements with the "walking sticks on the line" as Miss Hill called them, whereas Alex who until then had the confidence of someone who enjoyed drawing, now had the despair of having been told, "Unless you write with the proper hand, you will never get anywhere in life."

In the final three quarters of an hour of afternoon school, during which Miss Hill read a story called "The King of the Golden River", the like of which normally he enjoyed, all Alex could do was feel sorry for himself. He shut out the story from his mind and concentrated instead on how miserable he was and how lonely.

The final act of the school day seemed entirely meaningless to him and served only to underline his unhappy sense of isolation. Miss Hill told the class to stand for a prayer. With the bright sun of three-thirty in the afternoon during permanent British Summer Time gleaming through the high windows, she read from a little prayer book:

'Lighten our darkness, we beseech thee, O Lord; and by thy great mercy defend us from all perils and dangers of this night...'

Alex was not very much experienced in praying with others and picked up the sense of corporate wartime fear. There was plenty of danger about. Although no bombs actually fell here, the siren went off frequently enough as other people had to brace themselves for whatever they would find when they came out of the shelters after the all clear. Yet what was uppermost in his mind was what his father had said to him before he left to catch the coach on Sunday, "Learn all you can at school: if you've had an education more things are possible for you." On the showing of the last two hours, there were no possibilities for Alex's self-advancement at all.

He proceeded out of the room near the end of the last file as the initial of his surname demanded, followed by James Vaughan and Roy Wheeler. As the door was reached, they pushed past him, and he was the last one through the door. A backward glance gave him a glimpse of Miss Hill sinking into the chair behind her desk and resting her head on her arms. None of the children in her class yet knew that she was new this term, sent to replace a male teacher who had been called up, or that she lived in Didcot whence she intended to travel on the train each day since she looked after her elderly parents there, or that she had been kept up most of last night as a result of bombs, jettisoned from an enemy plane hit by anti-aircraft fire while attacking the West Midlands and off course, falling on the street where she lived. Her satin blouse was her Sunday best, kept in a different place from the chest of drawers containing her everyday wear that was soaked by the fireman's hose being used next door after bomb blast had taken out her bedroom window.

Edna was imitating an ostrich at the gate, stretching her neck over the heads of the other mothers as she looked for Alex who seemed to be taking a long time coming out of the building. She became annoyed when she saw him. The other children ran to their mothers with tales of new things on their lips, but Alex was moving slowly with his mouth turned down at the corners to make the face that often encouraged George to say to him, "Give us a ride on your lip!"

Instead of saying, "What's wrong?" as he hoped she would and expecting to be told why he was sad, all she could think of was the challenging question, "What's the matter with you, then?" This could only evince his miserable answer, "Oh, nothing."

Edna was relieved not to be compelled to spend emotional energy on him that afternoon. She had opened the letter from the solicitor in Wimbledon that came by the second post, in which she had learnt that hopes of repairing the damage to the house in Raynes Park had receded. She was compelled to remain as an evacuee and a weekend wife to George. The sight of Alex snivelling across the playground on his own was not calculated to help her out of her despair and she had few resources of strength left.

A symptom of her desperation, as they reached the pavement opposite the house, was her decision to begin to teach Alex how to cross the road safely in hopes that at some future time she would not need to accompany him to and from school. Standing on the kerb with his hand firmly held in hers, she said,

"Look up the road. Is there anything coming?"

"Yes. A lorry and a horse and cart."

"Now look the other way, down the road. Is there anything coming that way?"

"Yes. Two men on bikes and a bus."

"Look the other way again. Is there anything coming now?"

"The horse and cart is still coming, followed by a car."

"And the other way?"

"I can't see past the bus."

At this point, Edna realized that the time was not right for any more education that afternoon and that he was no higher than the tops of the bus wheels as they passed. So she dragged him with her behind the bus, knowing that the car on the other side of the road could not accelerate because of the milk cart it was following. As she dodged behind the milk cart, the driver of the car had ample leisure to sound his motor horn at her as she jumped from the kerb up to the front step of Joyce's house. Alex landed on his knee beside her and had to have ointment put on the graze. The fact that the flat, round tin Edna opened was labelled "Germolene" produced an interesting train of thought in his mind, and the question to his mother,

"Haven't we got any Englolene?"

This made her smile at him. At last, the load was lightened for both of them and, when she had taken her coat and hat off, Edna sat down to cuddle him for a little while. For once she did not tell him not to suck his thumb.

VI

Later on, when Graham, Joyce, John, Edna and Alex sat at the kitchen table for their high tea, the inevitable question was asked. It was Graham who asked it.

"How did you get on at school, Alex?"

"I got on all right with the reading, Uncle Graham."

"Did you make any friends?"

"Not really, Auntie Joyce."

By this time all at the table had realized that there had been something wrong with Alex's first day at school and wanted to find out what it was. John tried next.

"Were the lessons easy?"

"The tables were all right: all you had to do was keep on saying them."

"Give us one of them now, then."

"Once two is two, two twos are four, three twos are six, four twos are eight. That's enough isn't it!"

"That's very good, Alex."

"Yes, but it doesn't mean anything, does it?"

"It does. Look . . ." John reached for the jar in which Joyce collected copper coins and set out some pennies - the big old ones with Britannia ruling the waves on them. "Here are two pennies. Here are two more, so that's four. Then two more: six. Another two: that makes eight, and so on."

"All it is is counting, then!"

"That's right."

"Why didn't Miss Hill say so, then?"

No one had an answer to that. Joyce asked the telling question,

"Did you do any writing?"

Then she wished she had not.

"I didn't like that much."

"Why?"

This time it was his mother who asked.

"Because she wouldn't let me use my left hand and made me use the wrong one. It wouldn't work at all and all I got was an untidy mess on the paper. When I did it with the right hand - this hand, I mean," - at this point he waved his left hand - "I drew some nice Js. But with the wrong hand I couldn't do anything properly. She said I would never get anywhere in life if I didn't use my wrong hand."

Edna assumed the countenance of Britannia rising from the pennies, wielding her fork like a trident.

"I'll come in and see the headmistress again in the morning, Alex. They can't mess you about like that! I won't let them!"

"Thank you, Mum," sniffed Alex, and was glad when John started telling them about what had happened at his school. It didn't sound much better to Alex. Perhaps all schools were the same.

"When will I be able to stop going to school?" Alex asked.

"Not before you're fourteen, sonny," said Graham, "and if the war's finished by then, they've promised to make it when you're fifteen!"

John was Buttons to Edna's fairy godmother.

"It gets a bit better as you learn the dodges, Alex."

"'Ow long have you been in the service?" asked his father, and at last there was some welcome laughter.

Later on, from his divan in the living room, he heard Edna say to Joyce as they went upstairs, "I don't know what gets into people like Alex's teacher! Little Hitlers, all of them!" This was an encouraging saying to him as he lay in bed awake, frightened of the morning and dreading his return to Miss Hill's classroom. He went to sleep after the dread had produced a clear image in his mind of Miss Hill, wobbling deliciously under her satin blouse, with her grey skirt discarded, her hair sleeked down on one side and a little moustache, raising her right hand in the appropriate salute, and mouthing "Achtung". Fantasy and fear often go together.

VII

Edna did go to the school in the morning at twenty past eight with a sleepy Alex trailing behind her. She made straight for Miss Cook's door and hammered upon it with her fist. The wood and glass were unharmed. The side of Edna's fist hurt all day. Miss Cook appeared behind her in the corridor, wearing her hat and carrying her Gladstone bag and umbrella.

"Good morning. Mrs Ryland, isn't it? What can I do for you?"

"You can tell your Miss Hill to let Alex use his left hand for writing," said Edna with more truculence than she had ever heard from her own lips, though this was by no means the first quarrel she had picked with authority since she came of age.

"Won't she let him, though?" asked Miss Cook as she unlocked her door. "Come in and sit down while I go and see her."

Edna and Alex went into the classroom and sat down on a desk this time, preferring to avoid the cold stone step that was in this room as well as the infants'. After a few minutes, a smiling Miss Cook returned and asked Alex to go to his classroom to see Miss Hill. She did it so sensitively that he forgot to be frightened for long enough to comply with her wishes.

When he had gone, Miss Cook told Edna,

"Yesterday was very difficult. Miss Hill is new to us, replacing a young man who has been called up for war service. She was late in for the half hour's induction I was supposed to give her on her first morning on account of an unusual air raid at Didcot where she lives and I was not able fully to explain this school's policy to her. I decided some years ago to abandon that old-fashioned compulsion to use the right hand only. There have been plenty of left-handed geniuses. Let us hope your Alexander will turn out to be one, Mrs Ryland!"

"I do hope not," said Edna. "Clever people are so difficult to live with."

"Maybe they are," replied Miss Cook. "I haven't met many!"

Meanwhile, Miss Hill opened the classroom door for Alex, smiled at him, and told him that she had been thinking about yesterday and had decided that he should use the hand with which he was more comfortable to do his written work. Alex was more than relieved, and he even smiled at her.

"Go outside for a minute or two, now, Alexander," she said. "We have assembly in the hall first thing this morning, and I haven't practised the hymn tune on the piano yet. Off you go!"

Alex did not know what had happened, but he was very sorry to see that Miss Hill's mother had dried out and pressed the clothes she usually wore in school after the firemen had finished with the house next door. The plain, straight dress she was wearing today had very little to enthral him compared with yesterday's attractions.

During assembly, Alex learnt that Jesus wanted him for a sunbeam, and decided that whoever he was, he couldn't have him as such. It was a silly idea to suggest that he could. Likewise a few mornings later he decided that he bore little resemblance to a "pure, clear light" either and wasn't going to be anybody's "little candle". He found out that these fatuous songs were called hymns and the penny dropped from when he was outside the chapel at the end of Helen Road with his father on a Sunday afternoon months ago. He decided that hymns had no part in his sense of mystery. In fact they spoilt it for him. This was sad, because mystery was important.

He warmed, in contrast, to the lovely sound of Miss Cook's voice at the end of the assembly as she said:

". . . defend us in the same with thy mighty power; and grant that this day we fall into no sin, neither run into any kind of danger; but that all our doings may be ordered by thy governance, to do always that is righteous in thy sight; through Jesus Christ our Lord."

He had not the slightest idea what these words meant in detail, but they spoke to him of deep peace, so it didn't matter to him that he had never heard of sin. The inconsistency between now and his annoyance the afternoon before, when another prayer that he might be kept from danger only made him resentful, passed by him.

As he took his place at his desk a few minutes later, he asked Isabel,

"Did you like that song we sang in the hall?"

"Not the words, but I like to sing. It cheers me up."

Alex found that this was a widely prevalent attitude but for his part he liked the words of songs to mean something. Those songs on the wireless meant a great deal. It was a pity that all they conveyed was sadness, though.

"Why did we have to stand on those green spots in the hall?" Isabel asked him.

"I expect it's so that we don't catch colds from each other."

While one of the trusties who sat in a front desk was giving out the reading books, Miss Hill quietly made Alex and Isabel change places in the double desk they shared to avoid the inevitable clash of elbows now that Alex was going to use his left hand with impunity. She was not unbearably tired as she had been the day before, and she smiled quietly to herself as she thought of five-year-old Isabel giving Alex the elbow. The straight-laced element in her soon reminded her of her proper responsibilities and she called the class to order for a recapitulation of Nat running through the pictures in the reading book to see the fun.

"How was school, boy?" asked George on Saturday morning.

"Not bad at all," said Alex.

Edna had already told him the real story.

4

George, Edna and Alex had kept up their theatre-going in order to give Graham, Joyce and John a chance to be on their own for at least some time each week. On the Saturday after Alex had started at school, the variety show they went to see took on a special quality. A well-known comedian called Sid Field was top of the bill and Alex rolled about in his seat in the upper circle, helpless from what he said and did. His parents' laughter was infectious too. Alex could not tell why it was funny when the straight man observed that the comedian's Astrakhan overcoat was very long, and the comedian replied, "Yes, if it were any longer it would look silly!" But it was, and what particularly appealed to him was a well-painted set depicting the inside of a grocer's shop that looked just like the Oxford branch of the Home and Colonial. There was a long ladder with its upper end leaning on the top shelf behind the counter. Sid Field was the shopkeeper. Customers came in and asked for a pound of sugar. He made some remark about it being rationed and hard to get, while climbing right to the top of the ladder to obtain it. After doing this three times, he stopped at the top of the ladder with the third bag of sugar in his hand, looking round to say to the latest customer in the shop,

"I suppose you want a pound of sugar, too, don't you."

The new customer replied, "No, thank you."

The comedian-grocer began the long descent of the ladder, drawing out the process for as long as possible. He handed the pound of sugar to the previous customer, took the money and dealt with the ration book. Turning back to the latest entrant, he asked, "Well, madam, what can I get you?"

The answer was, "I want half a pound."

As the grocer painstakingly ascended the ladder again, the lights blacked out, the whole of the audience were convulsed with mirth, and Alex remembered what laughing was. So did Edna, and so did George. So did everybody else in the theatre.

Later on, Alex tried to explain this sketch and its impact to Joyce and Graham. No one would have dreamed of saying, "You had to be there" about a reported joke that no one else saw the point of in 1941, but it was true. He had skipped all the way home through the blackout with a hand held by each of his parents and occasionally they had shouted out together, "I want half a pound!" A policeman by the station entrance envied them their cheerfulness that evening as they bounded together past him. Even when the air raid warning sounded at the same time as they reached the front gate they did not quieten down.

For a couple of hours that afternoon they had forgotten they had been bombed out and behaved as they fancied they would have if there been no Hitler and peace and prosperity had been assured for all forever. All through the evening meal Alex kept repeating the punchline and, time and time again, George and Edna began to laugh once more. In the end they realized why they were laughing and gradually stopped. They were more kind to each other that evening than they had been for a long time. George put his arm round Edna as they sat on the sofa and she welcomed it, even though Graham and Joyce were in the room.

II

On Sunday morning, something planned over the garden fence on Monday took effect. Mrs Wilson and her two daughters who lived next door took Alex with them to St Frideswide's Church. Sergeant-Major Wilson had been home recently for a seventy-two hour pass, which, once travelling time had been deducted, gave him forty-eight hours with his family. Mrs Wilson knew how valuable such time was for a couple and what tension arose when children had to be built into it, so she offered to take Alex off George and Edna's hands for an hour or so.

He did not remember ever going to church before. He knew he must have been, because one of the things that had not been lost in the blitz was his baptism certificate. Edna had shown it to him and let him examine it for himself. He had perused it very carefully. It was printed on a white card that assured all its readers that it had originated in Great Britain. The card was headed Memorial of Baptism in very ornate lettering, although Edna assured him that it was a certificate not a memorial; a memorial was something else which he wouldn't understand yet, she said. This confused him because he knew "full well" (another of Edna's little phrases) what a war memorial was and Edna was quite right: he did not understand the connection between a large stone cross with a sword and some names on it and whatever his baptism might be. The card was decorated with gold, blue, green and red leaves and flowers and, in places, what looked like carrots. It was signed by a man called Thomas Parry in green ink to match the rest of the card, affirming that he was the Vicar of St James's Church, Myatt's Park, London, SE5. Edna explained that the church was not far from Flodden Road in Camberwell, where George and Edna had been living in lodgings when he was born.

He had been allowed to hold it until he started to crease it and then Edna took it back like the holy relic it was, to be protected under the front cover of George's World's Cruise book where it was kept with other valuable papers. Edna told him that he was sick all over her after the christening and that she had managed to keep one or two snapshots taken at the party in their landlady's garden. These pictures were kept in Edna's handbag, which was how they had been preserved, along with one Alex always hated of himself aged about eighteen months, dressed in a matching overcoat and long trousers together with what he could only recognize as a flying helmet and, worse still, around his middle a leather contraption with round bells on it from which reins hung down behind him. The expression on his face was of a child who had put a whole tomato in his mouth and did not know what subsequent action to take. Worst of all, Edna was fond of passing this photograph round and he really wished she wouldn't. Why didn't she get someone to take a photo of him now and pass that round? It was what he looked like at present that was important. John had comforted him by saying that at least he had clothes on in that picture: Joyce had one of him that was very embarrassing indeed.

Alex was thinking all this as he held Mrs Wilson's hand to cross the road to the church. In the middle of the road, he remembered one important result of his christening - and that was that he had collected two people he liked as his godparents as Edna's snapshots recorded. They were people George and Edna had known for years: a twice-born atheist called Arthur - always known as Art - and his wife, whose name was Jen.

Art was a good deal older than George and Edna. He was a very remarkable man. He had been born in King's Cross and not been involved at all in the elementary education set up by the School Boards ten years earlier. He became a regular soldier and fought in the Boer War and the Great War. Early on in his time in the army, he had taught himself, and subsequently many of his comrades in arms, to read. Part of Alex's impatience with the reading book used in his first week at school was the result of cheerful quarter hours with Uncle Art. Alex had no idea what a godparent was and nobody had ever tried to tell him, but he was very attached to Art and Jen, and was sorry he had not seen them in all the time he had been living in Oxford.

His reverie was interrupted by arrival at the church door.

"What's that smell?" he asked Mary, the elder Wilson daughter, while Mrs Wilson herself took possession of two small books for each of them, including Alex himself.

"This is what's known as a high church and they use something called incense at the services. You'll see what it is when they start: it's burnt in a thing on the end of a chain and it gives off smoke which leaves this smell in the building all the time."

Alex did not listen to all the intelligent girl with a coveted place at the High School told him, but began to puzzle in his mind why they called it a high church. Once through the door, he had gone down three steps, and from outside it did not look very tall. The roof of the school round the corner was much higher.

Mrs Wilson sent Mary into a pew first, followed by the other girl, Martha, then Alex, and sat at the end of the row herself, so he could not ask for further explanation. Alex was given the book bound in green and the red one was put on the little ledge in front of him.

"You'll need the green one first, so keep hold of it while I sort myself out," she told him.

Rummages in her handbag produced three of the multi-sided threepenny pieces with the plant called thrift on the obverse then in use and she put one in front of each of her girls and of Alex.

"Leave that where it is, Alex, and I'll tell you what to do with it when the time comes."

Alex's mind raced again, What time? Would they all be turned into frogs unless they all paid somebody threepence? His mind went along such devious routes because from where he was sitting, he could not see much. By craning his neck he could see a sort of up-ended wooden box at a distance, with something that looked like the enlarged lid of a jam jar some way above it. Between the lid and the box a white carving of human figure hung by its arms on pieces of crossed wood.

He turned to ask Mrs Wilson what the figure was, but saw that she was kneeling down on a little cushion she had in front of her ("Oh! I've got one as well!" he realized) with her hands in front of her closed eyes. So he asked Martha for information.

"That's Jesus," she said. "A lot of wicked people took his clothes off him and hung him on a cross to die."

There was no time for her to give an interpretation of this sadness, even if her seven-year-old intelligence had been up to it, because the sizeable congregation stood up as the choir procession was heard entering. Alex realized that this poor man was the one who wanted him for a sunbeam to shine for him each day as the others had sung at school - and he wouldn't.

The organ, which had been played quietly up till now, became loud, and there was something that Alex could recognize as a strong tune. Mrs Wilson took the green book from his hand, turned quickly to one of the songs in it and gave it back to him, pointing with her gloved finger at the right hand page where some little print divided into shapes like house bricks was to be seen. He soon realized that these were the words the others all round him had begun to sing. The singing sounded better than what had happened at school, because there it was only children's voices, and it certainly was more tuneful in here than it had been when heard outside that chapel a long time ago when he had walked back from the allotment with his father. He could not follow the words and he could not see anything beyond the knotty wood the pew in front was made of, or Mrs Wilson's best coat on his left, or Martha's on his right. When he turned round to find out if he could see anything behind, Mrs Wilson gently but firmly turned him back.

Then they all knelt down, leaving Alex still standing. He could see, between the backs of the people in front of him, a group of people dressed differently from all the others standing in front of something the same shape as Auntie Joyce's sideboard with a green tablecloth hanging from it. One of the people had a garment hanging down his back and front which was made of the same green stuff and he was saying a lot of words as a fairly quick pace, the same kind of words he noticed as Miss Cook used in the school hall before lessons and Miss Hill used at the end of the schoolday. When the man turned round and stood at one end of the sideboard with a large book in his hand, everyone sat down, and Mrs Wilson lifted Alex on to her knee. This meant he was able to see properly and take in a lot more: two big boys holding candles on long sticks, some more candles - he counted six of them - at the back of the sideboard and one or two elderly men standing about dressed in the same black and white things as the boys with the candles.

When the man with the book finished what he was reading - it had many long words in it - he went to the other end of the altar and began to say something which made everybody stand up to listen to it and mumble something in reply to what he read out. Then, while he seemed to be reading a story, Alex was cooped up between pew and best coats again, but he could see the smoke which Mary had told him about rising up to the roof and that gave him enough to ponder upon until they all started to sing again, for the purposes of which Mrs Wilson took his green book away, and gave him the red one open, pointing once more to the relevant words, one of which was God, yes, "one God", and they went on singing for ages, singing, but observing no particular tune as it seemed, although the melody did go up and down in places on a regular pattern.

At the end of it, there was silence. The man who had been talking before said something else, Mrs Wilson waved her hand up in front of her face, and then brought it down again, and everyone sat down. The man was in the upturned box under the jam pot lid with his back turned to Jesus, and he said a lot more things. Alex noticed that while he spoke both his eyes twitched in a wild fashion. The others were listening attentively to his words. Where he was, Alex found it hard to hear most of it. He heard words like "hope for peace", and "end of all conflict" and stopped listening and started wondering again at the words "fullness of time", which the man uttered with some emphasis. Bottles were full, cups and glasses were full, but how could time be full? By the time Alex had turned this idea over in his mind several times, thereby emptying it, the man had finished.

They all got up to use the green book again and, while they were doing so, an elderly man in a smart suit came round with a green bag and took away all the threepenny bits. Then they knelt for ages while the man spoke many more words in a monotone until everybody moved with apparent relief to sit down. After that, the people got up row by row to walk up to where the man who had talked so much was standing facing them with something round in his hand. Mrs Wilson went in her turn, leaving Alex to sit with Martha and Mary who were both very still with their eyes closed.

"What are you doing?" he asked Martha in a whisper.

"Praying for Daddy," she answered.

Alex left her to do that, and realized that all the prayers he had been witness to since he went to school last Tuesday, and here in church now, were expressions of great longing for something everyone wanted and could not yet have. What George had said to him when he asked him if he believed in God came back to him with some force. Remembering it then, he never forgot it afterwards: about hoping there is a God when there are miles of sea between you and the bottom, and it connected in his mind with the phrase the man in the box had used, "peace in the fullness of time".

Then Mrs Wilson and all the others were back in their places. More words followed, then another hymn. The man's voice again, using the word "peace" once more. There was some loud organ music, and all the members of the choir followed the boys and old men wearing black and white down between the people. After kneeling down again for a little while, Mrs Wilson and the girls stood with Alex to join the slow moving queue for the church door. All the people seemed to have much to say to each other. What Alex overheard was mainly news about relatives away in the armed services.

When they were at last outside the church, Alex asked,

"Why did the man who talked to us keep on making those funny movements with his eyes, Mrs Wilson?"

"It's something very sad. Alex. He was a priest in London, near the docks where the ships are loaded and unloaded, and his parish was severely bombed. He stayed there with his people as the bombs fell night after night and he did his best to help the rescue parties. After several weeks of this he had what people call a nervous breakdown. Our priest here was a younger man and went to be a chaplain in the Air Force, so Father Watson was asked to come here, so that he could get well again and we could be looked after. He is well again now, but he has been left with that nervous tic as it is called. Some children are very cruel and make fun of him, but you wouldn't, would you, Alex?"

"We were bombed out, Mrs Wilson."

"I know, Alex. Your Mum told me all about it."

III

For some reason or other, Edna had not been able to obtain tickets for the New Theatre the following Saturday, so it was decided when George arrived on Friday night that they would have a day out instead. Consultation with Graham and Joyce revealed that Boar's Hill was a very pleasant spot to visit in the early autumn because there was such a wonderful view from the top over as many counties as you could shake a stick at, enhanced by the sight of the autumn colours.

"That sounds good," said George. "We'll go there."

"I'll make some sandwiches to take," said Edna.

"There's a Thermos flask in the cupboard in the scullery," put in Joyce.

So next morning, George woke Alex and told him to get up quickly because they were going out for the day.

"Where are we going?"

"Oh, some boring place,"George told him in a loud voice so that Edna should hear, and she responded with her over-loud laugh in the kitchen as she spread a concoction she had provided out of the huge tin of National Dried Egg, which both families dipped into as and when there was need. The sandwiches were put in a brown paper bag from the greengrocer's, and there was a stale rock cake each left over from Wednesday when Joyce had asked Mrs White in for tea. All this was put in a small shopping bag, together with milky tea in the Thermos.

George put on his sports jacket and helped Alex into his coat, which he had to wear although the sun was shining over the garden, while Edna produced the new green 'box' coat, complete with its CC41 label, for which she had been saving up her clothing coupons. She decided to put it on today, despite the temperature the day before having still been in the sixties Fahrenheit (no one's anti-German feeling ever stretched to changing the name by which temperatures were still measured then). Joyce came down in her dressing gown to see them off, cheerfully commenting,

"I hope you all have a good day. Have you got everything you need?"

They had made sure that there was a bus due at ten to nine. They were astonished to see it coming over the canal bridge and had to rush across the road to beat it to the stop. George dryly commented as they made their way upstairs,

"I wonder if this old rattletrap will get us there!"

"Don't you know there's a war on?" said the bus conductor.

"Wouldn't be here if there wasn't!" said George through his clenched dentures.

Alex climbed along the lengthy seat to the window side and he sat next to Edna as the bus wound its way through the villages until it reached the hill where they were going. It took a very long time and there were many exhortations to him not to fidget and commands to him to wait when he said that he needed what his father had taught him to call a "Jimmy Widdle".

Relief was soon given. The bus driver had made every attempt to take his vehicle up the lower contours of the steep hill with as much horsepower from the engine as he could call upon. Suddenly, after two or three agonizing minutes for the engine during which it was heard complaining, it cut out and the bus lurched violently as the brakes were applied to stop it rolling backwards downhill. After an attempt to start it up again, the driver was heard getting out and slamming his door. He came round to the conductor and told him,

"I might be able to get it to start again if the gentlemen among the passengers would be so good as to give it a push."

Several young servicemen on weekend passes were on the bus with their girlfriends and they alighted to do what the driver asked while he went back to his cab. The upstairs passengers had heard all this and, very reasonably, the conductor asked them to get off the bus while the attempt to start it was made. They all made their way downstairs and Alex shot off to some bushes beside the road to attend to his acute need, only to find Edna when he had finished crouching behind the next bush with the box coat carefully held up by George to prevent her being seen while she did the same.

When comfort had been restored, they saw that there had been little success in bringing the bus engine back to life. A dozen or so youngish men had pushed it several yards, but there was no effective spark. George went forward to help.

"George, your hernia!" shouted Edna.

"Never mind that! We can't wait here all day for a breakdown truck that might not come," and he went to join in, with Alex running after him.

The sound of Chatham cockney being loudly spoken captured the attention of the Oxfordshire souls who were pushing if men, and encouraging the pushing if women. One of the lads, said,

"Yeah, come on George, you can add weight at least if not muscle!"

This "got George's goat", as he later commented, and he put his hands on the stern of the bus to give it a good shove with the others while it went uphill at an unimaginable speed. The driver put it in gear and the engine caught, bringing gratification to all concerned.

"Well done, George!" shouted one of the girls.

"Hero of the hour!" one of the better dressed ones called out.

"Let's all get back on before it stalls again," said George to hide his embarrassment, though his red face made that difficult. Edna was the first on the bus dragging Alex with unnecessary force, he thought, up the stairs.

Once they were all back in their seats, the driver took the bus away gently with all the passengers' hearts in their mouths and made it to their destination. Edna took her coat off.

"I'm much too hot in this," she said. "I wish you hadn't made an exhibition of yourself, George."

"You help where you can," he said, miserably.

As they got off the bus, the conductor said to him, "We need to carry a mechanic with us these days."

"If it was a matter of turbines, I'd have known what to do," said George.

"Navy?" asked the conductor.

"Used to be," replied George.

"Good to meet you, Chief! Thanks for what you did."

"Think nothing of it, Chief. All in a day's work."

"I hope there'll be no ill effects," said the conductor, looking at Edna.

"No, I don't expect so. It happened a long time ago now, on the Danae."

Edna grew more impatient as the conductor revealed that he too had been on the World's Cruise in the engine room of another ship and before the reminiscences could begin in earnest, dragged George away. George remembered his marital and paternal responsibilities and complied, though not all that meekly.

Boar's Hill was a lovely place and they looked at the views in several directions it afforded before they sat on one of the seats provided to eat the sandwiches and rock cakes and drink the tea. They had to pass the flask to each other as they had not brought any cups and Alex burnt his mouth on the hot liquid, "Because you would be selfish and take it first," said Edna.

They were forbidden access to the very top of the hill and could see that it was occupied by men who from time to time took long turns with large versions of what Alex had seen people using at the New Theatre. George explained to him that they were members of the Observer Corps and that the things they were looking through were powerful binoculars, which made far off things seem close.

"What are they looking out for?" asked Alex.

"Jerry," George told him.

"Will he come this afternoon?"

"I shouldn't think so, boy," was his welcome reassurance. "Even bomber crews like a day off now and again."

"Another drop of tea?" asked Edna.

"I've got a better idea," said George, looking down at a friendly roof, having observed what it covered as they walked up. A pleasant hour was spent looking at the view in the garden of the pub, with Alex allowed to wander away as long as he could still see his parents and his parents finding that their characters did have at least some compatibility, though it had been damaged by the Sunday night to Friday night parting each week.

At about three o'clock, they were asked to leave the garden and they walked round the hill again until it was time to catch the bus back to the city. It was the same one, and the same crew, and George and the conductor exchanged friendly greetings and called each other "Chief" again, once when they got on, a second time when George showed the return ticket and finally when they got off. The old inadequately maintained bus found no difficulty going downhill and by six o'clock they were going past the Majestic cinema just before they reached their final stop.

"That's where all those poor devils from Stepney had to stay - you remember Joyce telling us about them?"

"I suppose we've got a lot to be thankful for," said George.

"Had a good day?" asked Graham. "You don't mind helping me turn over the allotment to-morrow, do you?"

"Mind your hernia," said Edna.

George smiled, hitching up the truss he had worn for twelve years now.

"You help where you can," he said cheerfully.

IV

One day a couple of weeks later, Edna was in need of distraction and met Alex from school at half past three and took him to the cinema with her. Because they arrived in the middle of the programme, they saw the main film first. It was in black and white with Ruritanian princes and occasional outbursts of song, which fitted his criterion that all songs must perforce be sad, even if sung with a smile on the face. There was a newsreel. The Russians were fighting back hard against Hitler's invaders and were being helped by supplies from Britain sent with great difficulty via a place called Murmansk. A great deal of coverage was given to General Rommel, even though he was on Hitler's side and was causing much concern to our armies in the North African desert.

The lasting impression on Alex's consciousness, however, was from the other film. It was a Western in Technicolor; a story of settlers in Red Indian country. One of its takes was of little houses in which the settlers lived being set on fire, followed by a long shot of them burning away to nothing. Edna looked down to see him quietly weeping, but she was enjoying the story so hoped that he would soon get over it as he did for the time being. The destruction was later avenged when certain wigwams were set on fire by the people who had built the little houses in the first place. He did spend some time wondering why it was all right to set Indian wigwams alight whereas burning settlers' houses gave him such distress. Whatever the answer to that dilemma might have been, the image of the houses on fire stayed in his mind. During the course of the evening the distress returned and the tears began again.

"What's the matter with you?" asked Edna.

"Them little houses," he said.

"You're not still moping about that, are you? That's the last time I take you to the pictures."

"I am. And I don't mind if you don't if that's what they are all like."

"Don't be so silly. It's only a story you saw."

"But stories are about what's real, aren't they?"

"Sometimes, I suppose: but not always, and not that one!"

"Why not that one?"

"Oh, I don't know. But if you are going to go round like a dying duck in a thunderstorm after being given a treat, I haven't got much time for you!"

"Perhaps you haven't got much time for me anyway!" was his the final desperate outburst.

Joyce looked up from her book, "I'm sure that's not what Mum meant, Alex."

Alex looked at Edna and saw no reason to change his mind. It was decided that it was his bedtime and that he'd better go and wash. He did so - very perfunctorily. The fact that Edna did not check up on him suggested that his suspicions about her were confirmed. She came to tuck him in without saying anything beyond what was necessary to fulfil the task, and then put the light out right away without asking him as she usually did, whether he wanted to look at his books for a while before he went to sleep. The little houses on fire stayed in his mind for a long time and he did not understand how doing what Edna wanted to do had turned into a treat for him.

V

Many of Alex's formative experiences seemed to have happened on Oxford buses and in relation to the anger he provoked in his mother against him. One of the more significant ones occurred preparatory to one of her last aimless perambulations in the city before she had to accept that her way of life had changed and that there was nothing she could do to change it back.

Christmas had come and gone again and George's days off were over. A week of Alex's school holidays was left. Edna insisted on going out on a wet day. As she dressed Alex in his outdoor clothes she muttered that she could not stay in all the time looking at these four walls. Alex glanced round him to see rather more than that: the living room door was open and he could see at least two more walls by the staircase, and there were several others within easy reach of anyone who went through the door. Before he could say anything Edna pulled his scarf about him with such ferocity that he was too winded to speak.

"It really is dreadful out there, Edna. Do you really have to go?" said Joyce.

"Yes. I want to go and collect my shoes from the menders before I wear out my best ones and I want to call on that corset-maker Mrs Wilson told me about the other day."

"That could all keep until a better day, couldn't it? Alex will be back at school soon and you could go much easier on your own."

"Maybe. But we are both about ready for going out now, so we might as well get on. See you later, Joyce."

"Well, if you must go . . . Remember there's a nice stew on for dinner at one o'clock!"

By this time Edna and Alex were in the street and making for the bus stop, both within close reach of a different sort of personal stew of their own.

Because of the wet, the bus was full up. The conductor said there was no room upstairs and they had to stand as far as the station where several passengers got off. Edna sat down on the seat next to the window with Alex beside her by the downstairs gangway. When the bus stopped next, more wet people got on and came to stand in the crowded gangway, one of whom being an elderly woman with two large bags. Edna saw her and dragged Alex over to sit on her lap so that she might have his seat. He was apprehensive about this because he remembered another time that he had sat on her lap when she had not wanted him to and when the results had been unpleasant. Once he and the old woman were in position, he was clamped tight by his mother, and said,

"I don't think old people should be allowed on buses!"

Edna found great difficulty in smacking his face from where she was sitting. After trying to several times, she was reduced to hissing in his ear,

"That was very rude! Now apologise to the lady."

"No."

Edna began desperately to shake him up and down. This meant a measure of discomfort for the old lady as well and she turned to Edna and said,

"It really doesn't matter, dear. It's no wonder he regrets having to give up his seat on this filthy morning. He's tall for his age isn't he?"

"I've done my best to teach him some manners," Edna muttered, now sweating with embarrassment at the way things had gone.

"Don't you worry at all. I'm getting off at Carfax and then he can have his seat back."

"We are getting off there too," said Edna.

"You said we were going to St Giles," put in Alex.

"Well, I changed my mind," replied Edna, doing her best to squeeze her son lifeless before he should cause any more disquiet. The conductor called out that it was Carfax next stop, because nobody could see through the vapour on the windows.

"Good-bye, dear," said the old lady as she got up. "No one ever said bringing up children was easy - and I've had six."

Edna pushed Alex clumsily before her off the bus.

"Now you've got your socks wet!" she yelled as he fell off the bus into a puddle. "And you've splashed my only pair of lisle stockings! Good God, what more trouble are you going to cause to-day?"

At this she took off her glove and started to belabour her son ineffectively with it before dragging him down Cornmarket towards the Cadena once more.

"I'm taking you in here because I need a sit down; not because you deserve to be bought a drink. I've a good mind not to let you have one at all. Don't say a word. You've said more than enough this morning already. Just keep your silly little trap shut until I say you can talk again!"

With her coffee in front of her and a small glass of orange before Alex, mother and child sat at a table pretending that they were nothing to do with each other, taking no notice of anyone else who was near them. Alex saw Edna bring out her handkerchief from her handbag and apply it surreptitiously to take away her tears. He had been told to be silent, so no words were possible. He was still angry with a child's unfocused rage. He did not see his father much any more. His mother was always so miserable. The one special friend he had made at school was not acceptable to her. Once she found out that he was from Bermondsey she had told him not to mix with boys like that. He got on well with Joyce, but that relationship had become strained when he had been poking his hands down the sides of the big armchair in the front room when he had found a little orange-covered book with a sort of star on the front and the letters NESW at intervals around the star and inside the book thousands of small numbers in columns and boxes. He had given this to Graham and he had turned to John and told him off for hiding his logarithm book and claiming to have lost it so as to get out of his homework. John had, naturally, turned against him, and taken all the Meccano magazines back. "You cheap little sneak," he had said to him. And now, just because some old woman wanted his seat on the bus, Edna was in one of her sulks. So everyone was against him, except his Dad, and he wouldn't be back until another four days had dragged by.

Edna in due time put the wet handkerchief back in her handbag and stood up.

"Come on," she said to Alex. "We can't stay here all day or we'll miss out on Joyce's stew."

She marched him out into the rain with his thick overcoat getting heavier with the moisture it attracted by the time they reached a small street where Edna collected her shoes and then laboured on to the house in Jericho where the lady who fashioned excellent corsets would have been found if Edna had made an appointment and she hadn't still been at her daughter's in Witney. She had gone there for a rest, as Edna learned from a talkative neighbour. They walked back to Carfax once more, and waited for the Botley bus. It was half-past twelve now and three hours had done a fair amount to cool both tempers.

Fortunately there were few passengers this time and finding a seat downstairs was simple. The conductor was an amiable soul who made remarks about all his passengers being like drowned rats but that it didn't matter now there was no absorbent cloth left to upholster the seats. The force of this opinion was soon felt, as all of them slid about when their wet coats reached the shiny seat covers.

In fact, this was the salvation of the horrible morning for Alex. He slid down on to the floor and Edna had to drag him up again which, unaccountably in Alex's eyes, made her laugh, and then cry again, and then laugh once more. Alex was astonished to find her cuddling him as he sat by her, kissing the top of his cap, wet though it was. Alex could not understand any of this erratic behaviour, but was glad this part of it was happening. Edna laughing was much easier to cope with than Edna angry with him.

As she squeezed the life out of him again, but with a different motive, she said to him:

"You are a little pest, but you're all I've got, aren't you?"

She made to kiss him again, but put lipstick on his coat sleeve instead, which made her rueful again.

"I shall have to do something about your coat, won't I?" she said, "It's much too small for you now."

They got home at five to one, which just gave them time to rub their faces with towels before Graham came over from the dairy and they sat down to eat the warming and relaxing stew which had bubbled on the Kitchener stove for the last three hours to fill all the rooms with a smell such as to make the four of them, Alex included after the idea had been explained to him, pretend they were the Bisto Kids.

That afternoon, Alex repeatedly drew dark figures walking through the rain. Since there were so many of them depicting a woman with her hand raised in anger towards a child, he decided they should make their way to the fire-grate while no one was in the room. He realized that his father could not say that these were not bad. There were in fact well drawn, but their purpose, he realized, had been to draw out pain. The pain had been acute and he had no way to explain that to anyone in words since he had brought it on himself. He decided that he would do what he ought to assist irksome old people, if only out of sense of self-preservation.

Edna was fond of telling people who admired Alex's drawings that she could not draw a straight line and so she had no comparable consolation available. Her son watched her as she fitfully dozed in an armchair, recognizing that she felt lonely and lost too, and wishing that he could have helped her. At his age he was not able to recognize the resentment that was growing in her. She had long since stopped asking any deity that might listen to her, "Why me?" and defended herself with self-assertiveness whenever she had the chance. Even Joyce and Graham could do no more than watch what was happening to her and share her hope that George would not be late this Friday evening.

VI

When school opened again, Alex was glad to be out of the house for six hours in the day. He realized for himself what his mother meant by looking at the four walls.

In each classroom there was a coal fire, well guarded with black painted railings and topped with a brass bar that it was someone's early morning task to keep polished and remove all the little finger marks accumulated each day as the children found some pretext to come to the teacher's desk and linger momentarily in the warmth. By now Alex's precocity in reading had been matched by what went on the classroom and the writing skills were being obtained in due sequence. Everyone in Miss Hill's class could print with a controlled hand now and could do adequately in arithmetic (which nobody in those days called mathematics until the tasks had become much more involved). Miss Hill still used the imperative mood often, but she was respected and obeyed more or less willingly by all but one or two.

Alex had been the narrator in the class nativity play before Christmas and this had gained him some standing with the others because he had been the only one to wear his Sunday best instead of masquerading as a shepherd in a dressing gown and a tablecloth or a king in someone's old curtains and a cardboard crown, thereby looking a bit silly. Isabel, who sat next to him, had not warmed to being an angel in a sequinned frock and cardboard wings. In fact, she felt very cold during rehearsals. Alex, however, in his white shirt and his pullover above his usual corduroy shorts and long socks was as warm as any boy was allowed to be indoors in those years. He seemed to have the most comprehensible speaking part, too. He had to read from what was called a parchment, but was in reality a piece of ordinary paper, which Miss Hill had singed round the edges and hung a large blob of sealing wax from with a bit of ribbon. When he had read from the paper, the parents and other children had listened. The poor lad who was the innkeeper was hard to hear. Isabel, when she announced the improbable and incomprehensible coming event to the poor little girl who played the Virgin Mary and was the butt of vulgar jokes for many days, punctuated the whole performance with coughing, which she could not help since she was sickening for laryngitis. After the show, the seat next to Alex had been empty for the last two days before the holidays.

That had been last term. Miss Hill had looked for something topical for this term too, but kept her powder dry until February when Valentine's Day gave her the opportunity for some simple handwork, to which she hoped the children would respond. Accordingly on February the second, after a churchy assembly during which Miss Cook had held forth about the Presentation of Christ in the Temple, Miss Hill designed a large heart shape on the blackboard and decorated it with a lace edge, writing the saint's name in large copperplate above it.

She then told the children that on February the fourteenth people sent Valentine cards to those whom they liked best. She set the class the task of making valentines for the people they themselves liked the most, with the intention of them being given to these favoured persons on the day when it came. There was a good deal of giggling about this, but Miss Hill soon exercised control and the pieces of card were issued: "One each, and there are no others if you spoil yours!" A little more was done to decorate them on each of the next ten school days.

While they were designing their cards and thinking what to write on them, they were allowed to talk quietly. Isabel began to dedicate hers to her brother who was a good bit older than she was and had just gone into the army. Some of the children opted for their mothers. Alex decided that the person he liked best was George and dedicated his to "My Dad". He listed what he liked about him, and ended wistfully with, "I wish you were with us more often, but I see why you can't be". He printed it all without a mistake and managed to space the words so that they all kept within the confines of the heart shape without crossing its edge or the letters needing to be squeezed up. On the afternoon of the thirteenth, Miss Hill gave them each an envelope to fit the card and Alex brought his home to leave on the mantelpiece for George to find.

Fortunately such a card had already come through the post with a London postmark on it for Edna to open next morning, though she was not a little upset by George being singled out for Alex's affection at her expense, as it seemed. She was convinced in her own mind that she had done all she could to make Alex feel secure in this foreign place. She confided this to Joyce, who tried to reassure her by saying, "He's only a small boy as yet. See what he does when he's older."

Edna presumed she was speaking from experience and was somewhat consoled since John was now approaching fourteen. It was Joyce and Graham's concern for John that provoked the next event which was to affect the joined lives of these two families. It took place on the Saturday evening of the following week

VII

Alex was presumed asleep in George's arms after a marathon reading of yarns for which all the others except John, who was up in his room, had been present. Before Edna stood up to take him to his bed in the next room, Graham said, with Joyce nodding agreement,

"Look, George, Edna, there is something we both want to discuss with you."

Instead of acting upon her built-in instinct to prevent a child hearing anything that belonged in the field of adult concern, Edna left Alex where he was, and he heard most of the subsequent interesting discussion.

"What's all this, then?" asked George feeling apprehensive lest he was about to be asked to take Edna and Alex away.

"Don't worry," said Joyce. "It's only an idea in its early stages as yet, but we wanted to see what you might think about it."

"Go on, then," said George, "The suspense is hard to bear!" and laughed to hide his misgivings.

"Well," began Graham, "It's like this. The bombs seem to have been called off in London for a while now and, well, with John at what he calls a daft school here, we want to take him back to Motspur Park. Then he can go back to Rutlish School, where the teaching and discipline are better. Our tenant has written to us to say he does not want to stay there after this coming summer, and this makes it easier, and I would like to see if I could get my job back at the store."

"You'd be leaving here, then," said Edna, taking off her glasses to wipe her eyes.

"Yes," Graham said, "But there's a bit more to it if you wouldn't mind hearing the rest."

"No. Go on," said George, impatient to know it all.

"If I were to leave here, they'd want a Maintenance Engineer to take my place, and I was going to ask you, seeing how you can't get your house rebuilt within the foreseeable future, whether you'd like to take it on, and make life a bit easier for yourself. I know it's only a job in a dairy, and it doesn't have the prestige of what you are doing now, but you have been looking very drawn and tired lately with all the travelling and we both know how much Edna and the boy miss you when you're not here. The pay is not much less, this house goes with it, and it's not too bad a place to spend a few years in while the politicians and the generals get us back to rights."

"You mean you want me to change jobs with you, in other words."

"Neither of us had thought of it like that, George," put in Joyce, on the defensive. "That was your comment, not ours."

At this point, Alex had too serious a crick in his neck to allow him to pretend to be asleep any longer and Edna, hastily picking him up and taking him to his bed, called out, "Don't say any more till I get back!" Her words to Alex were no more than "Go to sleep quickly now," as she took his blue dressing gown off and pulled the bedcovers up to his chin. She put the boiled sweet she often gave him into his mouth with equal rapidity and rushed back to her husband and friends. As the sweet finished and he dozed off to sleep, Alex heard the voices through the wall in deep discussion, but heard no more until Sunday afternoon when it was discussed again openly, without any apparent misgivings about him or John hearing it all.

"I'll get in touch with the Amalgamated Engineering Union tomorrow, then, and see what they say about it, shall I?"

"That would be the best way, I think. If they say that it's feasible, then I could approach my bosses here, and we could both see what the store people think."

Alex liked the sound of the words "Amalgamated Engineering Union" and began to recite them as he sat drawing on the floor.

"What does it mean, Dad?" he broke an awkward silence by asking.

"Shush, Dad and Uncle Graham are talking," said Edna.

George turned to Alex and told him what it meant:

"A union exists to protect the interests of working men, and this one is for engineers like me and Uncle Graham. It's called 'amalgamated' because a long time ago it was not one union but several. D'you see?"

Before any more questions from Alex were possible the discussion began again and went round and round until it was time for tea - and then again until George went to pack his case and get on his way back to the seemingly quiet capital city.

As he was tucked in that night, Alex asked Edna,

"Are Uncle Graham and Auntie Joyce going to leave us here by ourselves, Mum?"

"We'll have to see," said Edna in the tone she used when he asked for something special for Christmas or his birthday. Alex went to sleep thinking that this was what Edna wanted as much as the Pattersons did. He wanted it too, if it meant that George would be living here as well.

VIII

In the springtime, Edna seemed to Alex more turned in upon herself. At first she had seemed pleased about the possibility of George coming to replace Graham here and having the house to herself. As the week-ends became warmer and Alex and his parents walked about the city as visitors used to in happier times, he overheard a great deal of what was meant to be kept from him.

One of the places George liked was Trinity College garden and he often led his family there in fine weather. Alex was nearer the ground than most people and met a tortoise for the first time. It had the appearance of being the owner of a particular stretch of border: its wrinkled face seemed timelessly wise to Alex as it blinked in the unaccustomed light after its hibernation. He was bold enough to pick it up by the shell and the accumulated contents of its bladder emptied in a stream upon the gravel path. Alex struggled not to drop the tortoise and George came to lend a hand from the seat where he and Edna had been discussing what might happen to them, glad of some relief and laughing. Alex looked up towards his mother while George placed the old tortoise back under the growing lupins and saw that her face was grim and her lips were chewing anxiously as she waited to resume the conversation.

"Go and see what else you can find," said George to Alex, "Only stay where we can see you, won't you?"

"All right, Dad," replied the boy and walked to where a girl in khaki jodhpurs and a green jersey much too thick for the late spring weather was taking dead flowers from the wisteria. A friendly conversation followed, in which the behaviour of the tortoise was discussed and Alex acquired information about the species that was unlikely to have come from home or school. He also learned what the Land Army was, that this young woman was in it, and that people like her could be recognized by their distinctive clothing. Her father was something to do with the college and she was helping out on a free weekend since most of the gardening staff was in the army.

When the wisteria looked once more like any other creeper on a college wall, Alex left his new acquaintance and went behind his parent's seat to hear Edna burst out,

"But after all we've worked for, to give it all up and leave without doing our level best to get it rebuilt seems so sad. We'll be back where we were when you first came out of the Navy."

"I'm not suggesting we burn our boats. There is no possibility of getting it rebuilt for a couple of years at least. The solicitor is quite firm about that. It doesn't mean that we are never going back: just that we aren't going back yet, that's all."

"Do you mean that, though. Or are you saying it just to keep me quiet?"

"Could I ever keep you quiet?" George said in a desperate attempt to make the mood lighter.

"No, that's why I'm having my say now, out of the way of Graham and Joyce, for whom it all seems to be more or less signed and sealed."

"It may seem signed and sealed, but it isn't. The firm may agree to his taking my job, and the dairy may see me as well suited as him to run their machinery, but there's all the wartime red tape to be untied about correct use of manpower and so on that all the bureaucrats talk about. It'll take a good long time to get all that sorted out."

"That's beside the point to me, George. What I mean is that their reasons for going back home are more or less the same as mine. I don't want to be stuck here where I don't belong. I came here expecting to stay for two weeks and then go back. Alex's chin was what brought me here and I don't want to stay here longer than I have to, with all the locals standing on street corners and eyeing me up and down as a Londoner as if I was dirt to them."

"Haven't you imagined that? You seem to get on well with Mrs Wilson and Mrs White."

"Yes, I do, but there are plenty of men in brown suits with watch-chains on street corners who say 'Ooh aar' as I go by and spit in the gutter while looking at me."

"I think you'll find they would have spat in the gutter anyway, whether you were there or not. There were plenty of people at home in Chatham who did that."

"But they didn't do it in Raynes Park, and I miss being there and want to go back. Sooner, not later!"

"There's no way of doing that, girl, just at present," said George, taking his hat off and fanning himself with it. "One thing I've got to tell you that I haven't up to now."

"What's that?"

"They've been understanding at the store, but there is a lot of tension there about me being away as soon as it shuts every Friday night. They open on Saturday, and the plant is maintained by people who weren't there when it was put in, and don't understand it as well as I am supposed to and they have to cover for me. Things are being said and the message is increasingly, 'Either come back full time, or we'll have to ask you to go.' I don't know how long I can fend off that kind of thing."

"Couldn't we move somewhere else then, to let you work as you used to?"

"I've thought all round that, but the only way to do it would be to sell our house and buy another one with a new mortgage, and who's going to buy a place with only a downstairs front room still standing, however desirable the area was before the war? There's something else, too. This old hernia of mine has been playing up a bit lately. The sawbones I went to see says that I have got to find something less demanding in terms of agility to do - and perhaps Graham's job would suit me in that respect. I don't want to be sacked on health grounds."

"So that's it," said Edna. "I've been on at you all these years to go and have the operation that would put it right, and you won't. Why won't you go and have it seen to now?"

"You wouldn't leave Alex in hospital overnight because of the bombs. Whatever Graham thinks, there are still a few of them falling in London, you know. That night in the coach station scared the life out of me; you remember where the London hospitals are? Sitting targets, all of them."

"Couldn't you have it done here?"

"Not very easily without living here, could I?"

Edna was quiet, and then jumped to her feet saying, "Good Lord, where's Alex?" only to find him standing three feet behind her. Then she added, "No good talking about it any more. It's getting cold here now. Let's go back, shall we?"

"It would be pleasant to be able to say 'Let's go home'," added George.

Edna blew her nose and only just caught her glasses in time before they fell on the pavement by the iron gates of the college. When sight and a measure of calm had returned, she took Alex by the hand and said to him,

“Look at all them funny old heads on the pillars over there.”

Although Alex was more interested in his parents’ and his own anxiety than a row of old emperors’ worn heads, for once he had the tact to reply,

“Yes, Mum. Funny ain’t they?”

George found he could still smile as he thought of telling his son and heir not to say “ain’t”, but he was being sensitive too.

On the bus going back to what was still their lodging house, all three of them quietly thought their own thoughts, each being miserable in their own way. Although he was longing to, Alex could not bring himself to ask George what red tape had to do with anything, nor what a bureaucrat might be.

5

Playground games were beginning to be more noticeable as the days became warmer. The five and six-year-olds in Miss Hill's class were not allowed to take part, but were expected to watch what the older ones did. No one seemed to teach these games, but they happened. When some arbitrarily chosen girl was put in the centre of a circle made by the others who went round her singing, "Poor Mary is a-weeping on a bright summer's day", Alex associated the song with all the others he had heard which, in their accumulation of distress, convinced him that the nature of songs was to express globally felt sadness. There was even a violent element: "The Farmer's in his Den" concluded with everyone heavily patting the child chosen as the bone wanted by the dog and this often allowed for heavy-handedness against its perpetrators' victim.

Relations between Edna and Joyce now seemed to be strained. They were very careful to be polite to each other now and the casual nature of their earlier chore-sharing had somewhat evaporated. George and Graham still got on with each other well enough: years in the mess deck had taught them how. They were working together at the dairy for two weeks, so that they could be assured of a smooth changeover when the time came. The time lapse between George leaving the London store and Graham going back to it was covered by the fiction of George being on leave. John was in a perpetual black mood about having to go back to a school where, as he put it, there were a lot of lines to toe. He was not as forthcoming with help to Alex as he had been, though he had almost forgotten about him finding his deliberately lost logarithm book.

At eight o'clock one morning at the end of July, a large green removal van with Carter Paterson painted on it was parked outside. The name of the town it came from had been blacked out at the beginning of the war lest it should help lost German parachutists find their way about, as George told Alex when he asked him about it. The furniture that had survived from Raynes Park was being delivered and the few pieces that Graham and Joyce were taking to Motspur Park picked up. The rest of the furniture and effects had been sold for a song or two to the Rylands as the new tenants of the house that went with the job. This meant that there would be beds for the three of them to sleep on still and some saucepans and plates and cutlery for them to use since their own had perished in the bombing. The removal men obligingly put what was to stay behind in the rooms where George and Edna wanted them. George had carefully arranged this with them unheard by Edna so that he could wear his truss in peace.

When Edna fetched Alex home for dinner, the arrangements had nearly all been made. Though not materially changed, the kitchen was oddly empty and the fact of George sitting down to eat there on a Monday, though it had happened twice already, was still strange. Graham's good-humoured remarks were missing and Edna's way of dishing food up lacked something of the finesse which Joyce always brought to it. George tried to be cheerful, but he reacted with an unusual silence to the tense feelings that emanated from Edna like a magnetic field. He sat at the table dressed as Alex had been seeing him in the last two weeks, though never before. He wore his working clothes: a khaki shirt beneath his overalls with a pair of Wellington boots positioned on the back doorstep ready for his return to work after his dinner. Alex thought he looked lost.

At five past one, Edna broke with routine.

"Are you ready to go back to school?" she asked Alex. Once she was assured he was, she took him, still in her apron, to the front door, and saw him across the road to find his own way back to school. The school was not far away, but she had never let him go by himself before. Once she had seen him safely across the main road, she shouted after him, almost as an afterthought,

"Don't come home on your own. I'll come and meet you! Don't forget!"

Round the corner he met his friend Roy, of whom Edna did not approve, and they kicked a stone between them as far as the kerb opposite the school entrance. This brought the comment from his friend in his authentic Cockney voice,

"Your Mum wouldn't have let you do that, would she? Not respectable, is it?"

After school Edna met him as arranged and told him on the way home that his bed had been moved upstairs to the room where she and George had been sleeping, and which would be his room from now on. George and she had moved into the front bedroom.

"What about John's room, then?" Alex asked.

"You never know: we might have lodgers!" replied Edna expressing the subconscious mental reflex of one convinced that many a true word is spoken as a sick joke.

Alex enjoyed taking possession of a room that was really his own. A year and a half of sleeping in the living room had been enough, he decided, especially since it had been shared with a canary whose personal hygiene was lacking on occasions. The canary had gone back to Motspur Park to chirp in more familiar surroundings. George, who had taken the risk of an unofficial two hours off work, had put Alex's books in a bookcase, despite their disparate sizes, and he could go there in the day time if he wanted to and get things out without having to negotiate his way round everybody else who used the living room in the manner its name suggested.

The curtains were the ones that had been there before. The old divan was still his bed and its green checked cover was the same, but there was a chest of drawers of his own with his clothes in it and his cupboard from downstairs was not the only place where he could stow his gear - a term he had learned early from his father.

When he went downstairs again the changed appearance of the living room gave him something of a shock. Some of the furniture he had not seen since they had left the old house was there: the sideboard, the extending table, the dining chairs, and the old Cossor wireless, which George had persuaded to work again. Edna's Singer hand sewing machine stood under the window on the tea trolley with its wooden cover on: Alex recognized it from the many times he had crawled round it a long time ago on the floor in a corner where it was kept while not being used. The mirror over the mantelpiece had survived intact, which Edna never ceased to marvel at:

"So we might get some good luck after all," was her repeated comment about it for a week or two.

In the front room Joyce's velvet curtains remained; so did the sofa and armchairs. The pictures from the living room had been brought into it, resting on the back of the sofa (always called the settee) waiting for George to put them on the wall after work. The Pattersons had left the carpet with its detached warps and woofs behind as additional reminders that there was a war on.

Alex went into the garden. The pie dish was still there but he had no use for it now. What caught his eye was that the shed door did not have its accustomed padlock in place. He tentatively reached for the doorknob, turned it and pushed open the door to see by the light of the sun through the little window something that really made it like home for him: George's old sea chest, with its black and white paint and brass handles, which were sometimes polished in times past, and George's name painted on the top. He ran his hands along the front of it and knew that this was a token of safety from the old house that had been restored to him.

Edna did not come to find him and he was sitting in the shed on a chair that had no back with his hand still resting on the black and white painted surface of the chest when George came into the garden just after six o'clock. George saw that the shed was open and came in too.

"Hullo," he said. "Found something you like there, eh?"

"I'm glad you've still got this, Dad."

"So am I - and the tools in it too. I'm glad we decided to keep it in the Anderson shelter last year. After tea we'll come out again and you can hold things ready while I screw the vice back in its place on the corner of the chest. This is a bigger shed than the one we had at home. I'd better not leave it unlocked, though, had I, or you'll be pinching all sorts of things - like your fingers!"

Alex shook his head in amused denial and they went in to find that Edna had tea ready for them on the living room table. The reason that she had not come looking for Alex was that she had made an apple pie as something special for their first evening as a family on their own together for a very long time.

"I hope you haven't burnt the custard," said George, and Edna went to brain him with a plate, thought better of it, and hugged him as he stood at the head of the table with Alex holding them together as near to their waists as he could reach.

II

Ever since Edna and Alex had been in the house, Alex had noticed that on certain days during the week a number of cattle went past the garden gate.

"Where are they going, those cows?" he once asked her.

"It's a dairy. They are going to be milked," was Edna's first answer, thinking on her feet. She had then hastily asked Joyce, who also asked Graham, to corroborate this statement of hers if ever Alex asked them where the cattle were going. She had sworn George to secrecy on the matter as well.

Like many of his generation, Alex had been a Cow & Gate baby and although he was no longer using the product had been aware of a good number of the tins it came in put to other uses in the old house before they came here. He had made the connection between cows and milk for himself and so was able to accept his mother's subterfuge for a surprisingly long time. When he had gone to school, it was easier for the pretence to be maintained, of course, because he no longer saw the beasts during term time. Although Alex was loth to provoke Edna's wrath, having done that with too great a frequency lately, the question of where the cattle were going arose once more in his mind now that it was summer again.

With the school holidays beginning, he spent a good deal of time in the garden. He would have liked to have spent some of that time in the shed, but George had restored the padlock and told him that he could only go into it when he was there too. There was also a new cupboard installed in it that was also locked and never opened unless George was there by himself. Whenever Alex asked George what the cupboard contained he was always given a jocular but firm refusal to answer truthfully. It was a very strongly built cupboard and he was sure it did not come from the shed that used to house the sea chest. Alex was more interested in the cupboard than the cows, but since no answer to the mystery about the former was given his mind returned to the unresolved difficulty about the latter. He had never seen the cows going back again after milking and besides, no cows were to be seen in any field close by. He had been on enough walks with either or both his parents to be sure of that.

The mystery soon solved itself, however. Now that George and Edna were under the same roof outside his working hours, she no longer felt any need to traipse around aimlessly with Alex in tow and this gave him more living space. It was raining a few days after his last ponderings upon this bovine conundrum and Alex was on his own in the living room drawing a battle scene. He was sitting at the small table under the window that looked out into the narrow passage between the back door and the brick wall dividing their garden from Mrs White's.

There was a sudden ferocious noise outside and at the same time the light changed from that of a sombre day to twilight. Alex looked up to see one of the cattle with its fore hooves on the top of the window frame and slobber from its mouth gathering on the window panes. He heard the terrified noises the poor beast was making. Alex expected the window to give way, threw aside his drawing, and rushed to the kitchen, where Edna looked as if she was doing her best to swallow the bottom of her apron which she had shoved in her mouth to stifle the worst of the piercing scream which was issuing from deep inside her. A man with a stick appeared behind the animal, senselessly hitting it hard and making its misery worse. Edna snatched Alex into the passage and slammed the door behind her. They made their way together up to his bedroom from which, since it was above the living room, they could see what was happening.

By the time they were there, other men had come into the garden and were throwing ropes to catch the animal's horns. With one man on either side of it, the beast was pulled down and led backwards until it was past the lavatory door where they could turn it round and take it away. Just as they had gone, George came running into the garden; he looked up to see his wife and child unharmed in the window and smiled with relief as he stopped and tried to recover his breath.

Edna and Alex went downstairs as he came into the kitchen.

"Thank God you're both all right," he said at once, still gasping, "Saw the bullocks coming in and then the commotion round our gate, so thought I'd better come over and see what was up! I must sit down."

And he did so, panting, at the kitchen table while Edna and Alex worried about him in their turn.

"Why was the cow so frightened of going to be milked, Dad?" Alex asked after the wheezing had become less acute. George looked at Edna, and Edna looked at George.

"Well? Why?"

"You might find this difficult to take in, boy but, well, it was not a cow, as a matter of fact, and it was not going to be milked."

"What was it going past for, then?"

"It was going to the slaughterhouse."

Edna looked away, as if to let George know he was on his own now.

"Slaughter is killing isn't it?"

"Yes, that's right."

"So they were going to kill it . . . and the others with it?"

"That's right."

"If it wasn't a cow, what was it?"

"A bullock: in this case a well-grown one."

"I don't know what a bullock is."

George looked desperately at Edna and she looked up at him trying not to smile at his predicament.

"A bullock is a young male, and a cow is female."

"So that's why it had no udders!" Alex burst out as a subsidiary question had been answered for him.

Edna's face was like a beetroot now, largely because of this taboo topic being raised in this way, but at the same time at amusement caused by the expression on George's face when he heard what Alex said. However, the speech that had come into George's mind under such provocation could not be denied emergence into the daylight, although its redundancy was plain to him even before he began to speak.

"Look," he said. "If we were cattle on a farm, then I would be a bullock, well, no, a bull, that's a full grown bullock; your mother would be a cow, and you would be a calf . . ."

The meretricious associations of the word "cow" were all too much for Edna and she spluttered while George dried up. She had just been frightened to death, as she put it, and now that they were all three safe her fear burst out in hysterical laughter which went on and on while neither her husband nor her son could think of anything to do to stop it. It was halted in the end by the manager of the slaughterhouse appearing at the door. He knocked apprehensively and when he saw they were sitting there opened the door for himself, wiped his feet and came in.

"I came to see if everything was all right, George. You're all safe, I hope."

"Yes, we'll live, Ben. I trust this sort of thing doesn't happen too often, though."

"It's never happened before, to my knowledge. He was a big beast, that one, larger than we usually have, and poor old Jim just didn't know what to do except hit it with a stick. Your ferns look a mess, don't they, and I'll see the painter comes over to put the window frame right. How it managed not to break the glass I'll never know!"

"Righto, then," replied George, "Thanks for coming round. I suppose I'd better be getting back myself. Bottling starts in a minute or two and I better be there in case the machine seizes up."

The embarrassed slaughterer left and George kissed Edna and patted Alex's shoulder.

"See you at dinner time," they all said at once.

Alex found his drawing book and carried on where he had left off.

III

Later in the day it stopped raining. George had been home to eat and gone back to work and when it was just after three o'clock Edna washed Alex's face and took him with her to the recreation ground, which all the locals called simply "the rec" for a concert to be given by an army band. They went out of the back gate, noticing that one of the bullock's horns had raked across it, through part of the cobbled yard between the house and the dairy and out into Henry Road, which had more of the dairy on the right and houses similar to their own on the other side. It was a short street and it ended in at the rec gates, through which they went. They occupied two of the chairs that had been arranged upstairs in the pavilion that overlooked the sports ground.

The sky was full of ominous dark clouds but the members of the band dutifully marched on in their khaki battle dress, broke ranks and took their places on the improvised bandstand. The bandmaster took his station, turned to the audience and saluted before he began the medley of songs from the shows that had been rehearsed and often played at other venues. Edna sang along with some of the tunes, as did several of the audience, mostly mothers and grandmothers with young children on holiday from school.

As the performance was woven together out of its component tunes, the clouds became lower and, from the height of the pavilion, Alex watched this meteorological phenomenon with great interest: the clouds became more dense and firm in their outline until lightning split the sky, thunder took over from the band's percussion section and rain suddenly emptied itself all over the bandstand canopy and into the balconies from which the audience was watching. The balconies soon emptied as the women and children made their way into the rooms of the pavilion from where they could still see whatever might be going on. The bandmaster kept conducting until he realized that no one could hear above the noise of the downpour and its accompaniment of thunder. Then he put his baton under his arm and waved a dismissal to the musicians who, picking up instruments and sheet music, ran headlong to the pavilion ground floor, with their uniforms taking on a blackish appearance as they were soaked in an instant.

"What a shame," said Edna. "I was enjoying that."

"So was I," said Alex. "The clouds were wonderful, weren't they?"

"The clouds? No! The music."

"I was watching the clouds . . . and the lightning!" And here Alex made his imitation of a thunderclap. Although some of the women standing there were amused, it made Edna profoundly uncomfortable. The discomfort was mollified when the bandmaster came upstairs to apologise for the swift curtailment of his programme.

"I am so sorry, ladies," he said. "But you will agree that all this is beyond anyone's control."

He then bowed in an old-fashioned way and smartly left.

The storm passed and the audience dispersed. At home (as it now certainly was) Edna went to get tea ready and Alex went upstairs to look at his books. He found the old one with the trees, which was still a favourite of his, and lay down on the bed to leaf through it. That amused him: he had only just heard of leafing through a book, but not all books were concerned with trees, were they? He must remember that to tell George at tea.

As he dozed off to sleep, the sky grew dark again in spite of double Summer Time and the thunder re-commenced while a great, lumbering beast with horns, walking on its hind legs, lunged towards Alex with head lowered, intent on pinning him to the garden gate. The beast slobbered as it came towards him and its eyes rolled wildly in time to the lolling of its tongue. The roaring that issued from its mouth was terrifying and Alex stood before the gate defenceless as the point of the horn came nearer to his stomach. He opened his mouth to yell and found pressure not on his stomach but his shoulder as Edna shook him awake,

"Come on. Tea's on the table and your Dad's waiting to start."

Edna was astonished by how eager he was to wash his hands in the bathroom and run downstairs. Once at the table, he hardly stopped talking and took a very long time to finish his food. He was pleased that George liked his joke about the leaves in the tree book.

He fell asleep again in an armchair very soon. In this dream the beast was being ridden by the bandmaster, who was using his baton to support the threat posed by the horns. This time it was George who rescued him and carried him "up the wooden hill". As it was still light, he meant to read a story, but the book soon fell from his grasp. He fell asleep with neither bulls nor bandmasters to disturb him until it was light again and by then they were memories not threats.

IV

George found that one of the benefits of taking over Graham's job was that he was also entitled to the leave he had accumulated. Edna's young sister Hetty had a husband whose job had taken him to Walney Island in what was described to Alex as The North.

They had not been there very long, and one of the reasons for the move was that Geoff, Hetty's recently and quietly acquired husband, had been in the Auxiliary Fire Service all through the London blitz and took advantage of his position as a civil servant in the Admiralty to angle for a move to a place out of range of the Luftwaffe. The organizers of submarine production at Barrow-in-Furness had a vacancy. Geoff applied for it and was relieved and glad to be appointed. So now Hetty wrote to Edna suggesting that she and George and Alex should come for a summer holiday by the sea for ten days. The place had all the attractions of Blackpool and Morecambe Bay: true, the beaches were defended from possible invaders with rolls of barbed wire, but it would be a change for them and the sea air would do them good.

At the station with Alex the following Saturday afternoon, trying to ignore the notice that asked him whether his journey were really necessary, George found that the train journey to Barrow was possible, although it would involve three changes: at Birmingham, Warrington and Carnforth and, if they were to get there by six in the evening as he hoped, they would have to be at Oxford station at four in the morning. Some of the changes would involve long waits and the booking clerk pointed out that there was no guarantee that all lines across the West Midlands would be open and accessible to a passenger train. George thought it would be worth it and bought the two and a half return tickets. When they were put on the brass ledge at the front of the booking booth for George to take, Alex stood on tiptoe to see that there were three tickets that were the same colour and shape.

"Is one of them the half ticket?" he asked.

"Yes. That one," said George, showing him the ticket that was for him.

"Why is it called a half, then?"

"Because you go for half the price of Mum and me."

"Won't my bum take up just as much room on a seat though?"

"Of course it will, especially the way you fidget."

"Why is my ticket a half, then?"

"So that poor and honest working men can take their families on trains from time to time."

"Are you a poor and honest working man, Dad?"

"Good God Almighty!" said George.

"What's He got to do with it?" said Alex, mentally using a capital letter for the deity as Miss Cook had taught them in assembly.

"He gives fathers the strength they need to cope with the questions asked them by their sons."

With that, they went home and told Edna the good news that she would see her sister and meet her new brother-in-law in a few days' time.

"All being well," added George, taking the reservations put into his mind by the booking clerk very seriously.

"Four in the morning though, George!"

"What about it? I'll tell you what: we'll go to sleep in our clothes, all ready, and then we can just get up at three, have our breakfast and go."

He meant it as a joke, but Edna thought it good sense. So they did it. All three slept on the big bed in the front room upstairs, still dressed, except that the only part of George to go to sleep after one o'clock was his arm because Alex was asleep lying on it. George did not want to wake him up or he would wake Edna and then he would be kept awake himself, because she had done nothing but worry about the journey out loud in the hour it had taken her to get to sleep at twelve.

So a bleary-eyed George was not displeased when the alarm clock went off, and he quickly shaved and re-packed his shaving tackle before locking the house securely as they went to the station, with Alex in awe of the stars in the sky and the silence in the main road.

V

After all the months with John's Meccano Magazines, of which Alex was sadly now deprived, actually to stand on a platform in the dark and see a fiery locomotive come into the station right in front of him was very thrilling indeed. George took him to inspect the great wheels and the pistons and, when they had got into the compartment and settled down, quietly explained how steam builds up to drive a piston, is condensed and then used again. As the train moved away, "There," he said, "you can feel the surges of the steam, can't you?"

Alex could and was delighted that George should share his enthusiasm for what the engine driver and fireman were achieving while they sat here in comparative comfort and a dim wartime light. The carriage itself was interesting too, with its rich upholstery, the leather strap at the window and the brass lugs that went with it to keep the window open or shut as desired. The blinds were down as blackout on the side of the carriage where there was no corridor. Above the seats were framed photographs of seaside places and a castle and a sort of fishing net hung between brackets, upon which George had settled the big brown case and Edna had put the little case together with the shopping bag with the sandwiches and the thermos flask. Joyce had forgotten to take this last object out of the kitchen cupboard when she left.

"Come on, now," said Edna. "Stop asking questions, and let Dad have some shut-eye. He didn't get much last night."

"Why not?" asked the still excited Alex.

George could see that Edna was about to tell him about Alex keeping him awake by lying on his arm and his stare dared her to say anything. She quickly registered this and said to Alex, "Oh, never mind. Get some sleep yourself. It will be a long day and you'll need it." Alex, perched by the window, realized that he would not be able to see anything until it was light and took her advice. This time George kept his arm firmly to his side, and smiled at Edna sitting opposite him.

"It may be a funny way of doing it," he said to her. "But it's good to be going on holiday."

"I hope so," said Edna.

The changes of train were all successfully accomplished and George, after sleeping in his seat for two hours, pointed out things of interest as they passed them. Going through the midlands landscape, they were saddened to see a great deal of urban destruction. George commented:

"Look at the mess the bombing's made of all the industrial plant. I wonder if we shall ever be in a position to fight back."

Later however, when they were passing through scenes of agriculture and wild land, morale improved under the inspiration of the bright sun on the landscape.

VI

Hetty's husband met them at Barrow station in a car. He had a broad smile, though Edna saw that his teeth were detached from each other and tobacco stained. She thought his expression was shifty and the broad shouldered suit he wore flashy. She withheld her confidence in him, sensing that he was too much of a smooth operator. Nor did she warm to his attentions to her as he helped her into the front seat of the car, leaving George and Alex to take their places in the back where there was plenty of room for legs and luggage alike. She kept her right knee well away from his hand whenever she saw it moving towards the gear stick.

As far as Alex was concerned, Geoff was a real uncle, not a self-appointed one, and very soon he and Alex were on good terms. When opportunity arose, Alex asked,

"What kind of car is this, Uncle Geoff?"

"It's a 1934 Morris Ten Four. Don't run away with the idea that it's mine! I'm allowed to use it to get around the various operations we have here - and don't ask me anything about those because they're all very secret. I can sometimes manage to squeeze an extra journey out of the petrol tank if I'm careful."

By this time they were crossing a strip of water to reach a village where he and Aunt Hetty lived near the sea. Alex had never knowingly seen the sea before. And there it was: grey under a cloudy sky past a beach made up of big grey stones that seemed to reflect it.

"On a clear day, you can see the Isle of Man," Geoff told them as he turned a corner into the road where they would be staying for the next ten days.

Hetty was tall and angular, unlike Edna, who was no longer overweight but still fleshed out. She had long hair, fashionably cut, with its length flowing out of the back of the roll which many women now wore because they could set it up for themselves without recourse to a hairdresser.

"Here you are then!" was her greeting and she came to kiss her sister, to comment on how tall Alex had become and to hug George, who had always had a soft spot for his little sister-in-law.

"We've put you and George in here, Edna, and Alex has a bed in the attic room." Their home was on one floor except for this little room built into the roof with a window that allowed a squint at the sea from one angle. Alex liked it and was pleased when George brought his clothes and a few of his books up so that he could make the room his own as he put them in the places assigned to them.

Food was ready on the table when he answered Hetty's call to come down and they all had a pleasant meal together. George expressed interest in the reason for Geoff being up here, knowing that naval shipbuilding was something that went on in the Barrow yards, but Geoff kept the information he was prepared to give very general.

"I'd like to take you round, George, but what we do here is so vital in combating the U-Boats that I'm not even allowed to tell myself where I'm going in the mornings!"

"Anyway," put in his wife, "whatever you do is a damned sight easier than being at the office all day and then being on called out for the Fire Service, isn't it, Geoff?"

She turned to Edna, and went on, "D'you know, he didn't take his fireman's boots off for three days and nights over one weekend in the worst of the blitz and then they had to be cut off."

George and Edna made sympathetic sounds in Geoff's direction as they ate.

Alex wanted to know more.

"What did you have to do then, Uncle?"

"I had to drive a big fire appliance as far as I could get it among the rubble, lend a hand with putting out fires, and after that we had to help as many people as we could."

A distant look came into his face as he finished and he attacked his sardines in order not to say anything else. Aunt Hetty gently patted Alex's arm as he sat next to her and said quietly,

"Promise me not to ask him any more. He saw a lot of very nasty things and he can't talk about it, any more than he can tell you about his work here, though for different reasons. It was my silly fault for bringing the subject up."

Alex felt sorry for a man who couldn't tell people about his achievements, but George's reaction to what he had said about the shipyards made him more appreciative about what might be in the locked new cupboard in the shed at home.

The silence was replaced by talk of family matters. Hetty produced the few photographs she had of her wedding day and told Edna all about re-styling one of her pre-war dresses for the occasion. Geoff asked if that was a picture of his wedding as well and, when reassured that it was, added apprehensively,

"I'm sorry it had to be a small occasion. We couldn't ask anyone to it because we did not know if we could keep the appointment ourselves even, on account of the raids and my fire service duties."

"How did you feel about that?" Edna asked, remembering her own wedding under not dissimilar circumstances.

"Well, our Dad's gone on, so there was no one to give me away and Geoff's family are all in Australia. It was for us two, anyway. I feel fine about it! We've got the bit of paper and the registrar's signature. What more do you want for legal happiness?"

After that, George carefully steered their conversation into other, less sensitive, areas than marital bliss in wartime.

"I have to be at work tomorrow," Geoff told them, "but there's the sea here and a few old bits of ruins that are worth a look at. Perhaps one day, George, you would like to take Alex into Barrow and just watch what's going on in a few places. Don't wear a leather overcoat and dark glasses under your trilby, though. I don't want to come and have to bail you out and Alex is far too young to be a spy!"

It was agreed that they would slough off the effects of the long journey the next day and then, while Hetty and Edna went their own way the day after, George would rediscover his maritime roots, even if it was a case of submarines rather than cruisers. What really mattered was to stop Jerry from sinking convoys. George wanted to believe that the allies were fighting back properly now. Information about that would be very heartening to him, especially in consideration of what he did most evenings after unlocking the secret cupboard in his shed when Alex had gone to bed and while Edna listened to the wireless in the living room. He hoped his little parcels of marine engine parts worked on the small lathe provided for the purpose and sent off each week in an approved manner were his small but vital contribution to the national war effort. In his own unofficial way, George was as patriotic as Horatio Nelson and as determined as the statesman from the past whom he had made his personal hero, William Pitt the Elder.

VII

The clouds were still low the next day, so all the Rylands and Hetty did was walk as far along the beach as they could to see and hear the Irish Sea pound on the stones. One or two vessels in the hazy distance were discerned and George told Alex they were probably making for Belfast where there were more naval facilities.

As he grew, with George as his mentor rather than the women at school, Alex had no problems with words like "facilities". Edna frowned on the way George treated their son, thinking that he would only be a little boy for a precious few years: there was time enough for all that grown-up stuff when he was of an age for it. Her own Edwardian childhood had been in a village called Luton, not far from Chatham, fairly uncomplicated, and with no enthusiasm for education after her poor mother died. George's world however, just three miles away, had been more demanding.

His mother had the same view about childhood as Edna: the two women from different generations were very like each other, though they never would admit it to themselves in their now rare meetings. His father, however, saw things differently and made sure that George learned all he could at the technical school - not just the things that would help him fulfil his immediate task of getting into the Navy as a craftsman, but others like a knowledge of English history and playing rugby football, both of which he was enthusiastic for and good at. George, and his younger brother later on, were both supported in the best kind of education then available to boys like them. Their father also made sure that their sister acquired the skills needed for office work rather than accepting her mother's pressure to go into domestic service, despite the claim that it was a girl's best preparation for the early marriage usually seen as inevitable.

George and Alex walked along the sea road, with occasional forays on to the beach to see whether one of them could still make stones skim and jump on the water and if the other could acquire the necessary acumen. After several minutes it was decided between them that George had forgotten how and Alex would never learn, but it was fun all the same. Edna and her sister, meanwhile, were exchanging each other's stories of the last two years, with Edna concluding that her sister was a social climber and that she herself was not all that sorry that they lived a long way apart. This was the sister to whom their father wanted Edna to devote her youth. Resentment still lingered and there was nothing that Hetty, who wanted to be reconciled, could do about it. She tried very hard during these days they had together, but Edna did not change her mind very much as a result. Alex kept a memory of them: Edna in her green utility box coat and his aunt in her fitted one, both wearing simple hats, walking at a distance behind him with linked arms but no real contact. Years later, when he was told what body language was, he found he already knew.

So Hetty was amused by George performing antics for his son to laugh at, entertained by him as she always was over the years since she had known him, and Edna felt uncomfortable until they went back to a lunch of sandwiches. Geoff did not come home for lunch, so dinner was eaten in the evening. Edna complained to George as he put the light out not long after it that she did not like going to bed on a full stomach.

"Why don't you lie on your side, then?" said George.

As she turned with her back to him, she felt safe when his arm went round her and slept in the warm comfort he had always given her.

VIII

"There she blows!" George called out as he and Alex stood on a road bridge looking into one of the basins being used for submarine tests. The great black shape burst upwards, expelling water from its tanks to settle on an even keel. Then it went rapidly down again as the water was taken back in. They watched this happen several times. Activity then stopped and the conning tower hatch opened for people to climb out and down. Another submarine moved almost without sound under the bridge on which they were standing to berth astern of the first one. George explained the manoeuvre to Alex and he mastered the nautical terms to his father's satisfaction. A large surface vessel was berthed where the inlet widened to meet the sea and George explained that this was called a submarine depot ship, not because it was a submarine itself but because it provided facilities (facilities again!) for submarines at sea so that they had a longer range to match that of the German U-Boats.

"Why do they call them that?"

"It's short for the German words for 'under sea boat', which is what they call their submarines."

"I see. But why do they need to go under water?"

"Their intention is to sink as many British merchant ships as they can before they are seen themselves, so that food for us and supplies for our troops don't reach us, and then they can win the war. Big submarines like those two are being developed to stop them by catching and sinking them."

"Where does all this happen?"

"Turn round," said George. "Over there behind the depot ship is the Irish Sea. Then there is Ireland, another stretch of land about half the size of England, Wales and Scotland together. After that there's three thousand miles of the Atlantic Ocean before you get to America, where these supplies are coming from. The Germans go out from the ports they have captured in France and Holland, which are about three hundred miles in the other direction: you know where they are from that atlas that John left behind for you. The U-Boats have started to hunt our ships in what they call wolf packs and we have got to find ways of intercepting them before they can attack."

George smiled to himself as he began to work out his definition of what "interception" was, and when Alex asked, he was very fluent in reply,

"It means getting in among them and sending the blighters to Davy Jones - and before you ask, Davy Jones's Locker is a term for the bottom of the sea."

He thought to himself, all the same, "I wish Geoff was allowed to be a bit forthcoming. Surely there's more to it than bigger submarines that can go farther than the old ones."

Both men had signed the Official Secrets Act and George, like the rest of his contemporaries who were not personally involved with such secrets, had to wait until the peace-time war films to know about Asdic and Sonar, or even longer to hear about Enigma and the codes that were broken at Bletchley Park.

With a sufficient number of rests on public seats and on the edges of horse troughs still conscientiously filled with water each day by the council workmen, Alex was very happy to spend the whole day like this. So it was that, towards five o'clock, they were walking past one of the shipyards when a hooter sounded on a building very close to them. The huge gates in front of the building slid open and hundreds of men rushed out to make their way to the lines of buses that stood on the other side of the road ready to take them to their homes and lodgings. George and Alex quickly jumped out of their way. Alex noticed that some of the men's clothes smelt as though they had been burning and that all were dressed in a way similar to George when he was at work in the dairy, except that instead of the old trilby hat he invariably wore they had flat caps a bit like his own, only with more cloth in the crown. It took a time for the men to find their buses and for engines to be started to take them away. Then the road became quiet again, except for the sound the riveters made in other buildings at some distance away.

"Why were there so many of them, Dad?"

"It takes a lot of manpower to build and refit ships - riveters, carpenters, metal-workers and engine fitters like me: and that's a shift coming off work. Prior to that there would be just as many who arrived to take over from all those and there's every chance that the shift that's there now will go on well into the night."

"Not much of a life, is it?"

"Not when it's on a large-scale like this and there's the national emergency to consider as well."

"National emergency?"

"The threat from Hitler to defeat us, occupy our country and subjugate us."

"Subjugate?"

"Put us under his yoke as if we were cattle."

"Like that poor beast that broke into our garden?"

"If you like. It matters a lot that he doesn't get the chance. Then, perhaps, we can get back to something like the life we were beginning to have before the war. His blitz took away a lot of what your mother and I had worked for and would have liked to pass on to you when we're gone."

"Why haven't I got a brother or a sister?"

This change of direction made George stop in mid-stride. Alex realized that he had to think out his answer and felt sorry he had asked when it eventually came as they stood together where a jetty overlooked some oily water churned up by the screw of a motor launch moving about between the quays.

"Your mother was very, very ill when you were born and the process took a long time and gave her a great deal of pain. So we were advised that you should be our only one - and I'm glad you are here."

Alex found George doing what he very rarely did nowadays, ever since people started commenting on how tall he was getting: he picked him up. Then he remembered his hernia and put him down again.

"Come on, he said, we'd better find our bus back to your aunt's place."

Going on a bus with George was much more relaxing than going with Edna and talk that interested Alex continued right up to Hetty's front door.

IX

The rest of the holiday was not so full of activity. George was glad to be away from his work and found books on the shelves, which he picked up and began to read. He slept a lot of the time because the intensity of his life had receded for a few days. Edna envied him his power to relax because she could not. She felt that Hetty was judging her for having kept her distance for so long and for still speaking with the local accent of their part of north Kent rather than refining her speech as her sister had. Her husband was obviously someone who had got on in life, not having suffered setbacks like George. She still blamed herself for not having supported George enough in his time in the Navy, particularly when they lived in Malta in the nineteen-twenties. One or two of their contemporaries who had remained in the service were officers now, but on the other hand, she thought grimly, three or four of them had been killed in action. Time to reflect upon their life was all very well but, like life itself, reflection on it was frightening. She was not enjoying her holiday because there was nothing to get on with. Moreover, it was quite obvious that Alex had enjoyed his day in Barrow looking at the ships far more than anything she could have offered him. Needless to say, the weather was appalling.

She heard Hetty at the front door and went to meet her, aware that she would be carrying a good deal of shopping. They went together into the kitchen and Hetty put the food she had bought in the larder.

"I thought we'd have a chicken for your last evening here," she said. "They'll even pluck and prepare them for you at the farm for a consideration. Saves us getting feathers all over everything and the stink of pulling out giblets."

"That'll be nice. Thank you," said her sister, with the unpleasant thought crossing her mind that the consideration she spoke of might not be monetary in Hetty's case.

"Look, I've bought this as a present for Alex, if he'd like it."

She put a paper bag on the table.

"It's a soldier suit. But the more I think about it since I saw it in the shop, I have misgivings about it."

She opened the bag and took out the two garments, a battledress top and long trousers.

"Yes, as I thought. It's French. So I can't give it to him, can I?"

Alex had appeared in the doorway while this was going on.

"But I'd like it," he said.

"You could never wear it where anyone else would see it," said Hetty.

"Why not?"

"Ask Dad to tell you about the Maginot Line," said Edna.

So he did.

"The French let us down," said George. "We all thought the French army would hold the Germans off alongside our army. We sent our expeditionary force across the Channel when war broke out expecting that their line of defences would hold. The Germans just bashed their way through the Ardennes forest in their tanks and went round the end of the line of forts. We were forced back on Dunkirk. The army got back home, but not the equipment. Mr Churchill was astonished at this and even dashed across to France to meet the French ministers while there was still time. Then a new government was set up in France under a First World War hero, give him his due, called Marshal Pétain, who made peace with the Germans. So we had to sink their fleet in the Mediterranean to keep it out of German hands, or we'd be in an even worse state than we still are. I told you about all that when it happened. Sorry, boy, but Aunt Hetty is right, though you ought to go and thank her for buying it for you, just the same."

Alex accepted all this because he had heard it from George, his reliable source. He went back to the kitchen.

"Thank you for buying me the soldier suit, Auntie Hetty, but Dad thinks you are right about me not having it. He's told me about what happened and about Marshal Pétain."

"Well, that's that, then. It'll do me as polishing cloths, perhaps. Now then, Edna, would you get the greens ready for us - and I'll scrape these lovely new potatoes I got at the farm."

Edna remembered her own foray after eggs and, bearing in mind her suspicious thought earlier, asked awkwardly, "How do you find getting food up here?"

"You soon get to know who grows it and not too many questions get asked. We thought of growing things in the garden ourselves, but Geoff's so busy at work and I don't known how to start."

The sisters kept each other at arm's length while they prepared the dinner together, on Edna's part because she was ashamed of herself for thinking ill of Hetty, and Hetty's because she had tried to get on with Edna and seemed to have failed. Then a bottle of sherry appeared and some glasses and Hetty put them on the sideboard ready for when Geoff came home. Some orange squash was in readiness for Alex, too. This made Edna feel inadequate again and she excused herself to do her hair and have a wash. George felt the need to go and tidy up as well. They met in the bedroom.

George sensed Edna's distress more acutely now than he had during the last nine days in Hetty's house and asked her outright,

"What's up, girl?"

"Oh, I don't know, but I'll be glad to be gone tomorrow. I can't take much more of Hetty's money and success."

"Then you do know. I wish you could have relaxed and enjoyed the time here a bit more. Is there anything else bothering you?"

"Yes, George, there is. You know that I've always had a good deal of pain every month since Alex was born. Well, just lately it has been terrible."

"How long is 'just lately'?"

"Well, I suppose since Joyce and Graham left."

"The last two months, then."

"Yes. I get so run down too. This last three days it has been really nasty."

"When we get home we'll make a doctor's appointment. You've had more than enough to worry about since the blitz, besides all you went through when the boy was born."

"Thanks, George."

"Good. Well we'll have to go and eat this dinner Hetty's been good enough to provide for us. I think that's Geoff coming in now."

"I expect they have a chicken whenever they want it."

Yes, girl, I expect they do. And we have a nice butcher's chop whenever we want one!"

"So we do."

"Come on then . . ."

The sherry bottle was opened and Geoff filled his wife's and her sister's and brother-in-law's glasses.

"Here's to your safe journey home," he said.

"Here's to your happiness together; it's the first chance we've had of properly wishing you two well," George said.

"All the best," said Alex, and before they began to laugh, everybody looked round to see where the voice came from. Drinking standing up, they had forgotten him down at their waist level.

As Edna sat through the meal in pain, the only thing that comforted her was that a taxi had been ordered for nine o'clock in the morning and that there was on this occasion a through train from Carnforth to Oxford. Only one change was needed and they would be home in time for tea.

6

August saw Edna becoming more anxious about herself. George spent as much time with her as he could, while keeping up with his evening commitment in the shed. He discovered that once the few undergraduates left in the university had gone down, there was plenty of opportunity for town people to use the punts on the river, so on a Sunday afternoon George, Edna and Alex made their way to the boathouse by Magdalen Bridge. George wore his flannels, as he called them, although they were made of light material fully cut in the style of the late thirties. He handed Edna, wearing a new cotton dress and a short matching jacket, into the punt and she leant back on the cushions in the bow. Alex sat next to her, while George took up his position in the stern, at first seated with a paddle and later standing up with the pole in his hands. He soon became very proficient in his autodidact's way, in the use of the punt pole, steering properly with the thrust without fishtailing. Except on the rare occasions when someone else came with them, they had to turn round and come back at Parson's Pleasure, where men were allowed to bathe in the river without swimming costumes. Because George's hernia sometimes caused him discomfort, he could not manage to push the punt on his own over the rollers that allowed them to by-pass the swimming place. Even Edna made ribald jokes about the elderly college fellows who were known to make use of the place for swimming and sunbathing. These afternoons were much enjoyed and remembered by Alex deep in his unconscious mind until more like them came to him fifteen years later.

George's hernia did not stop him doing things he wanted to do and Edna was astonished one evening as he came home from the dairy wheeling an old but serviceable sit-up-and-beg bicycle that he had bought for two pounds from someone in the dairy who was hard up. Once he had repaired one or two things it was in good condition again and he set about modifying it with the addition of a small saddle that he made and attached to the centre of the cross-bar for Alex to sit on, and a small crosspiece on which to rest his feet as if on stirrups. Instructions were given to Alex that he must always hold the handlebars with both hands and George added extra rubber grips for the purpose.

Edna had been to see the Scottish doctor in Holywell Street and had accepted her opinion that exploratory surgery at the Radcliffe

Infirmary was necessary. She also had to accept the waiting list. Both these factors had made her temper even shorter in respect of Alex, so George's plan was to take him on lengthy cycle rides either on Saturdays or Sundays in fine weather to give her some "peace and quiet" as she liked to express it. It also meant that George could have the exercise of which being confined to one workshop rather than a large plant had deprived him and he found that his hernia did not inhibit his cycling, whatever his wife might say.

Everyone was saying how tall Alex was, but he was only tall for a five-year-old and fitted on George's bike very well that year. Villages were explored, churches visited, tombstones deciphered, blackberries picked when the time came and quantities of them, left over from the ones they ate, were brought back for Edna to put into a pie for Sunday. George opined quietly to Alex that her fruit pies were better than the meat ones she made because the only stewing steak she was able to find was always sinewy and she never cut the sinew away. Alex was bound, equally confidentially, to agree.

A great deal of real communication went on between George and his father during these outings. When a tombstone declared something about its own time, George would set the life commemorated against the background of Clive of India, or William Pitt the Elder, Earl of Chatham (as, with the pride of his birthplace, he never forgot to call him), or the Duke of Wellington, or Lord Palmerston. Alex learned from George before ever he opened a history book about things like the expansion of the British Empire, the defeat of Napoleon, the value of naval power, the abolition of slavery, debtor's prisons, the plague and the fire of London. George carried his own syllabus in his head and never used it except in response to what Alex wanted to know. At another time he explained how metal expanded in hot weather, which was why lengths of a contemporary railway line had small gaps between them where they met; this was explained when Alex noticed the phenomenon once while they were waiting at a level crossing. Alex could not understand why the bicycle did not seem to get bigger as they went along in the heat. On this occasion, as on several others over the months when they went out on the bicycle, Alex came to respect George's integrity as a teacher whenever he replied that he did not know how to answer a question.

George became very tired doing all the pedalling, so there were frequent stops in the gardens of pleasant public houses. Alex was introduced to Smith's Crisps, which he delighted in saying while his front teeth were temporarily missing, and he was particularly fascinated by the little piece of blue paper in each packet that contained the salt. Once they followed the van which delivered the crisps out of a pub garden and Alex read on the back of it, "Please sound your horn: we wish to extend to you the courtesy of the road". He challenged George to overtake the van once he had explained what courtesy was.

"We're not going downhill," was George's breathless response to such confidence placed in his abilities.

Although George had spent his teenage years in a town, when he was a boy of Alex's age his mother had taken him back to live with her parents and brothers and sisters in the rural area of the Hundreds of Hoo during one of his father's nine-year tours of duty at sea. He understood the ways of the countryside, although he fancied that the lords of creation who owned and worked the rich Oxfordshire acres would not have thought much of what went on in Kent to the south of the Thames Estuary.

These outings were always far too short for Alex. Nevertheless, on the way home, he would often lean back against George, take his hands off the handlebars and tell him, "I'm going to ride no hands now, Dad," and fall asleep against his father's chest for a mile or two.

They usually found that Edna had enjoyed a few hours' sleep and she welcomed them back; but she never expressed much interest in what they had seen or done while they were out. Alex at first tried to tell her where they had been and what George had told him, but he soon realized that she was not responsive towards his news and after a few such outings no longer tried to interest her in it. She did not seem to want to cheer up, Alex thought.

II

While infantrymen, gunners and tank crews from the Scottish highlands and the English home counties were doing their best to cope with the heat of an Egyptian summer and being trained to bring General Montgomery's plans to fruition at El Alamein, Edna went for her tests in the Radcliffe Infirmary. Alex's days while she was away from home had been carefully arranged before she left. George took him to school riding the bike to make the process quicker. Once school was over, Mrs Wilson collected him and looked after him while George was still at the dairy. In the evenings and at the weekend, he was in George's sole charge. On the Sunday, George put on his best suit, found Alex's white shirt and a straight tie with horizontal stripes for him to wear and took him to visit Edna. They brought with them a bottle of lemon squash and the sort of sweets she liked. She embraced each of them in turn as she sat looking forlorn by her hospital bed and chairs were found for them. The talk was about nothing in particular for a while and then George told Alex to go out into the garden and see if he could find any more tortoises. He made the acquaintance of a friendly tabby cat, which let him stroke her for a while until she decided she would walk by herself after all.

George came out to look for him after a time, looking determined to be happy, Alex noticed.

"What's wrong with Mum?" Alex asked.

"Nobody seems to know, so they are doing one or two more tests and then sending her home on Wednesday evening. We'll come and fetch her after I've come back from work."

"She didn't seem very cheerful, did she?"

"No. Well, she wanted them to find out what was making her feel so lousy and put it right. Now, I suppose, she'll just go on feeling lousy. Come and say cheerio to her. The ward sister seems to want all the visitors to go now."

So they went in again and were very soon ushered away.

"Why did it smell so funny in there?" asked Alex.

George's mind was elsewhere but, in parallel with his real thoughts, he explained antiseptic and the discoveries of a man called Lister all the way along Walton Street and up to the Cornmarket. On the bus he told Alex all he knew about Florence Nightingale, which led to a more interesting discourse on the Crimean War, which lasted until the kettle had boiled. One of their forebears was known to have been a bugler as a boy soldier and had served in the campaign.

After tea, George wrote letters to his parents, to Hetty and to Edna's other sister, with many false starts and a good deal of complaint under his breath. He wrote few letters in his lifetime and did not relish such activity as an art form. The wireless was not put on, so Alex drew imagined scenes at Sebastopol and Inkermann and later received the accolade he desired, with George looking only at the side of the paper upon which he had drawn and saying, "Not bad at all, boy. Not bad at all!"

III

Alex found the hours between his own coming home from school and George's return from the dairy enjoyable and relaxed at Mrs Wilson's, particularly if Martha was there for part of the time. She went to a convent school and had some interesting books from which she worked at her homework. She showed him one that was about measuring spaces. It said that a man made a hole for his cat in the bottom edge of the back door through which it came into the house. The cat produced four kittens, of which the man gave three away to his friends and kept the fourth. Now that there was a kitten, should there be a smaller hole in addition to the normal sized one to enable it to come indoors?

"What do you think?" Martha asked.

"Can't the kitten come through the hole its mother uses?" Alex replied.

"Of course," said Martha and wrote that down in her book.

For Alex, however, the important thing was not that he got the answer right, but that he liked the drawings with which the question was set. The bottom of the gate was drawn with care to show the grained wood. One picture showed the grown cat sizing up the hole with her whiskers and the other showed the kitten doing the same in a diminutive hole. Neither of the drawings was bigger than three quarters of an inch square and all you needed to know in order to answer the question had been presented to you.

When Mary arrived home from the High School, she invariably did her piano practice before anything else, saying that it got school out of her system. The books from which she did her homework were more complicated than Martha's, though she was quite willing for Alex to browse through them.

"What are mathematics when they are at home?" he asked her.

"I suppose maths is really plural," she said, "The subject is in three parts: arithmetic: you know what that is, geometry, which is largely about measuring things, and algebra which is thinking things out logically."

Mary's reply raced ahead of him, but he replied, invoking what Martha's book had contained,

"So what we've been doing about the hole for the cats is geometry, then!"

"Not really," said Mary. "I must do my practice now."

She pulled out the piano stool and lifted the polished lid of the upright instrument to expose the keyboard. She rummaged in a leather bag, which interested Alex because it had one ordinary handle passing under a metal bar with small knobs at either end to keep it closed. Having decided which piece she would begin with, she arranged the music for it on the fretwork in front of the piano and, peering at the notes, began to play them. Alex listened with fascination as Mary took charge of the music and, after five minutes, was playing the piece very rapidly. What impressed Alex did not have the same effect on Mrs Wilson, because she came quickly into the room to tell Mary not to hurry her task but to do it properly.

Despite this exercise of parental discipline, Alex could not help comparing Mrs Wilson with his own mother. Only next door, despite the anxiety caused by a husband and father being away all the time and perhaps soon to be in grave danger, there was the kind of warm emotional security he wanted but did not receive from Edna. He was sure the Wilsons had more money than his parents, but that was because Mrs Wilson was a trained secretary who regularly received things in the post to type at home. This, added to what her husband earned, enabled the girls to be taught by people called nuns: Mary up to three years ago and Martha now. Susan Wilson had been provided with a convent education herself, so she was perfectly capable of knowing when her daughter was playing an adagio at twice its proper pace in order to shorten the time required for it.

On the Wednesday when these arrangements were in force George rushed through the back gate at five. Mrs Wilson saw him across the garden fence and told Alex it was time to go home. George was already washing his hair when Alex came indoors. He called down the stairs to say he would not be long and emerged in a short while with his best suit on again.

"How tidy are you?" he asked, and took a brush to Alex's head, smoothing down his fringe and then telling him to put his shoes up on a kitchen chair one by one for a wipe with a duster.

"That's all there's time for," he announced and they rushed to the bus stop. At Gloucester Green, George phoned from a telephone-box for a taxi to be at the Radcliffe in half an hour. They walked off briskly with George explaining the significance of buttons A and B to Alex and found Edna sitting ready in her coat and hat, very anxious to be on her way. She was holding a sealed brown envelope in her hands addressed to the doctor in Holywell Street and her small case was ready for George to pick up.

They cautiously and courteously said good-bye to the ward sister, took the opportunity to thank a young nurse who had been particularly kind and went out into the autumn evening to the waiting taxi. Edna got in first and then a folding seat was pulled out for Alex before George got in as well. They were home in ten minutes, and George did his best with a pound of sausages he had acquired, despite his lack of understanding of ration books, and boiled potatoes and some greens. After they had eaten Alex went to his room to read and his parents did nothing about him going to bed until gone ten.

It was once more George who got him up in the morning.

"Mum's going to have the morning in bed," he said.

This set the routine for the following month, until Edna spent three more weeks in the Radcliffe and then seemed slowly to recover.

IV

The pattern of their family life had been changed. Instead of George being away most of the time, now he was in evidence for Alex pretty well all the time that he was not at school. Edna was there too. She went shopping and she cooked meals, but she had her preoccupations and rarely said anything more than necessary for life's essentials.

"Be careful how you cross the road," was her main injunction to Alex, on the frequent occasions when she did not feel able to take him to school or collect him from it. It was agreed that if she was not at the school gate to meet him he was to come to the main road and wait in front of the shop for a reliable adult and ask him or her to see him across, while being left to assess reliability for himself. In this way Alex met his first American army officer, who not only brought him across the road but also knocked on the door to deliver her "well-mannered little boy" to an astonished Edna, whom he addressed as "Ma'am".

In the weeks that followed, the word Jeep came into every schoolboy's vocabulary and Miss Cook was at pains to make this announcement at assembly:

"Whilst some of our American guests in the city are accustomed to chewing gum at all times and find nothing objectionable in doing so, you are not to bring such gum into school, and you are certainly not to chew it while you are here. If you have chewing gum given to you, leave it at home."

Alex was with Edna in the Home and Colonial one day near the end of the long time it took her to recover from whatever they had done to her at the Radcliffe, and she started to talk to another woman whom she vaguely knew. Alex overheard their conversation, which began with Edna being complimented on how well she was looking, and Edna's reply that the other woman was very smartly dressed. To this the woman answered,

"All you need to do, Edna, is get yourself a Yank. They've got more money than they know what to do with. Very pleasant young men, some of them."

As the woman went away towards the empty bacon counter, she called back in a loud voice,

"They know how to treat a girl!"

As Edna blushed to her hair roots, Alex saw that she could not be described in any sense as a girl any more. She pulled Alex out of the shop and sought the earliest opportunity to sit down and fan herself with the evening paper she had bought in which to look at some advertisements.

Hence Alex's confusion when, not very long afterwards, a young American serviceman appeared at their evening meal (it had been upgraded for this purpose). He spoke in a very friendly manner to them all, was welcomed enthusiastically by George and took possession of the vacant back bedroom, where he stayed for four weeks, apart from Saturdays and Sundays when he went to see "The grand sights of your great country," as he put it. They all liked him and valued his amusing and informative contributions to their table talk. Alex had questions to ask him about the device on the buttons of his tunic, which seemed to be duplicated on his cap badge. His uniform seemed to be of better quality than the ones worn by the few English soldiers he had seen whose tunics were short and made out of rough cloth, buttoned up to the neck, whereas the American uniform consisted of a smart coat and a collar and tie all made out of soft material. If Alex had known about the difference between officers and other ranks in the British Army, he would not have seen this as so puzzling. Their lodger, as Edna called him when he was not there, was a junior officer, but the few ordinary soldiers in the American Army that Alex had seen about in the Oxford streets did not appear dressed very differently from him. George found everything the young man had to say fascinating. He had always wanted to go to the United States of America, as he delighted in calling his guest's country, but their

Lordships of the Admiralty had never sent any of the ships in which he served any nearer to that nation than the Panama Canal.

George explained to Alex, when he confided his misgivings as tactfully as he could to him in the light of what he had overheard in the Home and Colonial, that the young man was one of several Americans for whom accommodation had been sought in private houses while proper training facilities were being completed.

"What are they training for?" asked Alex.

"For The Second Front (there was no doubt about the capital letters in George's mind), which will open soon."

Edna came into the living room to find George and Alex both spread out on the floor with the atlas open for George to explain what the invasion of Europe might mean if it ever happened. She stood and listened and for a few minutes let herself hope that the war would all be over soon and they could go home.

". . . see: there's Stalingrad, where the Russians lifted the long German siege in February and since then have been pushing the Germans back where they came from and now they want us to attack the Germans not only up through Italy, down there. Look, that's Salerno, where some of our troops landed last month, and there's Rome, the capital of Italy, which they hope to take soon, but they've been held up at this place (here he put his finger where Monte Cassino was). The Russians want the Americans and us to attack somewhere else as well, perhaps in France over here, or down the river Rhine there. But the politicians and the generals say it can't be done yet. The fact that young Lootenant Zimmerman (George deliberately pronounced his rank in the way he did himself) and the other Americans are over here signifies that at last somebody means what they say and the war might be ended before we all get too old to remember what peace was like."

"Zimmerman sounds like a German name."

"It is. His family must have emigrated to America some time ago."

"What does emigrated mean?"

"It means that his family left Germany about three generations back and became settlers in America and have lived there ever since."

"What's a generation?"

"That'll do for one day," he said, looking up and catching Edna's appreciative eye. "Mum wants her sewing machine out and we're in the way."

V

On one of their forays down Binsey Lane on a Sunday morning, George replied in a friendly way to a bearded man who was leaning over a gate and greeted him with a smile and strange words.

"... And to you, sir," George replied.

"What did he say?" said Alex.

"He said, 'Good day, sir,' in Italian."

"Why is he wearing overalls?" Alex was still looking at the man as he turned round and left the gate. "And why has he got that big coloured circle sewn on his back?"

"He's an Italian prisoner of war and he has been brought here until we have finished fighting the Germans. This is one of their prison camps. He's as glad to have stopped fighting, as we shall be in due course. But that circle is there so that the guards can shoot at him if he tries to run away."

"He won't though, will he?" said Alex.

"Not if he's got any sense," said George. "And by the look of him, he has."

Miss Cook had already told the children in assembly what was happening in Binsey Lane and that they must be courteous to any Italians they met. Alex had found her to be a reliable source of information concerning military matters, but he needed to hear it from George before he really believed any of it. George did not know much about Italy at first hand, but had gathered much from the cheerful years he had passed with Edna in Malta. He told Alex what Malta was like, with its ancient churches and the headquarters of the Knights of St John of Jerusalem in part of which he and Edna had rented rooms.

"Who are the Knights of St John?" asked Alex.

"They were like monks, only they claimed they were serving God by fighting his battles against the Turks who turned them out of Jerusalem where they originally were for about three hundred years."

"They lost the battles, then?"

"Yes. First they moved to Cyprus, which is a big island in the eastern Mediterranean you remember from the atlas. Then they were pushed across to another fairly big island called Rhodes and, once they were expelled from there by the Turks, they settled on Malta in about the time King Henry VIII was ruling England."

"Were they still there when you were?"

"No, they'd been gone for about a hundred and twenty years by then. You remember I told you about Admiral Nelson and his enemy Napoleon?"

Alex nodded.

"Well, before Napoleon went to Egypt, where Nelson sank his fleet at the Battle of the Nile, the knights surrendered to him and the French, and that was really the end of their time there. We lived in their headquarters, but all that was left of them was a few souvenirs like bits of armour and things."

"Did you ever go to Italy, Dad?"

"Not to see much of it. The ship called in at Naples, I remember, but we didn't get ashore. Mum's been through Italy on the train to get back home when we had finished living there, so you'd better ask her about it."

"She never tells me things in the way you do."

George sensed dangerous waters ahead and changed the subject quickly. He said, "Anyhow, about that Italian prisoner. His country had been taken over about twenty years ago by some people called Fascists, led by a self-important little man called Benito Mussolini. He persuaded the King of Italy to give him almost total power in the country. The Italians called him Il Duce, which means more or less the same as what the Germans called Hitler, you know, The Leader. The Italian army was in North Africa when the war started and they were backed up soon by the Germans, but they lost the battle against our troops who fought their way westwards from Egypt. Now our troops are fighting up through Italy, as I told you. The Italians gave in, and did away with Mussolini, but the Germans persist in their fight and defeating them is going to take a lot longer, I'm afraid."

George looked down to see if Alex was still listening and was very pleased to find he was responding with great attention and that gave him a good deal of pleasure.

VI

Edna had not wanted to spend all her Saturday afternoons on the River Cherwell in a punt so, since the warm weather had persisted, it was decided that they would go to a municipal open-air swimming pool for their outing on one occasion. George thought that it would be a good idea to begin to teach Alex to swim in any case. Edna would not go in the water, but would watch the proceedings from the grass by the pool and provide a picnic tea for them when George and Alex had had enough.

George and Alex left Edna in the agreed place and went to the men's cubicles. They found a row of what looked like garden sheds, painted not merely stained, though the paint was looking flaky and in need of a fresh coat. Alex was told to go into one of them to change into the bathing costume that Edna had bought for him the day before and to leave his clothes on the seat. George went into the one next to it, and emerged in a pair of maroon woollen trunks held up by a white canvas belt joined over his stomach with a silver buckle which carried its maker's Italian name. Needless to say, his surgical appliance was hanging on a hook under his trousers. He explained to Alex, who was curious about the buckle, that his trunks were a souvenir from Malta where he had gone swimming a lot in places like St Paul's Bay. He had picked them up in the collapsed ruins of his bedroom when he went to inspect the bomb damage in Chestnut Road.

Despite pillage on an international scale currently taking place, the people in this locality were accepting of the rule of law and Alex was told simply to follow his father's example in turning a handle on the cubicle door that raised the word "engaged" into sight. George was confident that all their belongings would still be there when they came back. They took careful note of the numbers on the two doors and went to get in the water, both waving at Edna. For her part, she busied herself with the tea-things in preference to acknowledging that she had anything to do with the portly white-skinned and hairy-chested man with an incipient corporation. Nor did she acknowledge the boy who was equally white in comparison with other boys at the pool that afternoon in his costume, which marked him like a wasp with black and yellow horizontal stripes. In any case, George had left his glasses with his clothes and could not see what she might be doing.

George dived in from a springboard and Alex went in inch by inch from the steps at the side. After splashing around independently, trying to avoid others in the pool for a while, they met to stand in the shallow end and the instruction began.

"Hold the bar at the side with both hands and float out with your legs like this," said George, demonstrating the leg movements with his hands and arms.

Alex did what his father told him.

"Now kick your feet up and down."

Alex did that too and found that it kept him horizontal in the water. After a while, George said,

"Stand up now and turn round to face away from the side. That's it. Now lean forward with your arms out straight until you feel your legs lift, like this," and he made more arm movements.

Alex followed the instructions but the effect was not quite right because his head went under and his feet rose too far. George pulled him upright and then, after Alex had spluttered for a little while and complained that the water hurt his eyes, placed himself and Alex in deeper water where he could take both his son's hands and walk backwards in front of him, pulling him though the water.

"That's it," he said, "Now kick with your feet like you did before and, you'll see, it'll drive you along. You're getting along famously now!"

This was just beginning to happen when George saw that everyone else was scrambling out of the pool and a man in a uniform was gesticulating at him and demanding that he should follow their example. George picked Alex up quickly, carried him to the steps and clambered out of the water after him. They ran over to join Edna who had moved all their gear back to about ten yards from the pool. As they sat down by her they saw, when she pointed them out, three large army lorries parked by the gate. At least, Alex did. George ran to his cubicle to collect his glasses. As he sat down again, the tailgate of each lorry was lowered and thirty or so soldiers in denim overalls, tin hats and webbing, carrying rifles, lined up beside them. The soldiers began to double march into the park in single file, to line up again at the side of the pool from the deep end to where the four-foot mark was painted on the side.

Their sergeant stood by the shallow end and gave the word of command. They all jumped into the water: boots, tin helmets, rifles and all and made for the other side, kicking with their legs and doing their best to keep their weapons dry by raising one hand over their heads. Some succeeded; some did not. Then they put the rifles on the pool's edge and hauled themselves out of the water, standing there dripping unless, like some exhibitionists among them, they shook themselves like hilarious dogs.

George, Edna and Alex watched them do this several times. The sergeant good-naturedly encouraged those who had let their rifles go under the water not to do it again. After four attempts, they seemed to have mastered it, except three men, whom the sergeant separated out to be encouraged further, while some of the rest, permitted to sit down on the grass on the other side of the pool from the civilian spectators, discovered what the effect of chlorinated water on packets of cigarettes and boxes of matches was. A few other smokers were pleased to find that the driver of one of the lorries, with whom they had deposited their smoking requisites, had joined them and lit up accordingly. George was pleased to comment that their camaraderie was such as to let them to offer smokes to the others and cheer them up. He also admired the training technique and control exhibited by the sergeant, which reminded him of the skills he used to exercise himself long ago.

"If I jumped into a swimming pool with all my clothes on and my shoes, you'd tell me off, wouldn't you?" Alex commented.

"Yes. But you're not training to go ashore on a hostile beach with a lot of Jerries shooting at you!" said George

"Is that why they're doing it, then?"

"I imagine so. You know I told you about the hopes for a second front being opened in the west soon. Well, it looks as if this lot are in training for it. They couldn't ask the German gunners to wait while they sat down on the beach and put their uniforms back on with towels round their backsides, could they?"

The soldiers went behind the cubicles George and Alex had used, and emerged a few minutes later in dry battledress, with two or three others who had not gone into the water taking their wet things in bags back to the lorries. Before the soldiers left, they sat down on the grass in groups and carefully dried and oiled their rifles with materials that were given out.

Alex said to his parents,

"They all seem pretty cheerful, despite what they had to do."

"Poor young devils," said Edna. "If they didn't laugh, they'd cry."

"Yes. I hope not too many of them are lost when the time comes," added George.

There was a pensive silence.

"Let's have our sandwiches, then. Are you going to change first, George, or are you going to drip over everything?"

"Now, now!" smiled her husband, wagging his finger at her. "Come on, boy. We'd better do as we're told."

George instructed Alex into the mysteries of rolling his socks onto still damp feet and packaging his wet costume inside the less wet towel, after which they enjoyed their picnic with Edna, although the preponderance of beetroot was not entirely welcome. She even managed to smile outright when George eventually put into words what she had been thinking herself:

"I'm glad we saw them being trained. Gives us hope that we might start getting our own back one day not too far off. However," he went on, "I'm also glad that when we went ashore in whalers we only got our bare feet wet. Fancy having to carry all that kit as well as a rifle!"

Then he noticed he had said the wrong thing. Edna was not able to be anxious on behalf of the young soldiers without going back to feeling sorry for herself.

When the cake she had made had all gone - and George noticed that she ate a good deal of it herself for comfort - they packed up the things and made for the bus stop.

"Do you two think it's turned cold?" asked Edna. "Or is it only me?"

"I feel quite cold myself," George lied.

VII

"When you were in the Royal Navy, Mr Ryland, did you ever resent the decisions being made over your head?" asked the young American. George and Lieutenant Zimmerman were in the armchairs in front of the fire in the front room after the young man had eaten with the family one evening. No one had drawn the blackout curtains so there was no light on and Alex was sitting on the floor in front of George, so near the fire that his face seemed to burn, watching the flames licking around the coal and then becoming absorbed into the glow they created. Edna had suggested they go and talk somewhere other than round the table in the kitchen, volunteering to clear up without them so that she could get out her sewing machine again in the living room and finish the winter coat she was making for Alex.

"Of course I did. In fact for most of the time. You forget I wasn't an officer, like you. My decisions involved a choice of procedures already laid down by other people. The three buttons on my cuff meant that I had to hand things on, not think them up."

"I'm only just an officer and have no experience in things of a military nature at all. All I am is a trainee interrogator in case we capture a few Germans when we finally get going. I finished infantry training and then was picked for this course because I had had good grades in Spanish at high school. I'm not doing very well with learning the language of Goethe's Faust, or even of Hitler's Mein Kampf. In fact, I find it hard going in the extreme."

"But haven't you inherited something of what it was like to be German in the last century from your people?" asked George.

"They were businessmen in Württemburg, not Prussian soldiers. Besides, they stopped being German Americans twenty years ago and became American Americans. My father and mother speak Idaho indoors and at church they listen to Latin, but I've never heard a word of German in our family, even from my grandparents. I think they put our names in a helmet to choose the make-up of these courses. It sounds good, going to Oxford of all places, which even we country hicks have heard of, but I think any Kraut whom I interrogate is going to laugh uncontrollably. The old don who's supposed to be coaching me certainly does, even though he does it politely, up his sleeve."

"Go on. You're only three weeks into the course. You'll do it."

"Yeah. I don't have a choice in the matter anyway, do I? I'm sorry to let off my steam, but I'm away from my folks, and you mustn't mind if I make use of you, though that's presumptuous on my part."

"Any time you want to get something off your chest while you're here, you know where to come."

"Thank you, sir."

"You are welcome," George responded in his friendly way as Alex could see when he turned round from the fire to see its glow reflected on his father's kindly smile towards the young man.

"Can I ask you something now?" George went on.

"Of course."

"How do you Americans feel about being involved in this European war? Are you here just because they told you to come, or is it a matter of conviction?"

Zimmerman laughed before he said,

"I didn't have a choice, but there is something pretty evil going on in the Third Reich. Our church at home has pretty good relations with the synagogue and we've heard what's been happening with the deportations and confiscation of Jews' property and houses in Germany itself and all the occupied countries. Anyway, after Pearl Harbor, fighting Germany went with getting our revenge against Japan. You could say we're committed to the cause, politically and militarily, right through our nation. Certainly in our state there aren't many gainsayers. No family wanted to see its own sons go to war, but we thought the cause was just. We all went to see 'Mrs Miniver' at the movies."

"I didn't see that. Over here they said it was sentimental."

"Nothing like a good weepie to get the determination going! No, the bombing of the village church and the little ships at Dunkirk made it plain that, if you were standing up to the threat, we ought to stand with you. Once Greater Germany was in being after you'd been conquered, would Hitler really leave us unmolested? No he wouldn't!"

"What about when it's all over?" said George. "When Hitler's gone and Japan back in her own islands? The trouble is that last time, when President Wilson went out of office, America's unwillingness to be involved any more meant the effective end of the League of Nations. Personally, I think that some form of world government is the only answer, or we'll keep on having to fight dictators for ever and ever."

"I'm sure there's a lot in what you say. We can't do this every twenty years, can we?"

"Do you think your politicians will stay interested in Europe this time, then?"

"I think they've got to. I'm not so sure they'd take kindly to world government, though. We did fight a war of independence, didn't we? "

"Do you think you might go into politics yourself when this is over?"

"My rhetorical questions suggest it, don't they?" he laughed. "The only thing I can say now is, let's get it over and then see . . ."

By this time, Alex was sitting with his back to the fire, intent on following what was being said. He said nothing himself, but became aware that George had very definite opinions which, given the right company, he was willing to express with conviction. Alex did not have the vocabulary for all that, but what he heard was another base for the statue he was casting of his father. He had never heard him in the company of someone educated and intelligent before. He had enjoyed listening and was very resentful when the door burst open to admit Edna, whose first words were,

"Can I get anyone a cup of tea?" and her next speech was twofold, without catching her breath:

"Look at the curtains wide open. Don't you know there's a war on? (Alex sensed Lieutenant Zimmerman flinching). What's that boy doing there listening to all your talk? Come on, Alex. School in the morning: off to bed now. Wash your face properly."

"That's right," said the lieutenant, "School in the morning. I'd better wash my face too and see if I can concentrate for another couple of hours or so."

The tall American stood up and stretched and Alex did likewise. Then they both went out of the room. Edna pulled one of the curtains and George hurried round to pull the other one. When they met in the middle, George said to her, "I hope he'll be all right when the balloon goes up. He's very down in the mouth about it all."

"You mean Fred Zimmerman?"

"Yes. He says all the right things, but he says them with a fatal air. I hope he'll be safe when the time comes. Or, at least, that someone else will look after him."

"You can't take on the world's troubles, George," said Edna.

"No. I suppose there are enough round here one way or the other."

A few days later, the lieutenant came back unexpectedly, packed his things and said his farewells. He could not cope with language learning and was transferred back to his infantry unit. He seemed relieved and desperate at the same time. In a few days, Edna had a letter thanking her for her kind hospitality towards him and a postcard later from the Lake District, which contained no real news. George and Edna felt very sorry for him. He was at the age that any child they might have had when they were first married would have been. For a moment they forgot that all they had set out to do was raise their own income from the rent being paid for providing Americans with bed and board for a time. For many years the question was asked, "I wonder what did happen to poor Fred?" and they guessed at the answer, though no information came as to where, exactly, he met his end.

VIII

Arrangements were made for Christmas: George's mother and father were coming to stay for it and were going to arrive on Christmas Eve. Edna was very apprehensive because of the rough start to married life they had given her. So was George because he feared they might begin their campaign against her all over again. As for Alex, it had been such a long time since he had seen them that he could barely remember what they looked like.

George went to meet them at the station with Alex in tow and got off on the wrong foot because the train had already arrived. George recognized the short but upright figure of his father on the station steps, wearing his grey Homburg hat and his light coloured

Burberry raincoat, and broke into a run to meet him. Though he knew it was not the best thing to say, he began with an apology,

"I'm sorry. The timetable said two twenty-six and it's only twenty past now."

"Doesn't matter," said his father. "Mother's still in the station minding the luggage."

"You stay here with Alex," said George. "I'll go and find her."

Alex was left alone to look up at his grandfather and experience relief when he saw him smiling down.

"You're a lot bigger than you were when we last met, aren't you?" was the greeting offered to him.

"Yes," was all he could think of to say, and they stood side by side looking at the other side of the railway bridge with the faded Shanks's Pony poster on it that had encouraged people to walk to their destinations. They were both beginning to feel cold and had not found any common ground for conversation as yet.

The embarrassment was ended when George re-emerged from the station with two cases and his mother. The first thing Alex noticed about his grandmother was her large hat: black with a crumpled silk flower in front. She caught hold of Alex's shoulders and bent down to give him a kiss, which tickled his face.

"He's grown, hasn't he, son?" she said to George, who could not help himself saying, "Yes. Little boys do," in reply. The slight ground frost this caused soon passed, however, because Alex took charge of the situation. By this time they were near the road where they could see the railway bridge.

"That's where Mum and I saw a bus that was too big to go under have its top sliced off, Grandad."

This meant that both George's parents talked to their grandson, going on in front of him, each holding one of Alex's hands and he was left merely to struggle with the two cases behind them, feeling his truss slipping and hoping that Christmas would not last too long.

Edna had put her coat on and come to wait by the front hedge. When she saw them crossing the canal bridge, she came to meet them. She went to her mother-in-law to kiss her, and then to her father-in-law. She saw George, and took one of the cases from him.

George's mother, seeing this, said,

"Are you fully recovered now, Edna?"

"I can manage most things now," she replied and they were at the front gate, except there was no front gate any more: workmen had arrived one afternoon a while ago and taken it away, together with the railings that were under the privet hedge. All that remained of the gate was a small stump in the ground on which it used to swivel, the bracket where the top of it was and the end of the latch embedded in the party wall.

George breathlessly elbowed his way past Edna and Alex to be first at the open front door.

"Welcome to our home," he said, smiling apprehensively at his father. "It isn't much compared with yours, but it's a roof over our head until things look up a bit."

He then kicked himself mentally for being so diffident.

"Looks all right to me, son," remarked his mother, and followed him in.

George carried the case he still had upstairs and made for the back room where all signs of Fred had gone and there was a new counterpane on the bed. His mother came in behind him, smiling. George was surprised to see that she looked old now. She had taken her hat off and her wispy hair, held in a little bun, was pure white, though it was no more than grey the last time he saw it. Her face had become very lined and her teeth looked too big for her face. He put the case down where she could unpack it and was about to go and get the other one when she held his arm and said,

"George, one of the reasons we have come is to stop you feeling that we are going to carry on disliking Edna for ever. Please stop behaving so awkwardly. Just be yourself and everything will be fine. You two have been through a lot together in the last three years and we have not come to make things more difficult. Your father is very anxious that we put things right, but you know he will never reveal his feelings. He has asked me to say this to you."

Again, the discomfort was assuaged by Alex, who ran in to say,

"Gran, Mum says she's made the tea and would you like some now?"

"Tell Mum I'm coming right away and, yes, I would very much like a cup." Then, smiling at George again, "I meant what I said, son."

Leaving her coat and hat behind, she followed Alex downstairs.

George was bewildered. After twenty years of married life with Edna, his mother had never offered such an olive branch and here she was blurting all that out as soon as she arrived. He could not pretend that he was unhappy about it. He thought it very unlikely that his mother would say the same to Edna and he wondered why he should still feel like a schoolboy in her presence at the age of forty-two. He waited a bit. He was still fatigued by having carried both cases nearly all the way from the station and sat down on the small armchair by the window. He looked out on the untidy garden, past his shed and over the wall to the dairy where he spent his working hours and quietly said to anyone who was listening,

"Let it be true, what she said. That would be the best possible Christmas box." He felt a little better then and came downstairs.

His father and mother were in the kitchen, sitting at the table, in front of a cake made from hoarded ingredients. They were eating large slices with enjoyment and praising Edna for having made it so well. She looked up with a puzzled expression on her face and then smiled at George in such a way as to let him know that the speech had been made to her too. Moreover she had been able, after all these years, to accept it as genuine. He cut himself a large slice of cake.

"I see you haven't lost your appetite for good things," said his father, and all four laughed. Alex, in his room upstairs, heard them and was glad they were enjoying themselves.

Later, when George came back to Edna in the bedroom after putting a pillowcase with his presents in it for Alex at the bottom of his bed, she confirmed that George's mother had said the same to both of them.

"Let's hope it lasts," said George, as his teeth plopped into their nightly glass of water.

"I don't know whether it will or whether it won't. You can't suddenly start trusting someone who has not lifted a finger in friendship to you for all these years. I think I trust your father, but your mother still sets my teeth on edge."

"Even those teeth?" George laughed, pointing at the glass on the tallboy.

"Anyway," concluded Edna, "It's Christmas tomorrow and we'll take what they've said at face value for the present."

"Happy Christmas, girl," said George.

"We'll see."

IX

This year, George had spent a little more time than usual in secret in his shed making Alex a bus conductor's ticket machine, complete with a punch for the cardboard tickets he had made, and with a bell that rang very realistically. The tickets were supplied in an appropriate wooden holder. He had put what he called "tiddly work" on the front of the ticket machine around the letters that stood for Oxford City Omnibus Company. Alex was very pleased and went to play with it behind the front room settee on which his grandparents were sitting.

George's father offered a parcel about eight inches long to Edna: "From both of us, with love," he said.

She took it diffidently. Previously she had been accustomed to receiving purely useful presents from them. George looked up from observing Alex making imaginative use of his gift, and met Edna's eye. "Go on, see what it is," he mouthed at her while his parents were looking at her, waiting for her to do so.

She removed the wrapping paper to find a box with a jeweller's name on the lid and inside was a most elegant wristwatch made of silver with a thin leather strap.

"What a lovely watch," she said, and put it on, seeing as she did so the hallmarks on the silver. She stood up and embraced them both in a way she had never felt able to before and found her feelings reciprocated. George's father broke the silence this time.

"I'm glad you like it, my dear," something she had never been called by him before.

Alex was puzzled to hear that it had all gone quiet in the street outside the bus he had created in his mind and looked over the settee to see that all four were standing there with their arms round each other. He came and asked them for their fares and gave them their tickets.

The rest of Christmas day was spent happily. George and his father and Alex went for a walk, leaving Edna and her mother-in-law in the kitchen to see to the Christmas dinner, for which resources had been to some extent pooled, hence the weight of one of their cases. They went along the road to the school so that Alex could show his grandfather where he spent some of his days and the walk ended by coming in the back way so that George could briefly point out the architectural delights of the Victorian dairy. His father said they put him in mind of the old detention barracks, though the brick here was red, not London grey. Alex told him about the crazed bullock in the garden after they came through the gate and his grandfather said,

"Good Lord! Weren't you frightened?"

"Only a bit," he replied, and preened himself.

"I was, for certain," said his smiling father as they reached the door, but what he was smiling about was what he had seen though the steam on the kitchen window: his mother and his wife with glasses of port and lemon in their hands, talking to each other as though there had never been any tension between them. When their coats had been hung up on the hall stand in the front passage, a whisky bottle was produced for George and his father. Alex was allowed a smell of the whisky and a sip of the port, and then given a glass of fizzy lemonade. Three bottles would make a case heavy enough, but there had been six.

When evening came, they were in the front room again, with a warm fire and the blackout firmly in place. Alex realized that he could not spin out this happy day for very much longer and asked for a story.

"Grandad will tell you a story."

"No, George, you've heard all my yarns many times over."

"You tell one then, Dad."

"I don't know any. I only read them out of books, don't I?"

At school, Alex was fed on a diet of short poems by his new teacher since September and he asked,

"Do you know any poems, then?"

George replied with a little verse he thought suitable:

A flea and a fly, in a flue,
Were imprisoned,
So what could they do?
Said the flea, 'Let us fly,'
Said the fly, 'Let us flee,'
So they flew through a flaw in the flue."

They all applauded, and the laughter broke out.

"But what about one of your yarns, Dad?" said George.

"I can't remember much, nowadays," said the elderly man. "My plan to write them all down for you to read was foiled by that bloke who bombed your house."

"Yes. That was one of our saddest losses," put in Edna obsequiously on her part. "Is there any chance you could do it again for us, and for Alex, who hasn't heard them since he was a baby."

"No, dear. They're all gone now. I can remember bits and pieces, like when the two ships went round Cape Horn in a surprising calm and the ships' companies took turns to sing songs to each other."

"I wonder what the words were?" laughed George's mother, as she always did.

His father gave his well-rehearsed reply,

"They were perfectly respectable songs, Gilbert and Sullivan, bits from Chu Chin Chow and things like that. Nothing offensive at all, I assure you."

Then he remembered events from his time as a diver and underwater sights in harbour as he had un-fouled propellers and inspected hulls for damage. His family settled to listen to him. The adults had heard all his reminiscences before. They had temporarily overcome tension on previous occasions and now that the hostility had apparently been cancelled, and its cancellation accepted, the yarns he spun took on the nature of family cement.

Alex would always recount to his own friends in later years the tale George told him of his grandfather's time in a "down funnel up screw boat" that spent years protecting fishermen off Newfoundland at the time of Queen Victoria's diamond jubilee, during which time he had become the youngest Chief Stoker in the navy by virtue of his fists. But this Christmas night the old man was in no mood to boast, just to reminisce in the presence of part of his family where he had not hitherto felt at peace.

X

Boxing Day passed happily also. In the evening the air raid warning sounded, and George and Edna went all over the house seeing that the blackout was in place properly. There had not been many alarms of this kind lately and Oxford's reputation as a safe place had been preserved. Nevertheless, no one took any chances and all the occupants of the house waited with some concern until after about half an hour the all-clear sounded. George's father got out of the big armchair he had occupied and went out of the room. They heard him open the front door and go outside. Conversation began again without him and after a few minutes he came back in. He was pensive and only said one more thing in Alex's hearing that evening: "It's as quiet as the grave out there."

The old couple left the day after to go to see their daughter, George's sister, ten years his junior, who was working in an Admiralty office in Bath. Then they would go home for the New Year, where another daughter-in-law lived round the corner whose husband, George's brother, spent most of the war in Ceylon (as they called it then) working on dockyard installations.

Alex very much enjoyed his grandparents' Christmas present to him. It was Stephenson's "Treasure Island" and he could read it for himself, enjoying the full-page paintings that illustrated it. He still persuaded George to read bits of it to him, however, especially the chapter called "Heard in the Apple Barrel", which he delivered very entertainingly indeed with all the different voices.

In mid-January, George was on his way to work, when Edna called him back. A telegram had been brought and the boy waited for a reply. Edna watched while George opened it in the kitchen, then suddenly sat down and held the paper out for her to read. It said, with brutal simplicity,

"Dad died of a heart attack this morning. Please come. Mum."

So George, not wanting to shed tears till he had made arrangements, went to the dairy and told his assistant he would be away to bury his father and called the dairy's manager, who was still at home, on the telephone to tell him the same. Then he came back in order to change his clothes. While he was upstairs, Alex came down to the kitchen. It fell to Edna therefore to explain to him what had happened.

"So he won't be able to come and see us again," he said.

"That's right," Edna replied.

Edna made George a packet of sandwiches, because it had been before breakfast when the news came and as she gave them to him she said quietly,

"I see now why he made his peace with us."

George saw, too, and then he did weep. Alex thought he ought to as well, but only cried because George was unhappy. He had not been able to know his grandfather very well. He felt his father patting him on the head as he left for the coach station.

When George had gone, Edna did something unusual: she sat down in the kitchen and pulled Alex on her knee to cuddle him until she saw that it was twenty past eight and he had not had his porridge before he went to school. She felt sorry for Alex as well as herself. She had just begun to be able to like her father-in-law and he had been taken away. Alex had no grandfather at all now, since her father had died on his own after having estranged himself from all three of his daughters in his bereaved alcoholic loneliness eight years ago. Edna wept for universal misery, which had only a small connection with David Ryland's passing.

7

When George came back from his father's funeral, he was in a good deal of discomfort from his hernia. Other people would have called it pain. The Scottish doctor lectured him for having neglected it for all these years and told him that the truss he wore was worn out in any case. She strongly advised him to have the condition dealt with by surgery at the Radcliffe Infirmary:

"You'll not get better treatment, Mr Ryland."

George gave in and agreed to see the specialist there with a view to going into hospital as soon as possible. The powers at the dairy consented to him having sick leave at short notice when the opportunity arose. He was also advised by them not to refuse any chance to have it done quickly. If the European invasion began, as it might at any time, hospital beds all over the country would be at a premium. This was a common sense argument George had no reply to - and Edna in all her waking moments with him would not hear of him ducking the issue any longer.

"Who wants to go to bed with an old man who wears a truss?" was her own particular clincher, which left George wondering why she had not complained before about what he had been offering during the last fourteen years. All he said was, "I don't usually keep it on, do I?"

When they became aware that Alex had heard this exchange, they became embarrassed. He carried on drawing and only wondered briefly in passing why she should think that George needed his truss while he was asleep.

On January the twenty-fifth the letter came, offering him a bed in two days' time. So Edna ironed his most recently acquired pyjamas, leaving him the torn ones to wear for the following nights before he went, and he steeled himself for what he had been dreading all this time: an anaesthetic. It was his secret fear - and he had not owned up to it.

Edna took Alex to see him in hospital. He spent his time in a pre-occupied way during his family's visit. He had pieces of string with him and, sitting up in bed, demonstrated reef knots and bowlines and how to manufacture them to Alex as he joined them all together. Edna became exasperated and asked Alex to wait in the garden despite the fact that it was cold out there.

"I just want to talk seriously to Dad and then when I come out we'll go home."

So Alex hugged his father and told him to get well soon and did as he was told. No tortoise, no tabby cat. Evening frost on the only seat. Goose pimples on the knees - and then a purposeful Edna, out in a very short time.

"Come on, Alex. Sometimes I think your father is a blithering idiot!"

"He makes me laugh too," replied Alex, not really knowing what "blithering" might mean and misguidedly thinking idiots were funny.

When he came home from school next day, on his own as far as the shop and then with the guidance across the road of a lady who came out of it, there was George in the living room by the fire, in his pyjamas and big brown dressing gown.

"How did you get here?" asked Alex.

"I discharged myself," was the reply.

Alex went quickly to the kitchen where Edna was making tea for George.

"When did he go off bang?" Alex asked.

"It wasn't him who exploded. It was me, when he came home in a taxi half an hour ago refusing to have the operation after all and leaving the hospital with his clothes under his arm in a parcel done up with that bloody string he was playing with last night!"

"What's he going to do then?"

"He says he's going back to work tomorrow. He may find people there with other ideas about his future. Then where shall we be?"

II

The dairy management did have other ideas about George's future. They said they could not accept the risk of a man who was not in reasonable health working in a responsible post at the dairy. He had oversight of the sterilizing plant, to say the least, and if he suddenly had to leave the building and the machinery broke down, production would have to stop. His deputy could cope now and again, but the ultimate responsibility was his, they said. So, reluctantly they must let him go while thanking him for the excellent work he had done since he had been with them.

When he asked about the tied house, they said that since he had nowhere else to go, and had lost his only capital asset in the blitz, they would let him stay on in it for the time being. They would try to appoint a new engineer who had his own home and would not need the house. George would be required to pay what they called an economic rent. All this was said on the understanding that if they found that they did need the house he would have to vacate it. George accepted the terms and applied for a desk job a few miles away at Wheatley that he had seen advertised in the Oxford Mail, for an Engineering Supervisor of the plant being established in an American army hospital. That would mean a daily return bus ride, but the pay offered was good and he would be able to afford rather more than the economic rent on 56 Botley Road. Life looked as though it might get better if he got the job. Moreover, he would be glad to wear clean clothes at work and he hoped his days of grimy overalls were all over. He claimed that the new truss he acquired a week later worked wonders. He felt better than he had done for a long time.

As to Edna going to bed with George, one weekend there was to be a fun fair in the rec. Alex and a few other boys he knew from school, with Edna's knowledge, had gone down there to help put the fair up. This meant they were allowed a few free goes on the rides and the stalls. Alex won a Jacobean tumbler, as was said. He ran home all the way along Henry Road to show it to his parents and found them in their bed together in broad daylight. The main proceedings had finished and he heard them talking as he went up the stairs. They explained to him that they were both feeling tired and had taken the opportunity for a well-earned rest. He wondered why they had taken their clothes off to do that, as it was obvious that they had when they sat up to admire the heirloom he had won for them. But the thought of winning something else made him rush away and not give the matter a further thought.

Legitimate punters were now arriving at the fair and the stallholders and men on the rides did not need further assistance from juvenile volunteers. He and the other boys were paid sixpence each and realized that was the end of their period of employment. By the time Alex was home again, normal clothing had been resumed appropriate to a February day.

III

Alex found on Wednesday during the following week that tea was ready in the kitchen, but George and Edna were not in there to eat it as soon as George came home from work as was their usual practice. They were sitting at the living room table instead which bore no more than its usual diagonal runner and cut-glass bowl: Edna was crying and George had his elbows on the table and his head in his hands. In front of them was an open letter.

Alex came into the room quietly and sat down at the table with them. He did not know how to ask what was wrong. He could see that the letter was typewritten on paper that was printed at the top. He waited. Edna's sobs subsided eventually and George put out a hand to touch her shoulder. Then, looking up at Alex, he said,

"We're both upset, boy, because we've had bad news. This is a letter from Mr Marsh, our solicitor in Wimbledon. He says that we won't be able to repair our house as it's too badly damaged. The only thing we could possibly do would be to have it rebuilt from scratch. We certainly can't afford to do that and wouldn't be allowed to in the present circumstances anyway."

Edna picked up the letter and read it through again. Then she said,

"Life's so unfair to us. These Merton Council minutes he quotes says that tenders are out to repair the houses opposite, yet he tells us ours is beyond hope of it. We don't get any luck, George, do we?"

"So we can't go home, then," said Alex, not so much as a question to his mother and father but as the conclusion of their discussion with each other.

"No," George said. Then he stood up, went to the window and looked out at the dairy. Alex noticed that the backs of his hands were against his hips and his fingers drooped downwards. He looked very distressed. Then he stood up straight, squared his shoulders and turned to face Edna and Alex.

"Well," he said, "Now we know where we stand. We've got to stop hoping we could go back because we know now that we can't. We stay here as long as we have to and then work out what has to be done. What Mr Marsh has told us is spilt milk not to be cried over."

He tried to smile to comfort Edna, but knew he would have to wait a long time for any reassurance to affirm itself in her for whom this was the end of the world. It was for him, too, but his view of the universe was somewhat more informed than hers. She had no idea that there were other worlds besides her own. She did not want to know about them if there were, just then.

"We're caught, then, George, aren't we?"

"Yes. But we'll find a way through, I expect, in time."

IV

Remarkably, it was Edna who took decisive action first. She had noticed an advertisement in the paper for women to do valuable war work in a factory that had been empty along the main road from where they lived. So she started working there within a very few days, making detonators for shells. She intended to finish each working day in time to be at home when Alex came out of school, although taking him to school and going to meet him had been a thing of the past for some time.

Every time he left the house in the morning, there was a kind of automatic incantation from her,

"Look both ways before you cross the main road!"

This got on Alex's nerves. For some months now he had been allowed to go out by himself so long as he did not cross any roads apart from when he went to school. This meant he could go as far as the rec gates and he sometimes went through them as far as the river on the other side of the green space. One day he tried, instead of turning left and going direct to Henry Road, to walk across the dairy yard, but the disembodied voice of George himself, shouting like God from a third floor window that he was not allowed to be there, sent him scuttling back into the garden. Nevertheless, he became confident in the street by himself, and was often to be found out in it.

In response to his application, the people in charge of the new American army hospital at Wheatley sent transport to take George there to be interviewed for the vacant position. Edna had taken a great deal of trouble over ironing his shirt. He had his hair cut specially and took his best suit and his ex-navy tie to be cleaned. He went to Dunn's and bought a new trilby hat to show how determined he was to do all he could to obtain the post. He had ransacked Pear's Cyclopaedia for American information and discoursed learnedly about what he found to Alex as his captive and admiring audience in the evenings before the interview. Edna stayed in the room while all this was going on and unreservedly supported his endeavour. He came back decidedly hopeful and was like a caged bear during the three days it took for them to make up their minds and let him know.

George's morale was greatly improved at the end of those days. Another letter was waiting for him on the tea table. Edna had found it on the mat when she got in and thought it safe to put it there, as it bore no ominous London SW postmark. He opened it with his wife and son looking on.

Before he said anything, he took off his glasses and wiped his brow with the back of the hand in which he was holding them, with the open letter in his other one.

"Well," he said, "Sometimes you get some good luck, girl. I've got the job out at Wheatley. They want me to start in a week's time."

"Is that enough notice for the dairy?" asked Edna, before she allowed herself to be pleased.

"It'll have to be. They wanted me out in the first place, didn't they?"

She let herself smile in encouragement at him and said,

"Well done. We knew we had to stay here, but perhaps it won't be so bad after this."

"It might even begin to be good," George's euphoric mood allowed him to say. He crossed his fingers, nevertheless.

After tea, he wrote to the dairy management with his resignation, carefully pointing out that he had obtained other employment in the Oxford area and he would be glad to avail himself of their kind offer for him to remain in the tied house as long as it was still acceptable to them.

It really did seem as though there were fewer clouds to look for silver linings behind. George took his letter with him to put in the manager's office in the morning. His cheerfulness persisted:

"Only six more days as a bottle washer!" he said to Edna as he went back after dinner.

V

Alex had recently been allowed to cross the main road to go to the shop with a few pennies to spend if it was known to Edna where he was going. Alex was on such an errand on a Saturday in March.

Edna called from the kitchen as he went out,

"Look both ways . . ."

But he decided not to. He considered he had heard that command too often. He ran into the road.

Since the front door had been left open to allow him to come back in without bringing Edna from the kitchen, where she was immersed almost to the elbow in cake mix once again, she heard a commotion in the street. She washed her hands and, still holding the towel with which she was drying them, went to the front step. An army lorry was halted in the road, slewed to one side, and a crowd was interested in its front near side wheel. The driver was looking anguished at the edge of the crowd. He was a sergeant and seemed to be in his forties. Most of the people gathered were women, also of a certain age. Edna looked at the ground to see a small brown shoe lying between the feet of these women, one of whom was bending down.

Edna stood still on the step where the old iron gate had been, compulsively drying her hands for what seemed to her a long time. Then she realized that it was Alex's shoe she was looking fixedly at and, with a scream, ran forward to push two of the women aside.

"Steady on," said one of them. "You're not the only one who wants to see!"

"That's my son under there," shouted Edna, and knelt beside him. The front mudguard of the lorry had gouged its way through the flesh of the back of his left leg, and his head lay on the road, grazed from being dragged a little way as the driver had braked from a fairly slow speed.

"There was nothing I could do," the sergeant was saying to a policeman who had just then appeared and taken charge. "He didn't look, and just leapt out into the road. I can't help thinking of my own little boys."

Mrs Wilson had come out too; she had a telephone and went back quickly to ring for the ambulance and for George, once she had found the American hospital's number on the mantelpiece in Edna's kitchen.

The policeman had hoped never to use his St. John's training, but now he was glad he had received it. He kept Alex warm with his uniform tunic and gently restrained the unconscious child from twitching over-violently. He forbade everyone, including Edna, to move him. The bell on the ambulance was soon heard, coming from the direction of the station. The white vehicle turned round in the road and two elderly men came forward from it to take Alex very gently into the back. Edna identified herself and got in too, leaving Mrs Wilson in charge of the house, telling her where the keys were and to let George know where she was, not realizing that both those things had already been done.

The ambulance crew were very kind to her and very careful for her son as they sped past the station and Gloucester Green, along Walton Street and into the casualty entrance of the hospital where

Alex and Edna were both given attention: the former for a fractured skull and a lacerated leg and the latter for shock and self-accusatory guilt. The treatment for Alex's condition was in part the result of the researches of Howard Florey and Ernst Chain on the applications of penicillin in treating wounds, available particularly in Oxford where they had carried on their work. For Edna's condition there was strong tea, food at regular intervals and the presence of George who had already obtained such a good rapport with his new employers at the American hospital that they gave him plenty of freedom to come and go. He was often with her while she kept her vigil at night in the single room allotted to Alex until he should recover consciousness. Such an opportunity to be close to each other was at times a solace, and at other times a strain, because there was nothing they could say to each other to let reassurance replace anxiety. Silent embraces were a help, but words that made sense in these circumstances were lacking

VI

Alex himself, of course, was spared all the anxiety of the next three days. He woke up after seventy hours of unconsciousness, aware of how heavy his left leg felt and looking at a round, glass lampshade set in a plain, white ceiling. He heard voices, one of which was Edna's and the other that of a man he did not know. Edna's remarks were not audible to him, expressed as they were in between sniffs and whimpers appropriate to her acute anxiety. But he heard the man's voice very clearly. It said,

"He will recover consciousness, but you must prepare yourself for the possibility that he may not fully be in charge of his mental processes."

"You mean, he might be insane?" he heard Edna reply.

"I carefully avoided the term but, well, it is not impossible that he might need special care."

The next thing Alex heard was a long intake of breath, presumably from his mother. So he called out,

"Is that you, Mum?"

Then he heard a flurry of feet, one pair clumsy in high heels, and saw Edna, followed by a man in a white coat, pulling a curtain aside, looking at him and smiling with intense relief. She made as to hug him, but the doctor held her back from this until he had looked into Alex's eyes with a little light and taken his pulse. The doctor's face was serious as he set about his task, but he seemed to Alex to be more cheerful as his routines drew to a close. Edna's mouth was working anxiously as she hardly dared to hope for good news.

"I think you could embrace him now, Mrs Ryland, but be careful not to hurt his leg," the doctor said and left them alone together.

"Is this a hospital?" Alex asked.

"Yes. You're in the Radcliffe and they've given you the best possible care and attention. Tell me how you feel."

"Fine, only there are all these bandages round my leg and I feel a bit dopey."

"How many fingers have I got up?" asked Edna.

"Up where?" said Alex, and then realized that she was holding up her hand about a foot from his face. "Oh. Three."

"Thank God for that!" said Edna. "So you can hear and see perfectly well."

"Why shouldn't I?"

"Because three days ago, you went under an army lorry and hit your head severely on the road."

"How do you mean, severely?"

"I mean very hard."

"Did I? Is that why it's sore on my forehead when I touch it?" He did not persist with his experiment: it hurt too much.

"Yes, you walked on your head for a little way before the lorry driver could stop to let you out. You leg was caught between his wheel and his mudguard, which is why it's all bandaged up."

"Is it broken? My leg I mean, not the mudguard."

"No, but it's in bit of a mess, which is why they have bandaged it so thoroughly," Edna told him.

"Wouldn't be much use bandaging a mudguard, would it, in any case?" her son commented and she then began to wonder whether the dreadful possibility suggested earlier by the doctor had come about.

"Don't say silly things, Alex."

George came in then, his face beaming. He held up three fingers in front of Alex's face.

"I've already done that," said Edna.

"Hullo, Dad. Are you all right?"

"Yes, I'm fine, especially now you've come to. You can see and hear and speak, then?"

The use of so many interrogatives in the last ten minutes left the three of them exhausted. A companionable silence fell and remained until a starched apron appeared and the vivacious young face above it asked George and Edna,

"Would you mind just waiting outside for a few minutes while I see to the young man's leg dressing?"

George and Edna got up to leave Alex, and George, just in time, managed to stop himself patting him on the head as he often did in affectionate moments.

The nurse set to work, which astonished Alex, because no one other than his mother had ever approached him so intimately and Edna had not done so for some years now. The nurse unpinned the top of the bandage that covered his whole leg from groin to ankle and asked him to bend his leg while she rolled the bandage away from it. He was horrified by what he saw under the bandage: a mass of scab that appeared when his leg was lifted and one particular piece of it that appeared to the right side of his knee looked like one of the flower-headed upholstery nails on the single surviving dining chair that had been brought from Raynes Park. When the whole bandage was off, the nurse applied some lotion, which stung the uninjured parts of his leg a bit, and then she began putting a new dressing in place. She did all she had to do with amazing tenderness and Alex felt very comforted. She had made him feel that the damage to his leg was less severe than it looked because what she had done had eased the discomfort he had been feeling when he woke up.

The nurse pulled the sheet up and called George and Edna back.

"There, I've given him a new dressing. The wound's all very clean and there seems to be no infection."

She turned back to smile at Alex, leaving him wishing that his mother would smile at him more and bring him comfort, instead of leaving it to other people. The nurse's warm smile, he realized, was for his own reception only. She picked up the old bandage and left him with his mother and father who puzzled him by blowing their noses very hard and wiping their eyes. He also found that his mother was very keen to keep holding his hand, which was something she would never have done normally, but she did not smile at him, and that was what he would have liked.

VII

Alex was kept in hospital for three weeks, carefully observed as to his thought processes and his memory. George had a way of dealing with this that was very much to Alex's liking. At the American hospital, word soon got round that Mr Ryland's boy had been run over and piles of comic books appeared on his desk each day. George brought one or two of these for Alex to see every time he came in and subsequently questioned him carefully but unobtrusively, as if he were setting an intelligence test, about the stories in the strip cartoons. Lil' Abner turned out to be the feature in the comic books that most attracted Alex's attention and George read these strips carefully on the bus from Wheatley so as to be able to put questions about them to him after he had looked at them. Alex also spent many cheerful hours drawing cartoon characters from memory, but reminding himself of details as the need arose. All this made George able to say to Edna after a fortnight,

"That bang on the head doesn't seem to have done him too much harm, does it?"

To which Edna naturally replied, "Even so, he'd have been better off without it! And so would we."

The other children in the ward where Alex soon was were also glad to see George, who had realized that Alex could not possibly eat all the candy (George was not only learning American, but speaking it by now) that his American colleagues gave him for "his boy" and he shared it out fairly with them on the days when it had built up in a pile on his in-tray. The children soon came to know that he would arrive each evening at six and a corporate cry of greeting often went up as he came in. Edna remembered her basic nursing skills and lent her services to the staff, taking temperatures and feeling pulses, besides changing beds and emptying bedpans and bottles. Her main pre-occupation was of course her son, but she found she became interested in the other families and their stories. It gratified her to know that she was not the only evacuee who had stayed on and it was good to know that Oxford city people could be as friendly as those with whom she had now lost contact, largely through her own inertia, that were still in Raynes Park. She even used up her accrued coupons on a new costume, as a jacket and skirt were called at the time, made of very expensive-looking dogtooth patterned cloth. She even looked happy and was heard now and again to sing snatches of songs as she made beds and emptied bedpans. But she did not smile at Alex and that was his one regret during these days.

He never saw the nurse who saw to him on the day he recovered consciousness on one to one terms again. She frequently appeared as a comfort in between the threatening dreams he was having again. He was glad when another lady, after one of the sessions he was made to submit to involving electrodes on his head and being shown pictures to evoke a strong mental reaction, told Edna and George, that his mind was as normal as any of us could claim our own to be.

Alex had come to associate taxis with hospitals and hospitals with taxis, thereby suppressing the memory of an old journey that had re-appeared in his dreaming since the accident. One was ready to take him and his parents home when the declaration about his sound mind had been made. He was not allowed to walk on his leg yet and a very large pushchair was delivered in which Edna took him for walks.

"They can't really be walks though, can they?" he remarked during one of them. "You're the only one walking, Mum."

George's Americanisms had been passed on to Edna. "Don't I know it!" she said, "Next time you want to get close to a lorry, ask it to stop first!"

They had reached the low wall outside the factory where she would have been making detonators for shells had he not stepped out into the road that day and Edna gratefully sat down on it to get her breath back. Like their own house frontage, the wall had lost its iron-spiked railings, so that was perfectly possible.

When one of these excursions, made "to get some fresh air into your lungs" as Edna said to Alex, led to the school in which he had not been seen for six weeks, there was some severe embarrassment. Miss Cook greeted him as though he had actually died in the accident and had returned despite it. Miss Hill even kissed him on the forehead, which had fortunately healed by then, and his present teacher asked if she should set him some work to do at home. His mother assumed the shining armour worn by Viking women in a series in the comic books when she said that school work at home would not be necessary just yet as he had been told to keep to recreational reading, whatever that was. The teacher looked relieved because she would not have to mark what might have been set and virtuous because she had made the sacrificial offer. The music specialist who taught the tonic sol-far in each class in rotation was the most embarrassing with her little speech,

"When Miss Cook told me that if I came in here I would have a nice surprise, I thought I should see a beautiful butterfly on a windowsill but, instead of that, it's you, Alexander!"

Miss Cook, as uncomfortable as the recipient of this outburst, ushered Edna and Alex out and as they stood on the steps at the school door, said as the conclusion of a short exchange with Edna,

"We'll expect him back in for the second half of the summer term then, shall we? He'll be a lot stronger by then. Meanwhile, we'll keep in touch, Mrs Ryland."

Having the same need to repress the tendency to pat children on the head as George had had towards Alex, Miss Cook turned to go back into the school and Edna put her best foot forward to get home.

In doing so she fetched her ankle a crack on the back of Alex's pushchair. Alex heard a vulgar Anglo-Saxon expletive uttered in the full force of its consonants, but thought better of asking what it meant. He sensed that George would be better qualified to give him an explanation since he had heard him say it quietly in his shed when he thought he would not be overheard.

Edna was especially nervous as she took the pushchair across the road between the shop and the house, the place where the accident had happened. An American Jeep, which she had not noticed in her struggle to bring the wheels down the kerb, did manage to stop in time and George got out of it, glad of a lift home, but white with fear of what might have been. He used the word that Edna had uttered, but as a present participle in a sentence of rebuke to his beloved spouse. The GI driver hid his mirth in his forage cap and made hurried excuses for leaving.

There was no way of bringing the ice cream George carried home as a treat back to its solid state, so they drank it from glasses and marvelled at its unaccustomed taste. As they sat at the table relishing it, George said to Edna,

"I'm sorry I got so aeriated, but I hope none of us survived the blitz in order to be killed by lorries or Jeeps. Here, Major Feinstein insisted on me having these pork chops as well," and he went to fetch a greaseproof paper parcel from his overcoat pocket on the hall stand.

Alex expanded his vocabulary of cooking smells and tastes as well as his verbal one that day. He was beginning to think that all you needed to do to get people to be pleasant to you was to step out in front of a lorry. It was only when he began leg exercises supervised by a brutal woman in the outpatients' department that he was disabused of this idea.

VIII

In May 1944, Alex was walking fairly strongly and George decided that he would respond to the invitation of the major to bring his boy up to the hospital to meet the people with whom he worked. Edna took the opportunity of seeing whether she could have her job assembling detonators back while they were out, since Alex would soon be going back to school and she had heard that more detonators than ever were being demanded now, without the reason for the demand being given in as many words. George still sent off his weekly mystery parcels, so why shouldn't she do her bit to get her own back on the son of a gun (like George, she never forgot the sayings taken for granted in the Navy) who had dropped the bomb that made her homeless?

The Jeep was sent to pick George and Alex up at the time George would have caught the bus to go to Wheatley. Alex was dressed in his best clothes and Edna had made a fuss about his hair being tidy and his fingernails clean. The driver was one that George had never seen before, so he was able to carry out his intention of appearing as the dignified English father of a family without any memory of his vulgar outburst of a week or two ago detracting from it.

It was discovered in conversation that the driver was a Private First Class from a place he called Peoria, Illinois and when Alex remarked under his breath to George that that was a long-winded place to come from, it was explained to him again that the States of America were United, and that Peoria was a place in one of the states, which was called Illinois. He also learned that the President of the United States was called Roosevelt and that he had been elected on something called the New Deal, which had meant that a whole lot of people were enjoying the kind of life they had never had before. As a result of that, George reminded Alex, the Americans were in our country to help us win the war against Hitler and his little friends; then they would go on to avenge Pearl Harbour, where the Japanese had sunk a fleet of theirs over two years ago, help us get our own Empire back and set free our imprisoned servicemen in Singapore.

Alex soon became used to the wind eddying round the open sides of the canvas-topped vehicle, even if it did undo all Edna's careful work on his hair. He enjoyed seeing the city and then the hedges and villages go by. Eventually they drove into a place composed of single-storey brick huts and stopped while a man in a white helmet looked at George's identity card and the permit held up by the driver. After the man's careful scrutiny, he let them through the hospital entrance by raising a pole on a hinge, pressing down hard on the short end of it. During the time it took to reach the part of the hospital where George shared an office with Major Feinstein, Alex received an explanation of the documents that the guard had appeared anxious to see. The explanation included the words sabotage and saboteur.

"I got in without one, though. I might have been a saboteur for all he knew!"

"You might turn out to be," said George, "But you were let in because of this piece of paper attached to my card, which has your name on it as well as mine."

"What is a saboteur, anyway?"

"Someone who kicks his way in with his big feet and breaks things."

The lesson ended at George's office door and the driver went his way. Alex was introduced to Major Feinstein, who treated him with the utmost politeness after welcoming him with,

"So! You're Mr Ryland's boy. I've heard a lot about your troubles. I hope you are getting well again now."

"Thank you, I am much better now, sir. Thank you for all the books (George had explicitly told him not to say "comics") you and your colleagues sent for me - and for all the candy."

This was the right word, in George's mind, because he feared that "sweets" might mean something else in American, although he did not know and was later relieved to find that it did not.

"I expected to meet somebody whose teeth had all rotted away!" said the Major. "Now, Mr Ryland," he went on as efficiency clicked in, "We have to make a check on all our arrangements for the operating theatre. Did you find out if the lights are acceptable to the medics where we put them?"

George's working day gathered momentum. He used the telephone a lot, making jokes where he thought it was appropriate, and being very deferential when that was required. Alex was given a chair and a spare desk and more paper than he had ever seen to draw on, since George had proudly shown some of his drawings to the Major. When he tired of that, there were more comic books to read. Three times in the morning, George took him with him when he went to other parts of the camp and he saw that some of the soldiers did not walk round on their own, but marched in groups with someone pacing at their side, shouting incomprehensibly at them without them seeming to resent it. One of these groups was made up of men whose skin was dark brown.

George did not appear to have anything on his mind so on the basis of one or two of their conversations during their bicycle rides, Alex asked him,

"Are those men freed slaves?"

"Their great-grandfathers probably were."

"As a matter of fact, they don't seem very free, do they?"

"I'm afraid they aren't. Don't mention this back in the office, but they have a pretty rough time here. They are segregated - that means kept apart from the white soldiers - and they do pretty menial jobs around the place. Their corporals and sergeants are in theory equal to the others, but in practice they have to keep themselves to themselves or things get unpleasant for them."

"That's unfair on them, isn't it?"

"Yes, but some things have to be accepted until you can find a way of changing them and not enough people want change at present."

They had reached the building that contained the operating theatres now. George had no fear of anaesthetics for other people and checked a storeroom full of long canisters with dials attached to them with one of the officers while Alex watched.

Afterwards, on the way back to the office, Alex, who knew what hospitals were for after his protracted stay in one, asked,

"Why is there a hospital out here in the country? And why does it have so many operating theatres? Surely the people who live out here aren't all going to need operations at the same time?"

"You know I told you about the Second Front? You've drawn a lot of pictures of battles. What happens in battles?"

"People get killed?"

"Yes. And a lot are wounded. The idea is that when American soldiers are wounded and need proper care in hospital, like you did after you got run over, they will be brought here and given the right treatment without the long journey to America and back after recovery."

"They'd have to go back and fight again after all that?"

"If their wounds were cured, yes."

And Alex pondered on the unfairness of creation all the way back to the pile of comic books.

Over lunch he met Captain This, Captain That and Lieutenant The Other, who was a nice lady from New York with a winning smile. She readily accepted the compliments paid to her by the men present, including George. She gave Alex a half dollar piece to keep, she said, until he came to spend it in America. Someone else explained the significance of the Stars and Stripes on the flag displayed at the end of the mess hall. Yet another had a War of Independence button with thirteen stars on it, which he showed Alex and was pleased to find that Alex knew about that war and even more pleased to hear that it had been George who had told him.

Lunchtime was short but the food was excellent and Alex fell sound asleep in the Major's leather desk chair afterwards, at his invitation. George went about his tasks until mid-afternoon and then some cups appeared and some sandwiches and the Major returned together with another man who was more important called a colonel (Alex needed some help with spelling this later on). Central heating for next winter was discussed, with George taking notes of what was said and saying yes and no to the questions they asked him.

When this quizzing of George was over, they all stood up, the Major and the Colonel exchanged salutes ("Even without their caps on," George pointed out, later) and there was time for a little conversation, during which Alex was introduced. He hoped he did not let George down and sprinkled his answers to the inevitable crop of questions with deferential terms. George appeared to be pleased with him, and, when the Colonel had gone, the Major said it was OK (whatever that meant) for George to take him home now. Major Feinstein apologized for a Jeep not being available and remarked to George,

"Sometimes you can work it and sometimes you can't!"

He gave an order to Alex: "Now you be careful not to go singing and dancing in the road again!"

George brought Alex back on the bus an hour earlier than he usually came home himself. Alex had been given a bag to put the pencils and paper in. The comic books were offered, but George said there was a limit, although they both knew he would bring them for him himself over the next few days.

When they reached the house, they found Edna in a headscarf and an overall on under her coat coming from the other direction.

"They asked me if I'd do a shift today," she said. "I said I could - and I did! When Alex goes back to school, I'll go back regularly. They agreed."

As D Day came near, though unknown to them, the Rylands began to enjoy a measure of prosperity and content they had not had for several years. Alex was glad to walk to school again a week later. Edna had the good sense to trust him to cross the road by himself, though George had had to insist upon it in the ten minutes before he got out of bed that morning. When she went out to go to the factory there was no blood on the road and she looked forward to her day with the other women. Some of her reticence had fallen away lately now that she felt more at home in West Oxford. Having George with her all the time had given her back more than half the life she considered herself to have lost. She was worried about Alex being so skinny since his accident, but was assured at the hospital during one of his physiotherapy sessions that the provisions allowed by means of ration books were the result of careful planning on the part of dieticians. George had taken over Graham's old allotment and had used it carefully for growing vegetables and salad ingredients in season and there were several kind gifts that had once had feathers and beaks that came from a Wheatley direction, so Edna hoped to be able to feed him up.

IX

The back room had been let again, this time to a Polish man who had been in the Royal Air Force and his English wife. The Polish man did little other than laugh while he talked incomprehensibly in the presence of George and Edna and his wife tried to explain what he was laughing about. All they could do was be polite and take the weekly rent in cash, hoping that the dairy manager would not find out about this six-week arrangement.

From Alex's point of view, the presence of Mr and Mrs Zartovnish gave a new dimension to life. Mr Zartovnish made model aircraft out of kits while his wife was out at work as part of the therapy suggested to help him recover from what he had suffered in the cockpit of a real one some two years before. He had no use himself for the finished products: the making was the therapy. So, by the time their six weeks were over and the Zartovnishes had departed, Alex became the glad possessor of a Short Sunderland flying boat in its white livery, two Lancaster bombers and a Mustang, though the last named was out of scale with the others. He wanted to hang them on strings from the ceiling in his room as he knew others had done, but George thought that too many pinholes in the ceiling would not endear him to his former employers. He did not allow more than one of the Lancaster bombers to be displayed.

Mr Zartovnish excited interest on other grounds besides being a maker of models. Soon after he arrived, he had all his teeth pulled out, bled for several days and then submitted his raw mouth to the trials of the dentures that were made for him. George and Edna had both been through this process: in George's case because his teeth had decayed through being soft and in Edna's because of a popular scare supported by some unscrupulous dentists in the nineteen-twenties that she could neither spell nor pronounce. Alex's parents therefore had less sympathy than he did with their Polish guest's suffering. Alex's teeth had recently fallen out and grown again, so he did not really understand why there were so many dentures about, but neither of his parents seemed to want to answer many of his questions about these personal matters and he did not pursue the problem. Alex talked to Mrs Zartovnish about her husband's distress, which endeared him to her. This was how he came to be the recipient of the models, or they would have all gone elsewhere if they had survived at all.

From Mrs Zartovnish Alex also heard what had happened to bring her husband to England. His two brothers had been killed in the German invasion of their country, and the country house they owned had been destroyed when tanks went through the estate that went with it. He himself had escaped with others who had previously taken flying lessons and offered themselves to the RAF to fight a mutual enemy. He had narrowly avoided death in his fighter when bullets had gone right through its fuselage, wounding him in both his legs and making him unfit to fly any more. So he was invalided out.

"Just like my Dad from the Navy!" Alex put in.

Andrzej and Heather had met in the hospital where she was a physiotherapist and they had been married six months. Money was short, so they could not afford a house of their own and were going the rounds of available rented rooms for which Heather's salary paid.

When he felt he was confident enough with his new teeth to enter what might be called society again, Mr Zartovnish made a large model Spitfire, which he intended to fly. It was two feet long with a wingspan of twenty-one inches, made with a balsa frame covered in doped paper and given the livery of his own Polish 303 Squadron. Much time was spent by Alex in winding the propeller round in order to twist the gigantic rubber band that was intended to drive this beast through the air. Beast was its maker's word, not Alex's: Alex had great respect for it.

With Edna's agreement, Mr and Mrs Zartovnish and Alex took the model down to the rec. They carefully noted which way the wind was blowing and aligned the model accordingly. It was held up at stretched arms' length, with the propeller carefully restrained between Mr Zartovnish's thumb and forefinger. When he let go of the model, pushing it upwards and downwind, the propeller turned violently for about ten seconds and then the whole thing fell to the ground and the wings burst off the fuselage. Mrs Zartovnish gave Alex a censored translation of what her husband said. Alex heard for himself that the opinion expressed was loud and forthright. The translator led Alex to believe that he had said that it had not really behaved like a Spitfire after all, but something manufactured for the Luftwaffe by a firm whose name sounded very much like what Alex had heard said by both his parents in moments of extreme pressure. Since he had no further use for the broken model, Mr Zartovnish took it to the dustbins behind the pavilion and left it for anyone to take who wanted it. During the whole performance, the new teeth stood up very well to expletives in the Polish language alternating with the speaker's characteristic outbursts of laughter. The name Fokker is not easy to pronounce with a new set of full dentures.

The other enthusiasm that Mr Zartovnish had was for fishing. From the people he had met and told through his wife as interlocutor about the enjoyment he used to have beside his native lakes and rivers, he had access to several prime stretches of water in the neighbourhood and on one occasion he brought home a live rudd, saying that since George and Edna had no refrigerator, the fish must be kept alive in a bath full of water until such time as it was needed for the table. Edna had been prevailed upon to provide the zinc bath. The fish flopped about in the bath for several days in their bedroom until Mrs Zartovnish facilitated its escape into Osney lock while her husband was asleep. She reported, as he laughed and snorted, that he was relieved that this had happened because he had felt sorry for the poor thing himself.

When the couple left, Alex missed them for a long time and talked about them to anyone who would listen. Since there was none such at home, he regaled his friends at school with these tales, until the audience diminished only to Isabel Shergold, who was a captive audience by virtue of still having to share a desk with Alex and a very polite person. How much he missed this couple came home to Alex himself in an incident that happened a month or so after they had gone.

Alex had not completely recovered from his accident. There were days when Edna kept him home from school to rest, making arrangements to stay away from the factory to look after him. This was how the model flying boat was lost, to his great consternation. There was a draw-leaf table in front of the window in the front room. If you stood on it, Alex found, you could see over the hedge that had been allowed to grow up to replace the railings. Edna came in from going over to the shop and told Alex to climb up on the table to see a long low-loading lorry go by with an aeroplane wing on it. He got out of his chair and excitedly clambered on the table to watch this wonder go by. He jumped with excitement and then saw with sadness that he had broken the wing of the model flying boat with his foot and sat down to cry about it.

This made Edna inexplicably angry and she shouted at him.

"It's not my fault you stepped out into the road and it's not my fault you broke this sea-plane, or whatever it is. Mr Zartovnish isn't here any longer to mend it for you, so it can go into the rubbish!"

She took up the broken but beloved model and went to throw it in the dustbin in the garden.

The rest of the day was passed in mutual resentful antagonism by Alex and Edna. Only when George came home was it explained to him why she had behaved like that. Yesterday, the owners of the dairy had given George notice to get out of the house. It was generous, open-ended notice, but it was final. This had taken away all Edna's new-found confidence and her depression focused on Alex as it had four years ago when he had split his chin. George's determination to be strong to give her strength had also taken a severe knock.

"We're up against it, girl. But," he added through his clenched teeth, "we've come through so far."

Edna rescued the flying boat before the contents of the dustbin could be put out for collection. George glued it together again but because he did not have the wherewithal to repaint it, it had lost its pristine glory and besides, it now reminded Alex of what had become a dreadful day.

George wanted to strengthen Alex's leg without having to have days at home, which obviously frustrated Edna who spent a long time after their child had gone upstairs to bed complaining to him. He decided that the making of what he sent to the Admiralty in the greased paper packages could be put off for a couple of evenings.

He used the resulting free time in the shed to convert a bicycle frame he had acquired as a spare for the one he and Alex used on the country outings into a scooter for him. He cut the bicycle frame in pieces with a hacksaw to be converted into the base, upright and handlebars and completed the design with a wooden footboard and metal wheels taken from a discarded bottle trolley in the dairy, upon which he fitted tyres ingeniously fashioned from lengths of hosepipe.

Strict instructions were issued by George on the geographical range for Alex's use of this machine:

"Keep on the pavements. Don't go on the main road or Henry Road round the corner. When you are in the rec go only on the paths. Stop whenever other users of the pavement or path are going by you so as not to bump into them."

Edna had been told not to interfere in these arrangements, though her objections had not been easily overcome.

Going out on the scooter in the late afternoon after school and at times over the weekend was fun for the solitary Alex. Using it helped to strengthen his injured leg as his father intended. He did fall off once, but fortunately he was a good way into the recreation ground and there was nobody about to see what happened or the tears that followed. There was only one other scooter left over from pre-war in the neighbourhood and that now belonged to a girl two years younger than he was and was obviously for a little kid, so Alex was justly proud of what his father had given him: the gift amounted to one of independence such as he had never had before.

Alex was able to follow the sound of cheerful voices at the river one day and to find that he was looking at several older boys and two older girls who were swimming in the wide stream that was the boundary of the rec, taking turns to swing into a deep stretch of water by means of a rope hung over and secured to a safe branch of a tree. When one of the boys caught him watching with interest what happened to her dress when one of the girls took her turn at getting wet through, facing him as she swung back to the bank, Alex was shooed off very forcefully. Nevertheless, having seen enough to satisfy curiosity and feed his prurient imagination for quite a time, he haunted the spot for several hours of several warm days afterwards in hope of a repetition of the fascinating show.

8

Soon news of D Day was on everyone's lips. Alex went several times in June and July to the cinema with his parents, hoping that no little houses would be burnt in the features they were going to see. However, he saw newsreel pictures of plenty of houses of all sizes burnt out after the allied landings and the liberation of villages near Caen and the city itself. George was hard pressed to give Alex a biography of General de Gaulle when he had been received with a great welcome at Bayeux, but told him all about the tapestry instead. He did understand the Mulberry Harbour and the pipeline called PLUTO, when they were reported at the cinema and on the wireless. Explanations were willingly given and received with great interest.

Edna considered that she had been incautious about leaving one particular week's copy of Picture Post lying about before having looked at it herself. She was settling down to have one of her snoozes in the living room with Alex on a Saturday afternoon. He picked up the magazine and read the captions under pictures of young French women having their heads shaved in retribution for having slept with German soldiers during the occupation. Then he turned over to see a full page photograph of another woman with no clothes on at all, walking away through a jeering crowd. They had left her with her high-heeled shoes and she was walking upright, not shielding herself from anyone's gaze. She had far more dignity than any of her detractors. He showed it to Edna, whose reaction he did not understand.

"I don't want you looking at pictures like that," she said. "They will fill your mind with filthy thoughts and that will lead to a great deal of trouble."

"But why was sleeping with a German soldier so bad as to make the people so angry that they did that to her?"

"It's no business of yours, Alex. I shall be careful where I put the book in future and you're not to look at it without asking me if you can."

With that she abandoned her five minutes as she called it - though it was usually more than half an hour in the afternoon at weekends - and took the magazine away to her bedroom where he could not get at it. When she came down, she thought that some kind of explanation was necessary. It was not the one that Alex expected:

"Picture Post is a book for grown-ups, not for seven-year-olds. Dad and I read it because of the news about the war. Sometimes the pictures in there are very frightening and I don't want you upset by seeing them. What is going on in France is terrible and it's best that you listen to the news on the wireless or to what Dad tells you."

"But I saw several of the pictures in Picture Post in the newsreel at the cinema last time we went. Some of them were the same!"

"Don't start an argument now. Just do as you are told. I'll tell Dad what I have said to you, so don't go asking him if you can look at it, because he will say no as well."

Alex wondered why his mother's face had gone so red and why she kept fanning herself although the room was shady and cool. Then he went back to the comic book he was halfway through, but still kept seeing the image of the naked woman walking away with her head held high. He decided it was one of the most absorbing pictures he had ever seen: more intriguing than what the wet dress revealed of the girl at the river in the rec who was, of course, a lot younger than this woman. In addition, the boys and girls there had been happily enjoying what they had been doing, reserving their displeasure for himself as an intruder, while Alex recorded in his memory the ugly hatred shown on the faces of the people jeering at the French woman and was angry with them on her behalf, wishing he could have been there to act in her defence. He could not understand why there was no one to stand up for her: whenever things became violent in the school playground and someone was victimized, there was usually someone who would stand up against the bullies.

II

Precisely a week after D Day, any possible grounds for national complacency were brutally taken away when the flying bombs appeared and fell on London. It was known that the all-clear had not sounded all day on several occasions in the capital. Official reporting said nothing about flying bombs so as not to harm civilian morale, beyond recording the damage. There was worse news to come concerning these terror weapons, as everybody soon called them. On the eighth of September, when enemy action destroyed eight houses and damaged fifty in Chiswick, George explained to Alex that Chiswick was not far from where they used to live.

It was decided, since no one appeared safe from these weapons even on the other side of the Chiltern Hills from London, that air raid shelters were needed for the people whose homes were near the dairy. They were to be located in the gardens of the terrace in which George, Edna, Alex and their neighbours lived.

The dividing walls came down almost overnight. Large piles of breeze blocks were delivered in the dairy yard, footings were hastily dug and concrete floors poured. Then the breeze blocks were assembled into walls and roofs. Alex was free to come and go while all this was taking place and his imagination was seized by an integral part of these buildings, which was a seat that ran around inside each area of about eight feet by twelve feet, the area of each shelter, and there were thirty or so shelters altogether. In his mind's eye he saw ninety to a hundred people, including himself and his mother and father, cowering in the shelters while the sound of an exploding gas main deafened them; when they emerged they had nowhere left to live but the shelters themselves.

In fact the idea of gas mains exploding was an officially backed cover for this large scale destruction for the best part of two months, until the tenth of November when Mr Churchill told the House of Commons and the rest of the nation what many people had already seen for themselves and reported to their relations in their letters to them. George explained it all to Alex when he had digested the news himself.

"Hitler knows he's beaten," he said, "But a fatally wounded tiger fights to the last. His scientists developed the V1 flying bomb and then followed it up with the V2 rocket bomb. Our fighter pilots and anti-aircraft gunners have been stopping some of the V1s, but there is no way of stopping a rocket because it goes so fast and falls at the end of its trajectory. It also carries a great deal more explosive than the flying bomb. The Germans call them reprisal bombs - 'reprisal' in German begins with a V - hoping to get their own back for the American and British raids on their cities."

"They say you know when a V1 is going to fall," he went on, "because its engine cuts out and if you're underneath, you say your prayers. But these V2 bastards have knocked down a building before anyone heard them coming at all. Two thousand houses went like that in Croydon, which is also in Surrey, but over the other side from where we used to live."

Edna added her comment,

"Perhaps it's as well we couldn't get our house rebuilt. At least it means that it's not there for one of these things to get it."

"If we'd gone back there and it had got the house, it would've got us too," George hastily mumbled.

So the gardens disappeared and George's shed with them. The secret cupboard and the sea chest came indoors. Alex never saw the cupboard again after a day or two: George had arranged for the Admiralty to have it back, he told him after he had sworn him to secrecy, and Alex imagined half a dozen elderly gentlemen dressed in cocked hats and covered in gold lace calling for it to carry it away along Botley Road amid deferential onlookers.

All three of them barked their shins on or fell over the sea chest in the following days. Because it was too heavy with all the tools it contained to stow anywhere but the front hall, it remained there. Alex had remembered his old pie dish in time and rescued it for sentimental reasons before it could be taken away with all the garden topsoil that was being removed. It spent the best part of the next year on his bedroom floor, despite all Edna's efforts to persuade him to let her throw it away.

As it turned out, the shelters would have been more useful in the London suburbs. In west Oxford they had no other function than as places to hang new washing lines and store bicycles and the garden tools usually kept in the sheds they had replaced, together with Alex's home-made scooter. By the time the shelters were in being the scare had passed and no one saw fit to provide them with any doors at all, let alone such as would keep those inside safe from bomb blast.

A little while later, gates were put at the outside ends of the rows of shelters, because the residents complained that the houses were no longer secure from intrusion without them. When he came home on the evening after their gate reappeared, George looked out of the living room window and called to Edna,

"Here, girl! Look at this. In Raynes Park we only had one shelter when the bombs were falling all round us. In this place it's as quiet as the grave at night and we've got eight of the bloody things all to ourselves!"

III

Just before the Christmas holidays, Miss Cook made one of her special announcements in the school assembly. It went like this:

"You all know that, after the D Day landings in June on the coast of northern France, the allied troops made great advances into that country. Perhaps you do not know that the German army appears to have recovered some of its former strength and has been advancing rather than retreating into eastern France and Belgium for the last week. When we say our prayers, in a minute or two, we must pray that our men will be courageous in resisting them. But there is something important that I wanted to say this morning before the newspapers carried the news that I have just mentioned. I have been told that some of you, boys and girls alike, have seen the lorries carrying German prisoners of war through and out of the city by the main road here and have been shouting rude remarks at them. I know that for as long as many of you here can remember you have not been stopped from hating the Germans. Some of you who have been bombed out of where you used to live have a particular grievance against their leader and against them too. But these men we have recently caught sight of in our own streets are a defeated enemy with no more power to hurt us and it is our Christian duty to be gracious towards them as their vanquishers. It is enough that they have been captured by our men. They do not need the insults of children to make life worse for them."

Then she announced the hymn and Alex ignored it as he usually did. Yet he did recall that he had been standing in Botley Road with some eight or ten others when such a lorry passed and they saw some Germans crowded into its open back under the eye of their armed guards. There had been derisive hoots and dirt had been belatedly thrown towards them. This was the work of only three or four of their number. The rest felt sorry for them in their shabby uniforms, which cinema newsreels had shown to be splendid in the recent past, and were not sorry that the headmistress had spoken as she did. When she came to pray for the troops caught up what was to be called "the Battle of the Bulge", the Amen was more fulsome than it usually was, especially from the boys and girls whose fathers and elder brothers were in the army and might actually be in the Ardennes.

Alex said to his friend Isabel,

"I wonder if this means that we shall find out what peace is like soon."

"A lot more Germans will have to be captured first," the gentle girl replied.

"Or killed, I suppose," Alex added.

The war news soon faded into the task of multiplying unlikely sums in pounds shillings and pence by unreasonable numbers: "A shop is selling tables at £4 11s 7d each: how much would you have to pay for sixteen?" Alex was told off for being seen to write, "I would not want that many tables," in his work book. This was a cover for the ignorance resulting from his long absence from school. He kept quiet about it at home and no one in the school seemed very concerned to help him catch up. Later on, of course, George taught him, but only after Edna found he could not confirm that she had been short-changed when she was spoiling for a row with a man in the market from whom she had bought some remnants of cloth.

IV

The poignancy of the plight of prisoners of war was brought home to the Rylands next Monday morning when Edna called on Mrs White to return a plate that she had used to give her neighbours a rhubarb pie to eat over the weekend. Mrs White was plainly in tears and hardly able to manage to get to the back door. Edna knew that she had been a widow for a long time and that she had an only son called James who was in the army. Mrs White told Edna that she had heard last evening by telegram that her boy had been captured by the Japanese in Burma. She had read a popular newspaper's account earlier in the year after Anthony Eden's statement in parliament about how such prisoners had been treated and was very frightened. Edna went into her kitchen with her, refilled the kettle and put it back on the kitchen range while she listened to Mrs White's distress.

"I haven't seen Jim for three years now, not since his call-up papers came. He hasn't lived here since he finished his apprenticeship at Morris Garages before the war and moved to work in Birmingham. Please God he'll come home safely when it's all over."

Edna made the tea. As she and Edna drank, Mrs White talked and talked: about her husband, a stonemason who worked at the colleges, dead these fifteen years now; about Jim's childhood and youth; about her hopes for him and the nice girl he had taken up with before he went away. Edna listened, as Joyce had listened to her in her distress about bricks and mortar and as Mrs Wilson had when Alex was run over, which approached the distress which Mrs White was going through now.

Edna thought that it was fortunate that George was no longer at the dairy. He was out at Wheatley and would not need a midday meal. Alex took a sandwich and an apple to eat in the playground these days, so she could stay with Mrs White if she needed her until the time school was over. Normally she would herself had been at the factory, but the women had been told not to come in until Tuesday that week because a new type of detonator was going into production and the machines had to be re-jigged over the weekend and tested today.

Mrs White did need her so she sat and listened and went next door to find something from her own larder to make a meal for them both, though Mrs White ate little. Edna stayed while her neighbour dozed in an exhausted state until half past three. She left by Mrs White's front door to be at home for her son. She saw him coming down Ferry Hinksey Road jumping about and doing what George would call skylarking with other children.

"Nothing much wrong with him now, thank God," thought Edna, as she went in her own front door to be there when he came in.

This sense of gratitude evaporated fairly quickly. She told Alex about Jim White and his mother's distress about him being captured and her fears concerning the treatment he might receive from his captors.

"It's up to those who take prisoners to be gracious towards them," was his response, and all Edna's fear of having produced a precocious child returned from the dormant state into which she had pressed it since her early spring vigil in the Radcliffe waiting for him to recover consciousness.

"Why did you have to say that, you little know-all? What do you know about being taken prisoner, or grief at the chance of losing your only son?"

Alex was not a know-all and could not cope with this. He hid upstairs from his mother until he heard her slam her way into the front room. Then he hurried downstairs, went out of the back door to find his scooter and shot off on it through the dairy yard into Henry Road and the rec to wait for the time when George would be home. Although they glowered at each other over the table, neither of them told George why - at least, he didn't: maybe Edna did later. George was distressed to learn about Mrs White's boy.

"Good job he's too young for all this," George said, with a nod towards Alex.

"And that you're too old," she said, getting up to hug him. This very rarely happened outside their bedroom and in his embarrassment George smiled towards Alex, who made no attempt to interfere in his parents' closeness, which lasted an astonishingly long time. Their embrace had its own desperation and he knew about their anxiety caused by the notice given to them by the dairy.

V

"We are going to stay with Gran down home for the weekend," George told Alex.

"Why?" he asked, wondering if he would receive an honest and full reply.

"Because I haven't seen her since your Grandad died - and you and Mum haven't seen her for longer than that."

"Is it far?"

"A hundred miles or so: go and get the atlas and I'll show you where it is."

Alex brought the now dog-eared book to George and he found the Southern England page, as opposed to the France and The Low Countries opening they had recently spent a lot of time with.

"Look, you know we are here? Well, we go to London - look, the black line is the railway - and get off at a station called Paddington. Then we go across London, probably on the Underground, to another station called Victoria, and the train from there takes us to Gillingham where we get off. Then there's a bus ride and a bit of a walk."

"What do you mean by 'a bit of a walk'?"

"Further than you want to walk, but not far enough to kill you!"

"And why do you call it 'down home'?"

"Because near there is where Mum and I grew up. I was born in Rochester - there, and Mum was born in Chatham - there, see? I'm never sure which is which, but I think I'm a Kentishman rather than a Man of Kent. The River Medway - there - is the dividing line between the different sorts. I might have ended my short life there the night Mafeking was relieved, when Gran nearly dropped me off Rochester Bridge when she was trying to get through the crowd celebrating it."

"Mafeking?"

"Yes. Your godfather, Art, can tell you more about it because he was there at the time. A soldier called Baden-Powell with a small force was under siege there in the South African War and then the British Army beat the Boers and let him out."

"Bores? Why call them that?"

"It's spelt differently: Boer is a Dutch or, perhaps, Afrikaans word that means farmer. The Boers had settled there from Holland and during the Napoleonic Wars the British had taken and subsequently bought South Africa from the Dutch as a stopping place on the way to India - in those days the ships had to go all round Africa to reach it because there was no Suez Canal then. After the freeing of all slaves in the British Empire a hundred years ago, these farmers moved to a new place where they were not subject to British rule (here the atlas came out again and Alex was shown the Transvaal) and complications later arose about diamond mines and one thing and another led to war - and the relief of Mafeking was part of it."

"How come Gran nearly dropped you off the bridge?"

"She was frightened by the crowd, most of whom had had a few drinks. At least that's what she told me. I don't remember it myself being only a few months old! Anyway, we're going down there on Friday morning. I've got the day off from Wheatley. We come back Sunday afternoon."

So on Friday they were on the train to Paddington, George standing in the corridor with Alex sitting next to him on the suitcase and Edna sitting in the compartment beside them with the door jammed back, trying not to breath in too often since six out of the seven soldiers in there with her were smoking with the window shut. From where Alex was sitting on the case, he could see her face close by through the glass and thought she looked a bit green by the time they got to Reading. He also noticed that the soldiers, although they were British and not American, were wearing a different kind of uniform from the thick battle dress he had often seen. This one was of lighter material and looked as though it did not itch and would not be so hot to wear.

By the time they reached Slough, Edna had to give up her seat and open the window in the corridor. Alex heard her say under her breath to George as she did so,

"The things I have to go through for your bloody mother!"

Alex was put out by his reply, which he only half heard and was not sure about,

"You might be glad like me of a roof over your head come the autumn."

Eventually Paddington station came alongside the window and they got out of the train. They stood on the platform in a pale imitation of Frith's painting, though George had no silk hat or faun waistcoat, just his usual trilby and his three-piece suit with his mackintosh unbuttoned on top of it. They waited for the military men to leave the platform and then made their way down to the Underground, where Alex held Edna's hand firmly as he saw a train rush roaring from a tunnel and stop right in front of him, with the bottoms of its windows at the level of his eyes. He was very surprised that he was near such a monster and even more so to find he had to step into it. All this was explained by George when they sat down side by side with Edna opposite and the case in between George's and Edna's feet.

"This is called the Circle Line, because it goes in a ring all round the principal places of central, east and west London - and we get out at Victoria, as I told you, which is in the south-west. When you see Sloane Square on a sign at one of the stations, you'll know we're nearly there - and if I'm asleep wake me up!"

Here George put his head back and his hat fell over his eyes.

"He can't sleep in all this noise, can he, Mum?"

Even Edna, still fancying herself choked with second-hand tobacco smoke, had to smile in George's direction.

"No more questions now, Alex," she told him.

Alex kept his watching brief and then after fewer minutes than he expected shook George's arm,

"Sloane Square, Dad. Wake up!"

George made his hat fall sideways so that Edna could see his face but not Alex, and made an expression which conveyed his good-natured weariness with the present demands of fatherhood.

The next part of the journey, which was shorter than the first, was slow and in a dirty train. George explained the absence of a locomotive as they got on the train, and Alex was delighted when he remembered all the pictures of Southern Railway rolling stock he had seen in John's Meccano Magazines a long time ago and asked George to explain the mystery of conductor rails. His explanation enlightened all within earshot, even Edna, who commented,

"I never knew all that! Nor that you did."

"Goes with the job," said George, and this time did settle to go to sleep because he knew that Edna knew where they would get off. When they arrived there, Alex was puzzled by how much this station resembled some of the so-called underground stations they had gone through earlier, which were not under ground at all. George led them as they made their way up a good number of steps to find the bus to Rainham, which could either be a green one run by the Maidstone and District Company, or a brown one which would be from the Chatham and District. The green one came first, so they got on and went upstairs. The upper deck of this bus did not have long seats like the Oxford buses because there would be no low bridges for it to go under, but a gangway down the middle with seats on both sides. Alex was next to the window on the right hand side, Edna was with him on the double seat and George was behind them both. Looking out of the window he asked,

"What's that over there with window spaces very high up over the other buildings? Has it been bombed?"

George put his head between his wife's and son's to reply,

"That's called The Jezreels. A man believed God told him to build a tower up to heaven and began to do so, but the money ran out, and nobody saw fit to take it down."

Edna then put in,

"And just past it are some grass slopes called the Darland Banks, where we used to go blackberrying when we was kids. At the bottom of the slopes there's Luton where I lived when I was a girl, next door to the pub which was called 'The Wagon at Hail'."

Alex heard this as 'The Wag and a Tail' and thought that was its real name for a long time afterwards until he actually saw it for himself. Then George told him that they were going along part of a Roman road called Watling Street and a few minutes later they went down the stairs ready to get off the bus at the top of Twydall Lane.

George's mother lived at the bottom end of it and had stayed on in the house after her bereavement the year before and intended to continue to do so. George had more than hinted to her in a letter that they might be in a homeless state fairly soon, and she had assured him in her reply that her door would be open to him and his family. This short visit was, as George put it, "a toe in the water".

"If it's too bloody cold, we can find some other beach to paddle from," he added, and Edna sniffed.

It was a very long walk to Gran's house, Alex decided, after what seemed to him like an hour had passed, although it was only ten minutes by his father's turnip watch. George tried to lighten the load by leaning round Edna and pointing out his own familiar landmarks in the valley in front of them.

"Look there, boy, there's the River Medway."

Alex saw the strip of dark river and its further bank in front of which a large naval craft was making its way.

"Do you see the skeletons of the old barges sticking up out of the mud?"

"Where?"

"On the near bank of the river, look."

"I can't see them."

"What about those telegraph poles going through the gap in the orchards down there? That's the railway line the Golden Arrow express uses in peacetime to take the boat train to Dover."

"I can see some trees, but no telegraph poles."

George stopped trying to look towards Alex by craning round in front of Edna and, putting his mouth close to her nearside ear, expressed his anxiety under his breath:

"Maybe that bang on the head has done some damage after all or maybe he's never been able to see very far and no one asked him to look at distant things before. He looked at a lot of far off things when we used to go out on the bike, though."

"We must get his eyes tested next week, then," Edna quietly replied, allaying her fear of the next two days with pretence at being a practical woman.

At this point, the weary Alex walked into a tree that stood at the edge of the pavement. His exasperated mother remarked,

"He couldn't see what was right under his nose, let alone what's a long way off. Do look where you're going, for Christ's sake."

Whenever she invoked the thin man hanging on the cross in St Frideswide's Church, Alex expected his mother's thunderclouds to burst upon his head, so he now made every effort to walk upright, to look out in expectation of further hazards on this interminable walk and not to say anything provocative, or he knew he would arrive at his grandmother's with the imprint of Edna's glove on a painful ear, partially deaf as well as short-sighted. He was obviously not deaf or he would not have heard his father's quiet comment or his mother's whispered reply before he came in contact with the tree.

George realized there was no point in saying anything else because Edna would have liked to have postponed the coming night under her mother-in-law's roof that she was dreading. She was keeping quiet too.

Then, after another five minutes, they reached the terrace of ten-year-old houses behind front gardens in which Gran lived and saw her at her bay window looking out into the evening light to see her beloved firstborn son arriving with the woman he had married against her own expressed wishes and their only child who was, in her opinion, growing too tall for his strength.

"Doesn't she feed him?" she asked herself before she opened the door to be as warm towards them all as she felt able to be.

She had always made a god of her late husband when he was away for long periods at sea - which covered her lack of understanding of his attitude to life when he was at home with her - and she prayed to him for guidance now, to some extent receiving it as she opened the front door, smiled at, embraced and kissed all three in turn, saying exclusively to George as she looked at Alex,

"Is he fully recovered from his road accident now, son?"

"I think so," he replied.

His mother remembered that Alex had a mother also, and took her upstairs to show her the back bedroom where she had prepared beds for them.

"I'm sorry you're all in together, Edna. Sarah's here as well, so there isn't a great deal of room."

Edna simpered in reply and did her best to overcome antagonism as she looked out over the little garden that her father-in-law had lovingly tended in his latter years. The fact that her young sister-in-law would unexpectedly be here created a new problem, but Edna had made a mental resolution in spite of her real feelings to do her best to keep things on an even keel, especially if this was the only place where they could find shelter after the dairy took its house back.

VI

Louisa Ryland was sixty-six years old. She was little in stature and had not much weight about her, especially since she had neglected her eating since she had been widowed. Her face was lined, largely from a nervous complaint which years before had given her a twitch. That had been cured, but it left the creases in her cheek where it had happened and Alex had been warned not to comment upon them before his grandparents had last come to see them.

Years of coping on her own while her husband was contemplating God's wonders in the deep had made her self-sufficient enough, but her composure was expressed in polishing furniture and beating carpets rather than forming strong bonds with her children, which she left to their absent father's eloquent letters. Edna and she both realized that like poles repel and that her character and Edna's were very similar. George realized in his worst moments that he had married a prettier version of his mother.

However, here they were, and Louisa was in no position to say to her eldest child with his wife and son that they could not come and live with her until they brought their heads above water again.

George had told her that his present job at the American camp would only last until the end of the war against Nazi Germany - and that did not seem far off now. She was the only one in the family who could do anything for them and she had decided she ought to. Whether any of them would enjoy living together was another matter. Young Sarah would help for these two days, but she would be off before very long to join her husband in the Middle East where he was an administrator and George's brother would be in the Far East for a while yet, though his wife lived just round the corner from here.

As she stood in her own bedroom, waiting for Edna to finish putting her things where she wanted them in the other room, she looked up at the old photographer's portrait of herself and her husband with the three-year-old George. David was in uniform with his diver's badges on both sides of his jacket collar, standing upright in the centre, while she, in her full-length coat with its black collar setting off her high-necked blouse and her Gainsborough hat with feathers, was decorously presented on a garden seat. George, in a diminutive fore and aft sailor suit on the model of his father's topped with an incongruous Little Lord Fauntleroy collar and a huge Jack Tar's straw hat, was perched on the arm of the seat. It conveyed the tone of respectability she had wanted, though the scenery in the photographer's studio of great wrought iron gates set between monumental pillars was not very like the approach to their small house in Junction Road, which she would soon leave for her own parents' home in the country as soon as David had gone to sea again, that time to pursue his own respectability in a lodge of Freemasons, once more in Malta.

Edna scratched rather than knocked on her door to wake her from her memories,

"Hullo. I was miles away," she said.

"I expect it's nicer there," replied Edna, and stood aside while the older woman led the way downstairs to where George was ready with a pot of tea. Alex was sitting expectantly in front of a pile of scones put on the table a few minutes before they arrived.

George commented on his father's garden and his mother said that one of their neighbours had promised to keep an eye on it until further notice. George kept back from offering to look after it himself if they came to live here, but would have liked to do so.

Conversation was desultory and dealt with no important family issues while Alex was still at table and this gave him time to look round and notice that in two corners of the room, built in next to the fireplace on either side, there were tall cupboards with glass fronts in which fine china and large books were kept: the books on the shelves above and the china below.

"Can I get down?" he asked, when he had finished all the scones covered in butter and jam he thought he would be allowed to consume. George answered, as he always did whenever he remembered his old headmaster at Chatham Technical School,

"You can, my boy. The question is whether you may!"

And Alex replied, as usual on these occasions, taking the words from a play he had heard on Children's Hour about children in the English Civil War,

"May it please you, Papa, I wish to leave the table now."

"If your grandmother will permit," George responded, cheerfully taking up the idiom, and this gave Alex his opening:

"May I ask you something, Gran?"

"Yes, of course, Alex."

"Would you let me look at those books up there in that cupboard, please?"

"Of course. Get a chair from the kitchen to climb up on. I'll open the door of it while you are out there."

Edna looked apprehensive lest Alex should break something, but George took her hand under the table in friendly restraint.

Alex climbed up with his grandmother's help and looked with interest at the titles on the spines of the books. Some did not interest him at all, like The Universal Home Doctor; he had had enough from actual doctors in the last year; and they had a Pear's Cyclopaedia at home. It was the next one that caught his eye: Cassell's Illustrated History of England.

"Can I get this one down and look at it, please?"

She looked up from her awkward conversation to say,

"Of course. Be careful as you get off the chair with it," and rose from the table again to help him down, taking the book from him since it was heavy, and giving it back once the chair had been returned to the kitchen.

"Go in the front room, put the light on and read it in there, while we carry on talking out here."

Alex did as she suggested. He went into the other room and sat in a big armchair ready for the opening of a new chapter in his life.

The book was bound between thick boards covered in brown cloth with embossed Gothic letters in gold above and below the star of the Order of the Garter. The paper inside was thick and creamy in texture and the illustrations were most attractive to a boy who spent all the time he could with a pencil in his hand, drawing. On every page was at least one steel engraving and some of the pictures were full-page reproductions of historical paintings. The images that interested him most were the ones within the pages of printed text depicting some event, like the Empress Matilda escaping from Oxford Castle in 1141, or Oliver Cromwell dismissing the Rump Parliament in 1653. The local colour of something happening at Oxford Castle appealed to him and he was amused by the idea of a Rump Parliament. He decided to ask George what it might mean later on . . .

For the rest of his short evening he was fascinated by this book. The pictures showed the changes in costume from what Saxon men and women wore right through to one of the more extravagant of Mr Gladstone's collars and the history of facial hair from William the Conqueror's clean-shaven chin to the Third Marquess of Salisbury's full set. Military and naval uniforms also seized his attention. Wellington and Nelson took his eye and what George had told him about the Seven Years' War came to life for him when he saw the picture of General Wolfe's troops storming the Heights of Abraham. He hardly noticed George, who had come in on the pretext of seeing if all was well with him in order to withdraw for a moment from the tension in the next room. George decided not to disturb Alex because that book had fed his own imagination many years ago as well.

Alex looked up for a moment, just long enough to say,

"I'm enjoying this," and for George to respond,

"Good. So did I."

Then George was back again acting as mediator between his mother and his wife and nearly keeping the uncertain peace.

George's thirty-year-old sister let herself in then, home from her sojourn in Bath, and George busied himself with carrying her cases upstairs while she greeted her mother and renewed her tenuous acquaintance with Edna. They left Alex and the personalities of England's greatness for a little while longer and then decreed bed-time. They insisted that he let the book be put back in its place, but the effect of the demand was lessened by a firm promise that he could take it down again, if he asked Gran first, tomorrow morning.

Aunt Sarah was nice to him and, knowing he was coming, had bought him a book of his own by somebody called Hugh Lofting, which was about a Doctor who could speak the languages of animals. The illustrations, drawn and painted by the author, were almost as good as the ones in the big book, and Alex fell asleep while happily browsing through it. They found him, when they came to put the light out, with his hand resting on the coloured picture which showed the curvature of the moon's surface. Alex had noticed at least two things before he fell asleep: that Dr Dolittle wore collars like Mr Gladstone's and that a simple line could produce such a good effect in a drawing.

When it was time to leave on Sunday afternoon, Alex was a good way on in reading Aunt Sarah's present and his imagination was fully charged with material both from it and from the history book, influencing the drawings he did himself for a very long time to come. He made a point of drawing on both sides of the paper thereafter, so that George could say, "Not bad at all," twice in one go. This also meant that Edna would not tell him that he was wasting paper. Alex was learning to be diplomatic within his family, but the successful use of that skill was, he found, never certain. After the train left Gillingham station, Alex asked George about the Rump Parliament and sat back to be told all about Pride's Purge and the execution of Charles I, though the tale had to be broken off between Chatham and Rochester, where conversation turned to the nature of Norman fortifications and Short Sunderland flying boats, both of which were in evidence as the Medway was crossed.

"Is this the river Gran nearly dropped you in?"

And in the manner of speech often heard at work from his transatlantic colleagues, George replied, "Sure is!"

After a little more on Cromwell and what he did in Ireland, Alex remembered Dr Dolittle in the Moon, and it was brought out of the case for him to read while his parents talked quietly about future possibilities, not much of which interested Alex, beyond noticing that the talk was anxious and that both his parents were desperately worried.

VII

The eye test was quickly arranged in a shop in St. Aldate's that had a huge pair of golden spectacles hanging at right angles to its door. An elderly man took Alex and Edna into a darkened room and sat him in an enormous chair, which, to Alex's imagination, resembled the pilot's seat in a bomber. A heavy contraption was laid upon his ears and the bridge of his nose and the optician kept on putting in and taking out various bits of glass in metal circles, asking Alex if he could see the letters in front of him any better, first with one eye, then with the other and finally with both eyes together. Alex found this a strain, but answered all the man's questions as politely as he could for fear of one of Edna's outbursts after it was all over.

George had told him what to expect, having been through it several times himself since the Navy had dispensed with his services. Edna wore glasses too, but did not say anything to him on the bus coming in to the city. Since they had come home from Gran's it had been difficult to get any words from her at all. The only activity she had involved herself in was arranging this appointment and getting the school to agree to him having the morning off. She had done both these things on Mrs Wilson's telephone because she said she could not face meeting people.

Alex thought there was an inconsistency in this, because she had to go and meet Mrs Wilson and she had to meet the optician to tell him what had happened on the way to Gran's that had caused her to submit Alex to all this. He sat in the seat with the thin optician making elaborate gestures with the lenses as he changed them and behaving as though Alex were the hat he was about to produce a rabbit from like someone he had seen at the New Theatre when they used to go to the variety shows there. All the time, he heard Edna sniffing behind him and clicking her teeth together.

Eventually, Alex could read down as far of the sixth line of letters on the chart lit up before him and the optician declared that he was satisfied with his work.

"Your boy does, indeed, have a myopic condition, Mrs Ryland, but all that is needed is a pair of spectacles to correct it. I will be very pleased to supply you with them."

"A myopic condition" sounded awful to Alex. It may have sounded awful to Edna as well, but everything seemed awful to her at present, decided Alex, so there would be no use asking her if he was going to lose his sight altogether on the way home. The optician took Edna and Alex out into the front of the shop and Edna was asked to look at frames and choose a pair for her son.

"Can I choose, Mum?" Alex asked.

"No. It's a question of what I can afford."

"Can you afford those?" he asked, looking at a pair with wire fixings for the ears but tortoiseshell frames.

"Of course not. I'm not made of money!"

"But yours are like that and they look good. I'd like a pair the same as yours. Dad's got them too, only his have got straight sides rather than wire over his ears."

"Look, you'll have what I decide. Go and sit down over there."

By this time the elderly optician, who had amused as well as overawed Alex, had gone, and Edna was being attended to by a woman the same age as herself who seemed to Alex to be similarly burdened with the world's troubles. These two agreed between them that Alex should indeed have wire over his ears, but the rest of the frame should be of thin metal covered with a dark substance flecked with orange and yellow.

"Very good, madam," said the woman, "They take about a week to make up. Are you on the telephone?"

"No, but my neighbour, whose name is Mrs Wilson, said she would take a message for me if you rang her."

Edna gave Mrs Wilson's number to the woman and she carefully wrote it down.

"Very well, madam," she said again. "That will be done. Now, the cost is seven pounds. Will you pay now, or when you come to collect?"

"I'll pay now," said Edna, and did so, giving what Alex called from then on her death ray stare, like one of the characters in the comic books from Wheatley.

Going home was also a silent business. There was a toyshop near the optician's where Alex wanted to look at a display of Dinky toys in the window, but she would not let him linger and dragged him up to Carfax in a manner that reminded him of her reaction on the day he had sat on the eggs. Today he had committed no such misdemeanour beyond expressing a wish that he should not have to look like a dead fish in his new glasses.

At the tea table he asked George,

"What's a myopic condition, Dad?"

"It means you can't see things at a distance. Your new glasses will sort that out."

"Is that all?"

"Yes, what did you think it was?"

"I don't know, only it sounded terrible when the man said it to Mum."

"Didn't Mum tell you what it was?"

"I don't know why he has to bother his head with all these things," said Edna, with some vehemence. "The optician was talking to me not you."

"Yes, but I've got to wear the things, and go to school in them, and I don't want to be called 'four-eyes' by people at school like Ginger Thompson is - and his glasses are just the same as the ones you have chosen for me!"

Edna raised her hand towards him.

“That’s enough now,” said George, looking at Alex, but wanting to say it to Edna too.

“Why do you always have to make trouble?” asked Edna of her child.

“Best you go away and play,” said George.

Next time Alex saw Edna, half an hour later, she had obviously been crying. George looked like misery made flesh.

“What’s the matter?” said Alex to George.

“It’s a private matter between Mum and me,” was the only reply he received.

9

Uncle Geoff's painful recollections of his traumatic experiences in the Auxiliary Fire Service during the London blitz had receded somewhat by the time that his task in submarine development at Barrow shipyard was complete. He had no misgivings therefore, when the Admiralty called him back to London at the end of 1944 to work on other hush-hush projects. He and Aunt Hetty did not have a housing problem for long. They had chosen not to have children during the war and Hetty was free to take a job. She found one very soon, as housekeeper in a hotel in Leicester Square that had managed to avoid anything more than cosmetic damage so far, in spite of the Doodlebugs. This job carried a small flat with it, ample accommodation for a married couple, and they moved into it in January. They asked George and Edna to come and see them for a weekend. At the time the invitation was given, General Montgomery's troops had overrun the V1 launch sites in their advance on Antwerp. Although the V2 menace had largely had its teeth drawn by the beginning of 1945, there were still "a few strays", as the government minister charged with warding them off observed, and there was still danger in coming to London. Having saved her family from the bombing in 1940, Edna was in no mind to subject it to the final fling of Nazi terror weapons now, even for the sake of her sister, whom she did not like much in any case. So no answer was given for several weeks and then the invitation was accepted for a few days in the early part of May.

By then there had been a good number of developments in the European war, which made the thought of travelling more acceptable to Edna. Germany was being invaded by the British, Americans and French from the west and by the Russians from the east. During another visit to the cinema there was news of the liberation of Belsen. The pictures reminded Alex of that bullock which had fled from the slaughterhouse into the garden, which he had seen through the window before Edna took him to safety upstairs. Before the lights went down for the main feature, Alex asked George,

"Why are people sometimes so cruel to each other?"

"I wish I knew, boy. Then perhaps we could stop them."

After that, Alex had free access to Picture Post and no comment was made when he was seen with it.

Two days before George and Edna meant to travel to London, Alex was in Mrs Wilson's house, as he often was, and she and the girls had the six o'clock news on. They and Alex looked up from what they were each doing when they heard that Field Marshal Montgomery had signed a document in his headquarters on Lüneberg Heath, which meant that the German generals had surrendered to him. With the Russians actually in Berlin at the same time and Adolf Hitler dead, as the news on the wireless announced three days before, it would be only a matter of days for the whole European war to be over at last. Mary clapped her hands and said as much and Mrs Wilson quietly went to another room for a few moments to be on her own. When she came back, smiling and composed, Alex went home and told Edna, whose reaction was not so straightforward. Over the last months she had never put the news on when she was by herself and seemed to show little interest in what was going on. George came in a few minutes later and Alex was in no doubt about his reaction:

"Nothing to stop us going up to see Geoff and Hetty now, is there, girl?"

"No. But we were going anyway. We'd made our mind up."

George accepted this answer and Edna ironed the things she intended to take in the case. Geoff met them at Paddington and a taxi took them through central London past some buildings that were shored up with timber, and some that were now only shells, alongside others which were still standing and occupied but which, as George remarked, looked sadly in need of a coat of paint. Self-sown plants had grown in profusion in some of the ruins and were coming into flower, but the streets were clear for the buses and taxis and the few cars that were to be seen.

Hetty's hotel building stood proud among the survivors and the casualties around it. They left the taxi and stood at the door, looking around them. Edna kept commenting on how normal everyone looked in spite of what had been happening here on and off for years on end, but she was not pleased when George quietly said,

"Perhaps we should've stayed on too."

"But we didn't and that's that," was all she could think of to say, and she busied herself by adjusting her old, but still best, hat with the veil attached as she walked through the hotel entrance, greeted by the elderly doorman in his black and gold livery who did her good by calling her Ma'am as his hand went to the brim of his own hat.

Since Hetty would be busy for another hour, Geoff took them to the basement to see the exhibition arranged to show what a V1 was like, consisting of a specimen that had not damaged itself very much in its terminal plunge on a building nearby. They all felt the irony, even if they could not call it that, of a place that had been an air-raid shelter exhibiting this monster bomb as if it had been a war trophy. Alex would have been interested in it had it been a real aeroplane, but he had heard that many airmen regarded the flying bomb as a hybrid freak - words that George had explained to him - and gave it no more than a cursory inspection. George and Edna were showing signs of obvious distress in this ghoulish place underground and Geoff regretted his own curiosity that had made him bring them down here. He took them up in the lift to the flat on the top floor where they could see out over what remained of the roofs of London WC2 and down into the busy square below. They found themselves in a very comfortable living room, sumptuously furnished by the standards of George and Edna's own mixture of rescued and second-hand pieces of furniture. There was even a portrait of Edna's sister by an artist who lived round the corner and drank in the bar here. Geoff understandably said he did not care for it overmuch.

The original herself was not long in coming off duty, and she brought in a trolley with all sorts of good things to eat and drink prepared beforehand on it. They sat down to eat in the armchairs with the trolley between them and plates on napkins in their laps and Edna was determined to call the napkins serviettes, which caused Alex a little confusion for the space of about ten seconds until he found that smoked salmon was what he had been searching for all his life so far and George indulged a liking for Parma ham that he had forgotten he had. Edna made a meal of potted shrimps on tiny pieces of bread and then there was tinned fruit salad for everyone, just like that brought home from Wheatley by George, enhanced by the taste, new to Alex, of condensed milk. He found he did not enjoy what Hetty called real coffee, but the fizzy lemonade was entirely to his liking. He knew he had tasted it before, but could not remember when.

After they had eaten, George and Edna were shown their bedroom and Alex had another with a window under which there was an upholstered bench. When he stood on this, he found he could look out on Leicester Square itself.

The afternoon was spent on a walk with George to the Embankment, along the river to Parliament Square, briefly into the undamaged nave of Westminster Abbey, up sandbagged Whitehall, past the Admiralty to Trafalgar Square and along the Strand, with questions and explanations all the way. Something else to eat was provided back at the flat and Alex went to bed in the interesting room, leafing through a copy of Punch, which he had never seen before, until Edna and the others had stopped talking in the next room. He got out of bed and warily lifted the blackout curtain to look at the quiet dark outside.

II

George, Edna, Alex and Hetty had the wireless on over lunchtime the next day when it was announced that General Eisenhower's deputy, someone called General Bedell Smith, had received the unconditional surrender of the Germans from General Jödl, who had signed a joint document with him and generals from Britain, France and Russia at a place in France called Reims on the day before. As a result of this, all hostilities in Europe had ceased two hours ago at eleven o'clock. Another act of surrender was being signed this very day at the Soviet headquarters in recently occupied Berlin, again with representatives of the three other allies present.

Alex's parents and aunt looked at each other in silence and then he could see the tears begin to run down the women's faces and his father turn away for a moment before they all smiled and George said to him,

"Alex, the war's over!"

They watched Hetty get up and go to the kitchen and return with a bottle such as Alex had never seen before, standing in what looked like a silver bucket full of ice, with gold paper all round its neck, and the words "Moët et Chandon" printed on its label, which he was not able to say.

"They're French words and this is a drink called Champagne, which I've been keeping ready for today," Aunt Hetty explained.

"But you told me when we were on holiday a long time ago that the French had let us down!" Alex said to George, with the image of the woman without her clothes before the hostile crowd in France appearing involuntarily behind his eyes once more.

"They're all right now," said George. "They resisted the German occupation and then fought alongside our troops in their own country and across the Rhine. They certainly share the victory."

By this time the bottle was open and the glasses filled with not a drop wasted or splashed under Hetty's housekeeperly touch and the adults lifted their glasses and said "Happy days!" to each other, with Alex joining in with a half glass given him quickly by his aunt before anyone could argue.

"German surrender or not," said Hetty, "This place won't run itself, and there are rooms to get ready before the staff have the same idea as us! I'll see you later. Finish that bottle: there are five more for this evening when Geoff's home."

When Hetty had left, George and Edna fell into each other's arms again and Alex was brought into their embrace. After about five minutes, none of the three knew what to do. Alex felt he was in the way to some extent as he heard Edna whisper to George,

"We'll have to wait . . ."

A few minutes later Alex, feeling sleepy and not energetic at all, was poured into his jacket, a reach-me-down from John Patterson left behind at Oxford for when he should need it, and an attempt was made to repeat part of yesterday's walk with Edna coming too. There were so many people out of doors, all walking about happily, some arm in arm across the pavement so that George and his family had to flatten themselves against a wall or step into the road to avoid them. When the road itself started to be taken up by young servicemen and women in uniform, similarly linked arm in arm, they called the excursion off and went back to Hetty's flat. From inside, they heard people singing from time to time. George and Edna kept very quiet, thinking of the ruins in Raynes Park they were not able to rebuild, and wondering, without reference to each other, what was going to happen to them when the house they lived in was no longer available, which might now be at any time. Hitler was dead. The soldiers who had survived would come home. But there were still one or two things for George and Edna to sort out.

"We'll go back tomorrow, girl, and see what can be done."

"Is there anything we can do to us stop having to live with your mother?"

"I suppose I could tell the dairy that they can do what they like and we're not leaving."

"I suppose that will do a fat lot of good," said Edna.

Alex was given the impression that, even if he were not there now, they would still stay apart from each other, regardless of the feelings they both had after the champagne and before they had gone out. When Geoff had come in, Alex could not help noticing the contrast between his rather crestfallen mother and father and his exuberant uncle and aunt. He did not go to bed until ten and was left to his own devices over washing and cleaning his teeth. That had happened more often than not lately in any case and, after he had said goodnight, they did not come in to see him.

In the room he had been given the window was ajar behind the blackout curtain and he could hear, in contrast to last night, loud noises in the street. He did as before, stood on the padded bench and looked under the blackout. People were going wild outside, some dancing, nearly all singing, though not the same songs as each other. Allied flags were being waved. There were people in uniform, people not in uniform, someone with very little on at all, even people sitting on the roofs of beleaguered buses with bottles in their hands from which they drank frequently and deeply. They were all being happy together. Then Alex realized why this scene was totally different from anything he could remember: some of the street lamps were on, and the headlights on the vehicles were no longer covered up in any way. The downstairs windows of the buildings still occupied were fully lit with no blackout in front of them. He was enjoying all this and he wanted to respond to the happy shouts that were rising frequently to his ears as he occupied his fifth floor grandstand.

Then he felt Edna's hands on his shoulders. She quietly said,

"Into bed now, Alex. You don't want to watch a whole lot of drunken fools in the street."

He obeyed because he was tired and had had his small share of the five remaining bottles himself, but he did not consider people who were dancing because more than five years of war were over to be all that foolish. As he snuggled into his sheets, he called his mother "old misery guts," but he made sure she was safely out of earshot before he did.

His dreams were sparkling ones and the people involved were unstintingly cheerful. He had heard the phrase "uninhibited behaviour" on certain respectable lips used pejoratively about what they had seen outside during the afternoon. As he dreamed, he fancied he knew what the meaning of it would be for those who had come out of years of fearful shadow into a light that made them feel free and happy.

Then there was no more until George, shaved and dressed, gently shook him awake.

"Come on," he said, "Time to get up and go home. Be as quick and as quiet as you can."

He found his clothes and put them on, washed his face and cleaned his teeth in the bathroom and then found both his parents ready to leave. His uncle and aunt were nowhere about. They left immediately and not until they were in the street, making for the underground station, did Alex dare to ask,

"Why didn't we say good-bye to Aunt Hetty and Uncle Geoff?"

"We did that last night," replied George, quietly.

"Yes. For good and all," added Edna summoning all her supplies of vehemence.

Alex was not told the details about their great falling out. He was sorry not to see them again, because he liked them. He did not ask George any questions until they were on the train from Paddington - and only then in the hopes of cheering him up:

"Why is this line called the Great Western, Dad?"

"There you've got me," George replied. "But I imagine it's like Great Britain that became bigger when they added Scotland to England and Wales. The man who built it was called Isambard Kingdom Brunel and he wanted to build a railway line westwards to Bristol, which was to be followed up by a sea voyage to New York. He had some great iron ships built to sail out of Bristol, but the businessmen in Liverpool had a harbour that didn't silt up in the way the one at Bristol did and took his trade."

While George responded to his son with what he was able to call to mind out of a deep well as it were, rescuing himself for a little while from his deep misery, Edna who had no such resilience, feigned sleep in order to isolate herself. She had lost the elegance of yesterday, and George regularly looked up at her between his bits of information for Alex with a worried expression on his face. By the time the train left Reading, Alex himself went to sleep, to a certain extent deliberately, as he sensed his father's distress and could not understand it enough to be able to help. This journey laid down the rules that became more and more a feature of the family game in the coming years.

When Alex woke briefly at Didcot, he saw that his father was holding a handkerchief to his eyes and was glad for his sake that they were the only ones in the compartment now. He did not know about the thousands of displaced persons wandering about in central Europe, so he could be excused for wondering why his parents had to be so unhappy when everyone else was so glad that the war in Europe was over.

He thought it best not to show George or Edna that he was awake and resolutely kept still with his eyes shut. He heard George say to Edna,

"I wish you hadn't said those things to Hetty last night."

"I wasn't going to put up with her looking down on us like that."

"But she only said she was enjoying her new life and intended to keep her place at the hotel now the war is over."

"It was the way she said it, George, as if to pooh-pooh whatever we might be thinking of doing. She knows we're in such a fix over not being able to go back to our old life and just sat there smug, counting her own blessings and not caring a tinker's cuss about us."

"But I wish you hadn't called her a selfish bitch with no concern for her own flesh and blood. That's what got Geoff's goat and the reason for his being angry and telling us to be gone by the time they got up in the morning."

"If that's the way he's going to talk to me after all I did for Hetty when she was a girl and poor old Mum had died, then I'm glad to see the back of him, and her too, with her stuck up la-di-dah ways. Who does she think she is?"

"Well," replied George, "There's nothing we can do about it now. We can't go back and say we're sorry. It's such a pity, though."

"Sorry! Say sorry! I thought you would back me up George, but you didn't. You just let him say that and bundled me into the bedroom. Did you see the look on his face as we went? I don't care if we never see either of them again. They made it quite obvious they didn't want to see us!"

Alex heard Edna start to cry and then to sob. He opened his eyes and pretended to be waking up.

"Is it far to Oxford now?" he asked, to cover his pretence.

Edna stifled her crying, holding her handkerchief over her nose and mouth, and announced, "I must go along to the toilet," and left the compartment.

"Mum's upset," George said to Alex.

"You look a bit unhappy, too," his son replied.

"We'll be there soon," was all George could think of to say.

As the train was slowing down to come into the station, Edna pushed the sliding door back and came in to retrieve her small case from the luggage rack. George stood up next to her to grapple with the big one with one hand while he put his free arm round Edna's waist. Alex saw her flinch and move aside. So George got the case down with both hands, and looked grim as he slid the compartment door open again and the three of them left the train and stepped down to the platform without offering assistance to one another.

Peace in Europe had come, but the war was leaving scars hitherto unnoticed while the adrenalin was still needed. Now these scars were seen and fingered as their causes were sought. Hopes of erasing them were probably vain. All three Rylands went to bed unhappy in the house in Botley Road that night and each one was closed off from any consolation that could be offered by either of the other two.

III

A certain normalization began which affected what the shops could sell. Haines's shop over the road was suddenly selling bananas. Edna saw people on a Saturday morning leaving the shop impatiently tearing the skins off the ones they had bought, not wanting to delay the rediscovery of the lost taste until they reached their homes. She called Alex down from his room where he was putting his shoes on and, still wearing her pinafore despite her own criteria of respectability, took him over the road so that he should have a banana to taste before they were all sold out. She bought a bunch of six: two each, she thought, and kept them in the brown paper bag until they were indoors. She took one out of the bag, made Alex sit at the kitchen table and solemnly taught him how to peel it. She said,

"Go on then, have a bite."

Alex did, and the taste was fantastic to him. It was something he remembered, but was yet fresh to him. He must have tasted a banana before the dangers of the War in the Atlantic prevented their dispatch from the Caribbean, but the experience had been submerged in all that had happened since. He was so thrilled with this until now forbidden fruit that he agreed to save up the other one until dinnertime. No subsequent banana ever tasted as good as that one.

A later experience was not so happy. Haines's shop was also the origin of it. Ice cream was for sale there. Edna was anxious to produce some more happiness and had taken Alex to buy a cornet for him. Outside the shop, before they crossed the road to come back, she put it in his hand but did not tell him how to deal with it. He turned it upside down and was left with the empty cornet, feeling foolish and angry. Edna felt the same and exploded into her repertoire of disappointed words of rebuke. Alex tried to repair the damage he had caused by cramming the cornet into his mouth and saying how nice it was, but the scoop of ice cream in the gutter, which you could see from the front room window, remained for several hours. The rediscovery of that taste had to wait for several weeks since, as Mr Haines explained to Edna next day when she tried to make up for her own shortcomings, that delivery was a one-off and there would not be any more for some time.

Then there were the kites. Plenty of children in the books that Alex read had them and the illustrations of kite-flying were always cheerful. Word went round at school one afternoon that the stationer's shop further up Botley Road was selling them. Alex hurried home to ask Edna if she would buy him one, but she had not come home yet. He stood at the front door, hoping her return would not be delayed for very long. He saw boys and girls who lived nearby coming back with kites they had bought: gorgeous paper things in primary colours. Edna did not yet appear. Five or six more kites passed Alex in the hands of their delighted purchasers. Still no Edna. Then a bus stopped opposite and Edna emerged from behind it with her shopping bag. Alex did not dare to run across the road to meet her, but jumped about excitedly on the pavement as she approached him and he said,

"Mum, they've got kites at Williams's! Can I have one?"

Edna was still being conciliatory after the ice cream anger and replied, "Of course you can, but let me put this heavy bag indoors first."

When that had been done, she strode off like King Wenceslas, followed by Alex as her page, only to find Peter Simmonds from Alex's class and his mother going off with the last one.

Edna and Alex were as disappointed as each other. They walked back to the house hand in hand for once. Even so Edna, whose internal misery at the prospect of living in George's mother's house conditioned everything she did now, could not resist telling him not to scuff his sandals on the pavement as he walked along.

IV

There must be an article in a sociologist's file on the significance of Saturday afternoons in the development of family relationships. Alex was on his own at the table in the kitchen doing one of his drawings. George and Edna were in the front room dozing after a good meal, courtesy of the officers' mess at Wheatley. The washing up was stacked in the scullery sink to be done later. Someone knocked on the back door. A man and a woman stood outside. Alex opened the door, and the man asked to see George.

"Tell him it's Mr Robertson wants to see him."

Alex had heard of Mr Robertson and now knew what a Glasgow accent was.

Two or three days before, George had come home from Wheatley to find an unopened letter waiting and an anxious Edna, who had seen its telltale postmark. It was, as she feared and George expected, from the owners of the dairy. George read it out to Edna. It said that Mr Robertson who had taken George's job when he left, had been content up to now to come in each day from Headington where he rented a house. Circumstances had changed with the end of the war so that its landlord could not make it available to Mr Robertson after the month of August and this letter must be accepted as giving George three months' notice to leave his present address. Mr Robertson would be calling to talk to him in the next few days.

Edna had shooed Alex away and closed the kitchen door behind him. He had turned round and looked at it from the other side, realizing that he had never seen it closed before. He had been aware that George was waiting for him to move completely away and heard his first remark, which was,

"Why does every other engineer in England have to be a Scot?"

When he thought Alex had gone, although he had tiptoed back, George had said,

"Well. Now we know we've got until the end of August to get out."

"Can't we fight it?" said Edna.

"Do you think we would stand a chance of winning a court case? No. They've given us a good deal of leeway, three months, and we would have to have gone some time."

"Where will we go then?" asked Edna, knowing and dreading the answer.

"Down home is the only possibility for a while."

"At your mother's." This was not a question, but a statement of defeat.

"Yes, unless you can suggest anything else. Can you?"

Edna's father had died years before the war. She had just fallen out with her youngest sister and knew that the other one would have no room for them in her desirable but very small, undamaged bungalow in Essex and she had cut herself off from her since the war started.

"How long will we have to stay there, d'you think?"

"Until I've got a proper job and we can afford a mortgage. There will be something as compensation from the War Damage Commission, but don't count on it being very much. We've got two hundred in the bank and we'll need to keep that to tide us over. I don't want to stay at the ancestral hall any more than you do and I'll do my best to see that our time there is as short as possible."

Edna sat and cried for a while. Then she sniffed loudly and began to speak.

"George, I'll say this to get it off my chest. We ought to be grateful we're alive after the blitz and that Joyce and Graham took us in when we were bombed out and that Alex was not killed or had his brain damaged in that accident. Somehow though, I still feel that we've lost out in all this while others have been luckier. Old Bill Thompson who stayed in the Navy and became a commissioned shipwright spent the whole war in Chatham and has done very nicely. Joyce and Graham themselves are back in their old home and he's got your old job and they can afford all sorts of things we can't even think of. What've we got left after all this, George? Answer me that!"

"What about each other - and the boy?" asked George, very gently.

He got up, and Alex heard him go to the cupboard in the dresser where he kept his whisky bottle, find glasses and pour out what he called two tots, one each, as he put them on the table. Drinks that size, as Alex imagined them, bore no resemblance to little children. Edna drank quickly and felt a little bit better.

"My sister had an idea," he said. You know when you had gone to bed and so had Mum, Sal and I stayed talking for a bit and she asked me if I had ever thought of taking the exam for the Civil Service. She knows what she is talking about, because she's been in the Civil Service since she left night school and her husband Michael's on the way to becoming a Principal, whatever that means, but he went to university. If I got a job at Chatham Dockyard to keep the wolf from the door and we saved for a deposit, then we needn't be at Mum's very long if I passed the exam. What d'you think?"

"Sounds all right, George. D'you think you could do it - the exam I mean?"

"I could have a go. Then I'd give up engineering altogether and be able to wear my truss without anyone giving a flying fart about it. Meanwhile, I'd better see this Scottish bloke and sort it out with him. Will he want to buy the furniture, d'you think? If not we'll have to store it; it won't fit in at Mum's and she's far too house-proud to let it, even if it would!"

Edna had begun to cheer up and when Alex had opened the door to ask if there was anything to eat, they had seemed to him to have recovered some kind of balance.

By the time Mr and Mrs Robertson were on the doorstep now, Alex had suppressed the pain of what he had overheard then, but remembered the conversation of theirs in Aunt Hetty's flat. On the strength of that memory he blurted out to the Robertsons:

"My Dad says the dairy can do what they like and we're not leaving!"

"Perhaps you'd actually let me speak to him myself, sonny," was the best reply the visitor could think of, hoping that, despite his convictions as a Presbyterian, truth was not the prerogative of precocious babes and sucklings.

Alex went and found George, told him Mr and Mrs Robertson were here and also what he had just said himself, feeling he had done his bit to defend the family's interests but by no means sure that George would take it kindly. He was very surprised when George only laughed and said,

"Thanks for the confidence you have in me, boy. You stay here. I'll go and see them."

Then Alex and a shivering Edna heard George take the Robertsons into the living room and sit them at the table. They were there together for ten minutes, after which George brought them to meet Edna for the first time and Alex again, calling him "my misguided offspring", whatever that might mean. Mr Robertson was generous enough to laugh. It took half an hour to show them all the rooms and they left expressing interest in a good deal of the larger furniture, since their lodgings in Headington had been let to them furnished.

V

George encouraged Edna to make the most of their last summer in Oxford.

"There's no river to punt on in Gillingham," he reminded her and made sure that several Saturdays and Sundays in July and the first part of August were spent on the one they had here. Alex was allowed to use a paddle from time to time, but never when George was using the pole and doing it properly. A two-pound jam jar was trailed in the water for tiddlers, which sometimes obliged by accepting a free ride for a mile or so.

When it was wet once, George took Alex and Edna to the Ashmolean museum. She was not very interested in the pictures and made fun of the nude male figures in bronze and marble. The college quadrangles and gardens were explored again and George sowed a seed in Alex's mind by saying how pleasant it must be to spend three years here with nothing else to do but study the subject of your choice. When Edna remonstrated by saying that only toffs went to Oxford University, George became very thoughtful and commented,

"It might not be always like that, or even like that for much longer with this new Education Act that was brought in last year. Maybe boys from ordinary homes will stand a chance in future. If we're really going to have free medical services for all of us as the Beveridge report says, then why not free university education for as many of us as are capable of it?"

"Would I be capable of it, Dad?" Alex unthinkingly asked.

"Despite that bang on the head, you seem to be all about, to judge by the questions you ask. The real thing though is that working class boys and girls will be able to go to grammar schools free of charge - and then if they've got brains they can win scholarships paid for out of taxes to come here, or to other places like this."

"What about the poor devils that don't get into the grammar schools, though?" asked Edna.

"There're going to be as badly off as they've always been, I suppose."

They were in Tom Quad. George's last comment before they left it was,

"I shall miss coming into these places. The Georgian dockyard buildings at Chatham are impressive, but in a very different way. It won't be the same."

"They are named after you, though, Dad."

"That was another George as it happened. I'm not old enough to have that honour!"

VI

Alex had similar feelings to his father's in school at the end of the academic year. Edna had gone to Miss Cook to say that they were leaving the district at the end of August and that Alex would not be coming back in September. She knew the name of the school round the corner from where his grandmother lived and told Miss Cook that she assumed he would be accepted there. The Headmistress undertook to give her a testimonial to take with her to the head of that school. She said that it was always helpful to know something in detail about newcomers.

Edna had never encouraged Alex to bring friends home, so he was not particularly close to any one of his contemporaries, but on the last day of term he was given little gifts by one or two of them to remember them by. Isabel, who had sat next to him for four years without falling out with him, gave him an old fashioned silver sixpence from a bracelet she had. The boy whom Edna did not like him associating with gave him a regimental cap badge his brother had given him which was obviously one of his treasures. On the last afternoon many wished him well and he sat sadly in the front room for a while when he got home.

Then he remembered something and went up to his bedroom. He picked up the old pie dish. Its last function was to become a tin hat for a moment or two, and then Alex realized that you didn't need tin hats on this side of the world any more. He brought it downstairs and, taking it out to the path between the shelters, he flung it, spinning, at the back gate, watching its trajectory until it crashed and fell. After that, he went and picked it up and put it in the dustbin, which was kept in the last shelter on the right by the gate. He felt very grown up as he went back into the kitchen and determinedly stood up straight, squaring his shoulders, feeling able to face future uncertainties with new found courage.

VII

"Whereabouts is Hiroshima, Dad?" Alex asked George as they sat at table ten days later, after he and George had been listening to the news on the wireless together. Edna, as was usual for her now, had got up and laid the table in the kitchen when the news came on.

"On the Japanese island of Honshu, boy. At least, it used to be. There can't be much left of it after what has happened. The Yanks at the hospital say the atomic bomb killed thirty-five thousand people.

"Why kill so many people? Aren't we supposed to be stopping wickedness, us and the Americans?"

"All I can tell you is what they are saying out at Wheatley. Apparently the British and American scientists, hoping we would have it before Hitler did, have been developing this bomb for many years in a desert in America. One of our scientists - his name was Rutherford - began the process in the thirties when he discovered at Cambridge that you could split the atom. We all feared then that if they did split it, then everything else would start to break down. Perhaps it has now, though not in the way we thought it would. What the Yanks are saying (he repeated that, Alex noticed, as if he thought what they said might not be true) is that, if it had not been dropped, the Japanese would go on fighting to their last man and that would mean the end of a lot of our men too. This seemed to President Truman the best thing to do, they say."

"How did it manage to kill all those people? Even the V2s didn't get all that many."

"This bomb is more powerful than anything that has ever been used before. It creates an enormous heat as well as having the effect of a normal explosion. Then there's what's called radiation, which makes a lot of people who didn't die when it exploded very ill indeed."

"Do eat your tea, Alex," put in Edna. "And let Dad have his. I don't know why you have to enquire about these terrible things. You'll find out how horribly cruel the world is soon enough when you grow up without you wanting to know about what's happened thousands of miles away and doesn't affect you."

"It does affect me if it means that when I have grown up the war is still going on."

"Oh, go on, then," shouted Edna, and got up from the table. "I can't stand listening to any more of it. Let me know when you've finished, George, and I'll come back and wash up."

"No, girl. You just go and put your feet up and Alex and I will square up out here. He needs to know - though I can't cope with all this any more than you can."

Edna sniffed away to the living room and put the dance music on the wireless up very loud.

George relayed to his son what the Americans had told him earlier that day about the atom bomb and about their hopes that this would bring about the end of Japanese continuance of the war. He explained to him about what was called Bushido, and how it was different for people from another culture to see things our way. He also expressed his own fears. He knew as well as any informed civilian that the Russians had declared war on Japan now, but could not help telling Alex that it was expected that the next war would be with Russia, though he kicked himself for it.

"Will there always be wars then, Dad?"

"And rumours of wars," said George, dredging up the words from nearly thirty years ago when part of the routine for boy artificers in the Navy was being confirmed in the Church of England.

By this time they were at the scullery sink, whose window gave no light any more because of the air-raid shelters outside. George had Edna's pinafore on and was washing the plates, while Alex was doing his best to dry them with a tea towel. Alex looked up at his father from behind and thought he was looking little and old as he stooped with his hands in the low sink. He had been grey-haired for years and increasingly thin on top, but now in the obscurity of the little room denied its natural light he looked bent with many cares and, when he turned round to smile at Alex with what reassurance he could summon to give him, he appeared to Alex to have lost his usual vitality. For the first time that he could remember, Alex did not want to stay with his father. For a moment as he looked up, Alex feared that the war had crushed him in the way it had crushed Edna and he wondered for a moment how he would cope if that turned out to be true.

The mood soon passed. George took off the pinafore, Alex hung the tea towel up and they both went to join Edna. In desperation, or so it seemed to Alex, George went and found the board, the counters and the dice for a game of Snakes and Ladders. Edna reluctantly agreed to play, but when all she seemed to land on was the heads of successive long snakes, her mood became blacker and George felt more unable to be of any use to her. Alex seemed to be put on several ladders by his shakes of the dice and George hoped this was an omen for him. As in life, he for his part went down one long snake on the board and seemed to make very little progress thereafter. The thought of taking Edna and Alex to live at his mother's meant now to him that he had got nowhere since he had left the home she and his father had in the Naval Detention Barracks at Chatham when he joined H.M.S. Fisgard in 1917.

Edna was pleased to find that Alex did not argue when she declared it was time for him to go to bed. Alex was glad of a way of escape from the brooding atmosphere and thought about Joyce's canary, which used to be in his cage in this room. It had managed to keep cheerful despite being in prison all its life - but then what did it know of any other life?

Alex did what he did not usually do: he gave Edna a kiss on her cheek and said, as kindly as he could, "Goodnight, Mum." He did not even mind tonight when her reply was no more than,

"Make sure you wash behind your ears. I'll be up to see if you have."

As she said it, she had a look on her face that belonged to a woman who had forgotten how to be happy, even if she ever knew. Going upstairs, Alex had to find his handkerchief and blow his nose hard in order not to cry at the horror so far away of having to kill so many so as to finish a war and the horror at home of his parents' unhappiness, about which he could do nothing although he longed to be able to be of help. Sadness they cannot understand is hard for children to deal with. Edna was partly right.

VIII

With nearly three weeks still to go, Edna set about packing such china and glass as she had accumulated since coming to Botley Road. There was no more than would fill one large cardboard box. Alex was very keen that she should not forget his fairground Jacobean tumbler. George carefully checked over all his tools in his old black and white sea chest. Alex's books and toys were to be taken as they were in the cupboard that had been left behind by Joyce. Clothes fitted into two cabin trunks and a suitcase that George bought in what he called an old tot's shop. All this would be a part load along with the sea chest for Carter Paterson's who would bring the things down to Gillingham at some unspecified future time.

While the carrier's men were dealing with the sea chest's passage through the front door to the van on the day appointed for the move, both of them being older than he, George wryly gave thanks that hernias were not infectious. Once down the front step, they put the sea chest on rollers and made the job easy. That tickled George - a sea chest making its way over the rollers. He told Alex about it to amuse him, but unfortunately he had only seen the sea at Walney Island and had not learned to call waves rollers, so he did not get the joke.

When the neighbours saw the van had gone, they called to say their goodbyes. Edna was pleased that Mrs White came first, brimming over with the news that when Lord Mountbatten's amphibious force had taken Rangoon, all the prisoners of war kept there had been released, and Jim was among them. He would be repatriated as soon as possible. Then Mrs Wilson came to say that her husband would be in Germany for some time but she now knew for certain he was safe, which she had not for the last three months. The girls gave Edna a little clock to remember them by, and Alex a Doctor Dolittle book they knew he did not have. All George got was a kiss from each of the girls and from Mrs Wilson herself, but he seemed more pleased than anybody.

They were not going to hospital, but they did have a case each, so a taxi arrived to take them to Gloucester Green. George had decided that they would be sure to have a seat each on the Black and White Coach direct to Victoria. Travelling that way rather than by train, would save a lot of trouble and be a sentimental journey for him. Edna had agreed and added that it also cost a lot less.

Before they left, Martha produced a box camera, saying she had been saving the last film on a roll for this very occasion. She lined the Rylands up before the privet hedge, George in his best suit, Edna in the dogtooth tweed costume she had had made when Alex was in hospital and Alex himself in his white shirt with a tie and the grey school suit that used to belong to John. As she stood there Edna realized that this was the place where she had seen Alex's shoe under the lorry and was glad that Martha said they must all smile or she would have done the opposite. As soon as the shutter had clicked in the camera, the taxi stopped in front of them.

There was nothing left to do after the luggage had been stowed (Sea-going language came readily to George's mind in moments of stress). He opened the taxi door for Edna to get into the back seat and, in his preoccupation with what might lay ahead, went round to the other passenger door and settled himself next to her. Alex was left standing on the pavement. It was the taxi driver who told him to get in the front seat. The taxi was parked facing the oncoming traffic, so he said to him,

"Look both ways before you step into the road!"

This time he did.

10

Alex stood in the garden on the second day after their arrival in Gillingham with his father and grandmother. Edna had gone to bed with a sick headache.

"Do you think you could take it over while you are here, son?" Louisa said.

"Go on, Dad!" said Alex. "I'll help!"

"They certainly need to be pruned," George commented.

The roses had flowered well, but the dead heads outnumbered the budding hopefuls by about three to one.

"Yes. I can't leave all his years of work on it to go to wrack and ruin, can I? I'll help where I can."

Alex noticed that his grandmother's arm had gone round his father's waist in a proprietary fashion and that George quickly moved away. When he looked up, he saw that Edna was standing in the bedroom window with the expression on her face he had seen a lot of recently. She stood listless, leaning against the window frame with her mouth partly open and her eyes staring at George. That was why he evaded his mother's embrace. Alex already realized the sadness of a love so possessive that it tries to stop its object loving the people who were already loved before. Edna in the window in the evening light seemed to Alex like a fey apparition from an illustration by a man called Arthur Rackham in a book of tales he had looked at among the books at school. Alex feared his feeling that his mother was becoming more of a threat to family happiness than a component of it. He could remember how unhappy she was when they first went by themselves to Oxford without George and she had to accept Joyce's domestic arrangements. It was far worse now, here at Gran's house amid the smell of mothballs and lavender furniture polish and with George at home all the time with his nerves on edge.

George had written to apply for a job at the dockyard as he said he would, and had sent to the Civil Service Commission for application forms to take their examination. He was in a sort of dead man's gulch, as he put it, for the present. He even behaved out of character towards Alex on occasion. In the last months of the European war soldiers had sung a current hit song with nonsense words as they marched, and singers on the wireless made it a standard for a time. So it was that whenever Alex started to sing:

"Mares eat oats
And does eat oats
And little lambs eat ivy,"

he never got as far as "A kid'll eat ivy too, wouldn't you-oo?" because George, not Edna, would shout at him to be quiet.

While he was waiting for something to happen, and in order to get out of a house one hundred per cent overpopulated by female close relatives, George did take on the garden and was dead-heading and pruning one morning, bizarrely dressed in formal trousers which would no longer do up round his waist. He had bought them to wear when he had been asked to give away his older sister-in-law at her wedding since her father was no longer alive. An old shirt with no collar and a green cardigan out at the elbows completed the ensemble, along with his father's old lace-up rubber gardening boots from the shed, which were a bit too large, but would save his own shoes from the ravages of gardening after several days of wet weather. He had intended to wear his hat, but after it caught in the branches of the apple tree above the roses two or three times, he left it off.

Alex came out to be with him. George gave him a job. He was to take the basket that was on the ground at George's feet whenever it looked full up, and empty it out on the pile behind the tree at the bottom of the garden past where vegetables were growing. When he had done that three times or so and was waiting for it to be filled again, George began to speak to him in a weary tone such as he had not heard him use before.

"How are you getting on here? Are things all right between you and Gran?"

"Yes. She doesn't say much to me, but lets me get the history book down whenever I ask. She doesn't tell me off for touching things, as I thought she might do."

"What about Mum. How are things between you and her?"

"She's closed up altogether on me."

"You mean she doesn't talk to you?"

"Only to tell me to do things I would be doing anyway, like washing and cleaning my shoes. You know how quiet she has become."

"Only too well. Look, Alex; this can't be any more easy for you than it is for me or Mum. Tomorrow you'll start at the school round the corner. I don't know when I'll be able to go to work again and be with other people a bit during the day, but what worries me is that when we are both out, Mum and Gran will be left here together, getting on each other's nerves all day long. I was hoping your Aunt Sal would still be here to keep them apart, but Michael got a her a passage to go and join him sooner than she thought he could - and just because we're not very happy we mustn't begrudge other people a chance of it. I shouldn't be talking like this to you, but it's all bottled up inside me."

Then he grew anxious and went on,

"Please don't say I said all this to either Mum or Gran, will you? One day we'll have a place of our own again and live as people have a right to. But for now we've all got to put up with things as they are I suppose."

Alex realized that by now his father wasn't actually talking to him, but just talking to himself, or to God, if God were listening. He knew how distressed George was, but was at an eight-year-old's loss to know what to do to help.

"When the bike comes on the van, can we go out for a few rides around here?"

"I'm afraid you're a bit too big for that now. But yes, we could go out and look at nice places around, like Newington, which is only a short bus ride away, and to Rochester Cathedral and the castle there, of course. They make and test those flying boats you had a model of across the river from there and you can watch them take off from the water."

"That'd be good. When can we?"

"School tomorrow, but let's see what happens at the weekend."

By this time George had finished cutting and pruning in his father's beloved rose beds and looked with a small measure of pride at what he had been doing.

"Time to wash our hands before dinner," he said. "Thanks for your help - in more ways than one."

They put the secateurs and the basket away, locked the shed and went indoors. Edna came down to join them and Louisa. They ate their lunch in a monastic silence. Alex found that eating while three other people with full dentures were doing the same was funny. The only trouble was that he could not tell them what he was laughing at, and this made both Edna and Gran cross with him and left George no way of defending him from their rebukes and the charge of silliness. The dread sentence from Edna's lips was uttered:

"Tell him not to do it, Dad."

George looked at Alex, whose giggles were almost under control now, and only allowing his eyes to smile behind his glasses, uttered the words, time-honoured in all families,

"You heard what your mother said."

II

George took refuge in current affairs. Coping with another taciturn meal, he had got up from the table and put the wireless on for the six o'clock news and the family heard that an American battleship called USS Missouri had steamed into Tokyo harbour and high ranking officers from all the countries involved in the conflict had received the official Japanese surrender. Now the war really was all over. Louisa Ryland was not the sort to have champagne in her cupboard, but she had half a bottle of port and brought that out to celebrate the return of international peace.

When they had all, including Alex, had some in their glasses, Alex saw his grandmother get up and walk round the table to where Edna was and put her arms round her.

"I can't keep on saying this, Edna. I have tried on several occasions to make peace with you. When we came up to see you in Oxford before David died, and again when you came here earlier in the year, I tried to tell you that I really do want to bury the hatchet. It is about time we were able to accept each other and, as we are under the same roof for a time at least, I want to be able to make you welcome as my daughter-in-law. I didn't do it when I should have, but I want to now."

George put down the slice of bread and jam that had stayed motionless in front of his mouth as his mother said this and he and Alex waited in apprehensive silence to see how Edna would react.

Slowly she stood up and just as slowly put her arms out to draw Louisa to herself in an embrace. George could not see her face. Alex could not either. They could both see that George's mother had meant what she said and waited for Edna to put her reply into words.

The two women moved apart and with intense relief father and son saw that Edna was smiling at Louisa. Holding both her hands, she said,

"I'm very glad you said that. Now I can call you Mum after all these years."

They hugged each other again and, completely out of character, as George knew well, Louisa poured another glass of port for Edna and herself, then remembered that George and Alex were still there, gave George some, and a trickle in the bottom of a glass for Alex.

"David used to do this a lot when he was master of the lodge," she said, and raised her glass to George and to Edna as they sat together. "I drink to your future happiness and you finding fitting work and a home of your own in good time."

They responded and as the glasses were put down Edna said,

"And thank you for having us to stay here until such time as that happens."

Alex finished his little drop of port and thought he ought to say something too. What he came out with was,

"Isn't it good that the war's all over now?"

"Very good indeed, boy, very good indeed!" said George, and the laughter broke out.

III

When the table had been cleared and the washing-up done, Louisa went out to play cards with some friends as she always did on at least one evening a week. This left George and Edna on their own once Alex had gone upstairs.

"Does she mean it, d'you think?" asked Edna.

George looked at his wife in silence for a long time before he answered:

"I think she does. It's what my father wanted; she told me as much when they came to see us the Christmas before he died and again after his funeral. What she said then was that she longed to be able to get on with you, but didn't quite know how to go about it."

"That suggests that us not getting on was my fault, then, doesn't it?"

"You know it isn't, though, don't you?"

"They never gave me a chance at the first and that was why things went as they did. It's difficult to turn round and behave differently now."

"But . . . do you think it's worth a try? We have to be in her house for a while until we get ourselves sorted out. It needn't be too long. Even without the civil service, there might be a job in the drawing office in the dockyard that I could do and then, with a regular income again, we could borrow for a house."

"That would mean us staying round here, though, George."

"But we both came from round here in the first place . . ."

"Yes. But we left, and were glad to have done so. You have given your mother's address to the War Damage Commission, haven't you?"

"You know I have. You saw me post the letter."

"D'you think what they pay us will go towards a deposit on a house?"

"I sincerely hope so."

"Even if we don't go back to Wimbledon, we would be on our own again if that happened."

"All we can do is try to start again. Do you think you could turn the other cheek a bit when I'm out at work and you and Mum are here on your own together?"

"I can try," Edna said, "As long as I don't get slapped on both at once!"

The uncertain smiles that followed that remark led to a change of subject and possibilities for their future were discussed in circles and in spirals until Louisa came back and Edna made a cup of cocoa for the three of them. Peace was certainly kept until it was time to go to bed. There was even a deal of warmth between them, expressed in pleasant chatter.

IV

In the little room he had been given facing the top of the stairs next to Gran's - the one Aunt Sarah had when they were last here - Alex had gone to bed fairly early, consenting willingly to this on the grounds that he did have the new school to come to terms with in the morning. He had not been able to see inside it. When his parents had tried to take him to the school the day before there was no one to let them in, so it would all be new and strange to him. Yet, if things really were to be better between his mother and father and grandmother now, he thought that he would be able cope with whatever a new school might do. Children have a great capacity for hope.

V

People like George and Edna lost a good few landmarks at this time. Mr Churchill had lost the general election to Mr Attlee. President Roosevelt had died back in April and his place been taken by President Truman. Conventional warfare - bad enough in itself with the millions of violent deaths all over the world in the last six years - had been replaced by Britain and America possessing and using the ultimate terror weapon. Stalin was once more recognizable as an adversary rather than an ally. Things that appeared permanent were unpleasant: rationing, the lack of a home of their own and the discontinuance of George's well-paid and enjoyed work at the American hospital.

For Alex as well, the terrain was very different from what he had become used to. Junior schools would be very much the same as each other, he decided. There were people you got on with, people you didn't; teachers who were supportive, others who were officious. Soon men teachers would return to classrooms with enthralling editions of war stories to tell, having imposed a subconscious denial process upon their memories as a protection against the horrific things they had seen. Living in Gran's house brought new tensions. "Wipe your feet when you come in!" had replaced "Look both ways before you cross the road!" as Edna's principal injunction to him. He and George and Edna all tried to pretend that things were going well for them.

News bulletins on the wireless seemed universally gloomy and one day George summed it all up by saying after hearing one of them as they all sat at table,

"Perhaps nations are not meant to get on well with each other." No one could think of a reply to what he had said.

The local newspaper announced that the sodium lights installed on what they all called the top road were going to be switched on for the first time on an evening in October. George came home from the dockyard drawing office with red, white and blue caps he had bought on the way for them all to wear when they went up to watch. Edna and Louisa both needed persuasion to put them on but, when they looked out of the window to see the most respectable of their neighbours sporting similar versions of the national colours, they consented and all four walked up to Watling Street wearing patriotic colours in the half light of the late evening.

They stood with the others at the end of the lane under one of the tall lampposts, which Louisa had told them had been installed in September 1939 but never used till now. A glow in each light began as the darkened sky replaced the daylight and soon fizzed into a steady orange. All the people looked at each other with surprised expressions: the colours on their hats and scarves were not the same as when they left their homes: greens and browns replaced the colours they expected to see and the whites had taken on a neutral luminosity. Some brash souls began to sing:

> "There'll always be an England,
> An England proud and free . . ."

but most of the people present remained silent and the song did not last more than one verse, largely because most of the people could not remember any more, even if they had wanted to.

After those who raised their voices had lowered them, an eerie hush to match the forlorn colours descended on the small crowd and the people began to disperse in family groups and parties of friends. Any wider association between people who did not know each other was resisted. The four Rylands walked down the lane without the sense of an affirmation of peace that they hoped that the switching on of the lights would have brought them. Under the ordinary, old fashioned lamps which were also on now in their lane, you could see that the caps that they had taken off and held in their hands were the right colour after all, but the confidence they had been meant to represent had evaporated.

"School in the morning. Up you go to bed," Edna said to Alex after warming mugs of cocoa had been enjoyed. "Make sure you take your glasses off when you've finished reading!"

As he obeyed this fatuous injunction half an hour later, Alex brushed his hand against the scar on his chin and was relieved to find how small it had become.

Lying curled up in bed in a darkness not induced by blackout curtains, he started to review what had happened since the morning he had tried to rush out into the garden in Raynes Park all that time ago, but was relieved of most of the memory by losing the battle to stay awake.

Acknowledgements

Isabel Sullivan at the Surrey History Centre made a search on my behalf to discover important information about the London Blitz and about the nature of the housing in the area where my story begins. She drew attention to the fact that a 4/KG54 Junkers aircraft crashed on houses in Richmond Avenue on 20th September 1940 (The Blitz: Then and Now, ed. William Ramsey, Battle of Britain Prints International, 1988).

Susan Andrew at the Education, Leisure and Libraries Department in Merton Civic Centre provided me with information about the bomb damage in the Bushey Mead Estate, the relevant extract from the 1939 Electoral Register and a section of the minutes of the meeting of Merton and Morden UDC held on 14th February 1944 about possible repairs to bombed houses. She also made extracts available from Judith Goodman, Merton and Morden, A Pictorial History, Phillimore, 1995, and from E.M.Jowett, Raynes Park, A Social History, Merton Historical Society, 1987. A comparison of maps made in 1933 and 1952, as well as subsequent visual research, shows that 74 Chestnut Road was not rebuilt in its original form after the war.

Peggy Pyke-Lees knew where all that information was available and guided me to the sources. Philippa Kennard-Bent and Sheila Donaldson Walters read through my manuscript, making helpful comments and constructive suggestions. Mark and Magda Norris gave me information towards the cameo appearance of the Polish airman in Chapter 7.

Vanessa, my late and dear companion of nearly thirty-seven years, was most supportive of this endeavour and supplied the deliberately ambiguous title for the story. James Aitken Ballard believed in it and put it in the right place at the right time. Sally Lawrence, Henrietta Hopkins, Guy Hopkins and Sarah Ballard also gave me great support.

Angus Calder, The People's War, Jonathan Cape, 1969, provided an essential stabilizer to the process of remembering the involvement of men, women and children who had neither political nor military responsibility during the struggle against the axis powers.

To these and many others besides, I offer my sincere thanks.

REB

Printed in the United Kingdom
by Lightning Source UK Ltd.
108444UKS00001B/13-33

9 780954 728021